CW00549872

James Hadley Chase (born R…
born in London in 1906. He v
which time he was inspired by American …
and went on to write his own thrillers and gangster stories,
also set in the United States. He first found success with
*No Orchids for Miss Blandish* which was published in 1939
and was one of the most successful books of the thirties,
selling several million copies. George Orwell described it as
'a brilliant piece of writing with hardly a wasted word or a
jarring note anywhere'. It was subsequently dramatised and
performed on London's West End and also made into a film.
Chase went on to gain popularity for his numerous other
gangster stories, and by the end of the war he was one of
Britain's most successful thriller writers. During his career
he produced some ninety books, also writing under the
names of James L Dochery, Ambrose Grant and Raymond
Marshall. He travelled widely, though only visited the USA
late in life. He died in 1985 whilst in Switzerland.

JAMES HADLEY
# CHASE

MORE DEADLY THAN THE MALE

HOUSE OF
STRATUS

First published in 1946

Copyright by Hervey Raymond

This edition published in 2000 by The House of Stratus, an imprint of Stratus Books Ltd., 21 Beeching Park, Kelly Bray, Cornwall, PL17 8QS, UK.

www.houseofstratus.com

Typeset, printed and bound by The House of Stratus.

A catalogue record for this book is available from the British Library and the Library of Congress.

ISBN 1-84232-114-5

Cover design: Marc Burville-Riley
Cover image: Photonica

# 1

They were all there – Capone, Dillinger, Nelson, Karpis and Charlie Lucky. The table at which they sat was littered with poker chips, playing cards, whisky bottles and glasses. A green shaded lamp hung low over the table; its harsh light fell on their faces, while the rest of the room remained dark and shadowy.

Several men, almost invisible in the gloom and haze of tobacco smoke, lounged behind the group at the table. They were small men, with eyes like wet stones, swarthy complexions and granite faces.

The group at the table and the men in the shadows suddenly stiffened when George Fraser walked into the room. He stood a few feet from the table, his hands in his coat pockets, his jaw thrust forward and his eyes threatening and cold.

No one spoke; no one moved.

"If any of you guys wants to start something," George Fraser said, after a long pause, "I'll take care of his widow."

Very slowly, very cautiously, Capone laid his cards down on the table. "Hello, George," he said in a husky whisper.

George Fraser eyed him coldly. There were few men who would have had the nerve to walk alone into that back room and face five of the biggest and most dangerous bosses in the booze racket, but George Fraser was without nerves.

"It's time we had a little talk," he said, biting off each word. "You guys have been running this show too long. You're through – the lot of you. From now on, I'm taking over this territory, and I'm running it my way."

There followed another long pause, then Dillinger, his eyes glowing and his face white with rage, snarled, "Who said?"

George Fraser smiled. "I said," he returned, in his clipped, cold voice.

Dillinger made a growling noise deep in his throat and his hand flashed to his hip pocket.

Capone, sitting next to him, grabbed frantically at his wrist. His fat face was blue-white with fear. "Do you want to commit suicide?" he yelled. "You don't stand a chance with Fraser!"

Dillinger, swearing under his breath, tried to break Capone's grip, and the table rocked as the two men wrestled. A bottle of whisky toppled and smashed to pieces on the floor.

"Let him alone, Al," George Fraser called. "If he wants to play it that way, you'd better give him some air."

Capone shot a terrified look at George Fraser. The pale, set face and the eyes that were now like chips of ice completely unnerved him. He nearly fell over himself to get away from Dillinger.

"Look out!" he cried. "He's going to shoot!"

The other three at the table kicked their chairs away and jumped clear, while some of the men who had been standing in the shadows threw themselves on the floor.

Dillinger, alone at the table, sat motionless, glaring at George Fraser.

"Okay, Johnny," George Fraser said mockingly, "go for your gun. What are you waiting for?"

Dillinger rose slowly to his feet. He swept his chair out

*of the way and crouched.*

*"Bet you a hundred bucks I can put five slugs in your pumper before your rod shows," George Fraser said, letting his hands hang loosely at his sides.*

*Dillinger cursed him, and then his arm moved with the speed of a striking snake. A heavy, snub-nosed automatic jumped as if by magic into George Fraser's hand. The room rocked with the sound of gunfire.*

*Dillinger, his eyes wide and sightless, crashed to the floor and rolled over on his back.*

*"Take a look at him, Charlie," George Fraser said, his eyes on the group of men huddled against the wall.*

*Charlie Lucky, after a moment's hesitation, reached forward, pulled Dillinger's coat back and ripped open his shirt.*

*"Five slugs," he said, his voice cracking; "all in the same spot."*

"Good morning, Mr George," Ella said, putting a cup of watery tea on the bamboo table by the bed. "Did I wake you?"

"Hmm?" George Fraser asked. He looked up with blank astonishment at Ella in her frowsy blue uniform and her ridiculous cap perched on the top of her mouse-coloured hair. "Good Lord! You gave me quite a turn. I didn't hear you come in. I must've been dozing ..."

"It's ever such a lovely morning," Ella went on, crossing the drab little room, and pulling up the blind. "The sun's shining and there ain't a cloud in the sky."

George Fraser closed his eyes against the bright sunlight that streamed through the grimy window pane. The image he had been creating of himself as "Machine-gun Fraser", millionaire gangster, still gripped his imagination, and Ella's unexpected intrusion fuddled him.

"Shall I tidy up a bit?" Ella asked, her plain, shiny little face resigned as she surveyed the disordered room. "Coo, Mr George! Your socks are in the coal-scuttle."

George Fraser sighed. It was no good. He would have to leave the back room, the smell of cordite, the terrified faces of Capone, Nelson, Karpis and Charlie Lucky until later. He could always pick up his fantasy when Ella had gone.

"Oh, all right," he said, pushing the blankets from his shoulders and sitting up. "Only don't make too much noise. I've got a bit of a head this morning."

Ella looked at him hopefully. "Did you have any adventures last night?" she asked as she busied herself about the room.

George resisted the temptation to give her a fictitious account of his evening. He did not feel quite up to it this morning, and after the story he had told her the day before, which had been his best effort to date, he did not think it wise to risk an anticlimax.

"I can't tell you yet," he said. "A little later perhaps; but it's too secret right now."

Ella's face fell. She was thin, sharp-featured, wistful – a typical product of the East End slums. For three years she had been the general help at this boarding-house off the Edgware Road. Most mornings, providing he hadn't a hangover, George would keep her entranced with lurid tales of G-men, gangsters and their molls. He assured her that, when he lived in the States, he had known them all. At one time he had worked with Frank Kelly, the bank robber; at another time he had been the bodyguard of Toni Scarletti, the booze racketeer. His name was known and feared by all the big shots of the underworld, and he had experienced enough adventures to fill a dozen books.

These stories which George recounted so glibly were the figments of his extraordinary imagination. He had never been to America, let alone seen a gangster; but, being an avid reader of the lurid American pulp magazines, and having seen every gangster film ever made, he had acquired a remarkable knowledge of American crime. The gunmen as depicted by such magazines as *Front-Page Detective* and *True Confessions* completely obsessed him.

Like so many other men and women who live in a secret world of their own, George suffered from an acute inferiority complex. He had always lacked confidence in himself, and believed that whatever he planned to do was bound to end in failure.

This inferiority complex was the direct result of the treatment he had received in his early childhood from his parents. His birth had been an "accident", and his parents, music-hall artists by profession, had no place for a child in their rather selfish, extremely mobile lives. They regarded him as a calamity, and had made no attempt to conceal the fact from him. He was always the last to be considered, his babyhood was loveless, and at the earliest possible moment he was handed over to an elderly couple who had reluctantly taken on the role of foster parents in return for the much-needed addition to their meagre income. They were too old to be bothered with a small child, and it was not long before George realized that they considered him to be an unnecessary burden to them.

It says much for George's character that this unhappy, unwanted existence did not entirely affect his nature, but it certainly made him extremely shy and unnaturally sensitive. Because of his shyness he had a wretched time at school. As he grew older he became more reserved and repressed. He made no friends, and consequently had no outlet for his thoughts and desires. It was not surprising, then, that he became an introvert: as an antidote against loneliness and as a bolster to his drooping ego, he filled his mind with stories of adventure and violence, imagining himself as the hero of whatever story he happened to be reading. When he was at school he imagined himself as Bulldog Drummond; later, he saw himself as Jack Dempsey, and now, at the age of twenty-seven, he pictured himself as the all-powerful gang leader, amassing millions of dollars, terrorizing other mobs, racing the streets in a black armoured car, and being the idol of dazzling, beautifully dressed blondes.

For some time George Fraser had been content to live, in his mind, this rôle of a gangster; but these mental pictures became so vivid and exciting that he could no longer keep them to himself. Cautiously he tried them out on Ella, and was gratified to find that he had an immediately enthralled audience.

Ella had previously regarded George as just another boarder who seldom got up before eleven o'clock, and who expected a cup of tea just when she was occupied in making beds. But when George casually mentioned that he had lived in Chicago and had rubbed shoulders with most of the notorious Public Enemies, Ella was instantly intrigued. She went regularly to her local cinema, and was well acquainted with the savagery of American gangsters. Now here was someone, it seemed, who had actually met these men in the flesh, who had fought with and against them, and whose experiences were much more exciting and fantastic than the most exciting and fantastic film.

Ella was profoundly impressed. Not that George Fraser was impressive to look at. He had a tall, beefy, ungainly figure. His complexion was sallow and his eyes were big, blue and rather sad. In spite of his size, he could not entirely hide his timidity and shyness. If someone spoke to him suddenly he would change colour and become flustered, looking anywhere but at the person addressing him. His landlady, Mrs Rhodes, terrified him, and whenever he ran into her he would talk complete nonsense while endeavouring to escape, leaving her staring after him, completely bewildered.

In spite of his manner, the stories he had to tell fascinated Ella. Not for a moment did it cross her mind that George was deceiving her. When he told her that he had been forced to leave the States in a hurry and that even now, if a certain mob knew where he was, they would come after him, she spent restless nights in fear for him. She must not, he had warned her, tell anyone of his past. He was, he explained, doing important and secret work, and his life would be in danger if anyone so much as suspected what his activities were.

All this was so much nonsense. In actual fact, up to four months ago George Fraser had been a bank clerk. He had been with the bank for ten years, and he would have been quite satisfied to remain a bank clerk for the rest of his days, but it did not turn out that way. One evening he had wandered into a pub – he was always wandering into pubs – a few minutes before closing time. There he met a flashily dressed individual who had, rather obviously, been in the pub since it had opened. This individual proposed to do George a good turn. Lowering his voice, he conveyed to George the name of a horse that was certain to win the next day's two o'clock handicap.

Now, George was no gambler, nor was he interested in horse-racing, but he was flattered that his companion had mistaken him for a sportsman. He decided to have a flutter. The horse finished a length ahead of the field, and George received twenty pounds from a disgruntled bookmaker. He immediately jumped to the conclusion that he could make his fortune by backing horses. Before long he was in debt, and in desperation he turned to a money-lender to get him out of the mess. Then he couldn't pay the money-lender's charges, and the bank heard about it. George got the sack.

He was out of work for two miserable weeks, and he soon discovered that a discharged bank clerk was not a proposition an employer cared to consider. Things looked pretty black for George. He tramped the streets looking for work, and just as he was giving up hope, he obtained a job with the World-Wide Publishing Company. It wasn't much of a job, but, by now, George was glad to take anything.

He was, however, a little dismayed to find that the Company expected him to sell a set of children's books from door to door on a "commission only" basis.

George had no confidence in his ability to sell anything. But the sales manager assured him that he need not worry about that. They would train him, and by the time they were through with him he would be able to sell coals to Newcastle. George was introduced to Edgar Robinson, head of the group of salesmen on whose territory George was to work. Robinson, an odd, aggressive creature with a shock of black hair and a blotchy complexion took George aside and earnestly congratulated him on his good fortune to be working with him. What he did not know about selling the *Child's Self-Educator*, Robinson told him, could be written on his thumbnail. Every salesman who worked on his territory received personal tuition, and there was not a man trained by Edgar Robinson who was not earning at least ten pounds a week.

George became much more enthusiastic after he had heard this, and greatly encouraged when he realized that he was going to be shown how to obtain orders. He was, in fact, given an intensive two-day course in salesmanship along with the other applicants, and then he went out with Robinson and saw for himself how orders could be obtained.

A week later George was canvassing on his own, and by sheer hard work managed to earn three pounds ten shillings a week. He soon discovered that Robinson's stories about salesmen earning more than this amount was so much sales talk, but, as George knew that he was not likely to get anything else, he stuck to the job, and continued to make enough to keep himself going.

The job of calling from door to door was a great blow to George's pride. At first his shyness and timidity were a handicap. He would stand outside a house, screwing up his courage for such a time that people would become suspicious of him, and once one old lady telephoned for the police. Many people slammed the door in his face, while others were extremely rude to him. This treatment greatly increased his inferiority complex: there were moments when he suffered from moods of black depression, and he was driven more and more to rely on his fantasies of violence and adventure to sustain his bruised ego.

While Ella was tidying the room, George wrestled with his hangover. He had spent the previous evening at the King's Arms, and had drunk one too many beers. Feeling the tea might help him recover, he reached for the cup.

"Seen Leo this morning?" he asked, for something to say.

Ella gave the dressing-table a final flick and moved to the door.

"He's somewhere around," she said indifferently. She was plainly disappointed that George wasn't in a talkative mood. "The silly thing! Wot you see in that cat I can't imagine. Not that I don't like cats meself, but not an old stupid like Leo. Leo indeed! I wonder who gave 'im that name. As much like a lion as I am. 'E's frightened of 'is own shadow. I reckon it's crool to keep 'im alive. 'E never comes near anyone but you, Mr George. But I must say 'e does seem to 'ave taken a proper fancy to you, doesn't 'e?"

George's face lit up. "Animals like me," he said simply. "Poor old Leo! He must have had a pretty rotten time as a kitten, I should think. He's all right once he knows you."

Ella sniffed. "He's 'ad enough opportunity to know me," she returned, "but 'e bolts as soon as 'e sees me. 'E's daft, that's wot 'e is," and she reluctantly took herself off to make the ten beds and clean the ten bedrooms of the other boarders who had, three hours since, gone off to their various offices.

As soon as she had gone, George slipped out of bed and opened the door. He left it ajar, went over to the dressing-table, found his cigarette case and then returned to bed. He left his door ajar every morning, for as soon as Ella was out of the way, Leo would come to see him.

When George first came to the boarding-house, Leo had been as terrified of him as of everyone else. The room George took over had been vacant for some little time, and the cat had used it as a kind of sanctuary. Several times George, coming home late, had found Leo curled up on his bed. The moment he opened the door the cat had sprung from the bed and had shot past him out of the room, a terrified streak of black fur.

George had been sorry for Leo. He saw, with a startling flash of intuition, that Leo was very much like himself. The cat was big and imposing, but its soul was as timid as George's. He understood the cat's fear of strangers, and he made up his mind that he would win its confidence.

For two months George wooed Leo's affection. He

bought fish, which he left under his bed, he was always careful to enter his room slowly and without noise, and he would sit motionless if the cat ever visited him. It took a long time before Leo would stay with him. Even then the cat would spring away if he came near. But gradually, with inexhaustible patience, George won its affection. Now Leo came regularly every morning and kept him company.

This was a major triumph for George. He was not only flattered, but his interest, filling many hours of otherwise lonely boredom, developed into an intense love for the animal. He depended on Leo for company, and their association afforded an outlet for his own repressed affection.

While he was thinking about the cat, he felt a weight on the bed and, opening his eyes, he found Leo looking at him. The cat was a big black Persian with enormous yellow eyes and long whiskers. It stood on George's chest, padding with its paws while it sniffed delicately at George's face.

"Can't stay long, old boy," George said, stroking its head with tender fingers. "I've got work to do this morning. Come on, settle for a moment," and he pulled the cat down beside him.

He continued to talk to it, stroking and fondling it, feeling at peace with life, grateful to the cat for its company, lavishing on it the urgent, rather overpowering love which unconsciously he yearned for himself.

## 2

George Fraser wandered into the saloon bar of the King's Arms at ten minutes to one o'clock. He walked to his favourite corner at the far end of the long bar counter and propped himself up against the wall.

The bar was not particularly full, and after a moment or so, Gladys, the barmaid, a big, good-natured looking girl, detached herself from a group of men with whom she had been gossiping and came towards him, wiping the counter with a swab as she did so.

"How's yourself?" she asked, giving George a fleeting smile as she drew a pint of mild and bitter, which she set before him.

George tipped his hat and returned her smile. He liked Gladys. She had served him regularly for the past four months, and he had a vague feeling that she was interested in him. Anyway, George always felt at home with barmaids, considering them to be friendly, comfortable women, not likely to jeer at him nor to pass unkind remarks about him behind his back.

It gave him considerable pleasure to enter the saloon bar of the King's Arms and receive a pint of beer without actually asking for it, and for Gladys to inquire how he was. These trifling attentions made him feel that he was one of her special clients, and he regarded the King's Arms as a kind of second home.

"I'm fine," he said. "No need to ask how you are. You always look wonderful." He paid for his beer. "Don't know how you do it."

Gladys laughed. "Hard work agrees with me," she confessed, glancing in the mirror behind the bar. She patted her mass of dark, wavy hair and admired herself for a brief moment. "Your Mr Robinson was in last night. Oo's his new friend – young, white-faced feller with a scar? I haven't seen him around 'ere before."

George shook his head. "Don't ask me. Robo's always picking up waifs and strays. He can't bear his own company for more than five minutes." He winked and went on, "Case of a bad conscience, if you ask me."

"Well, I dunno about that," Gladys said, polishing that part of the counter within reach of her arm. "But this feller looked like a bad conscience if ever anyone did. 'E fair gave me the creeps."

"Go on." George's rather vacant blue eyes widened. "How's that?"

Gladys sniffed. "Something fishy about 'im. I wouldn't like to run into 'im in the dark."

George was mildly intrigued. "Oh, come off it," he said, smiling. "You're imagining things."

An impatient tapping on the counter reminded Gladys that she was neglecting her duties.

"Shan't be a jiffy," she said. "There's old Mr Henry. I mustn't keep 'im waiting."

George nodded understandingly. He was used to carrying on interrupted conversations with Gladys. It was understood between them that customers should not be kept waiting no matter how pressing the topic of discussion happened to be.

He glanced at Mr Henry, who was waiting impatiently

for a small whisky. Mr Henry, like George, was a regular customer of the King's Arms. He was a thin, red-faced little man, and he kept to himself. George often speculated what he did for a living. This morning, George decided that there was something rather mysterious about Mr Henry. He drank a little of his beer and relaxed against the wall.

*... Gladys served Mr Henry with a whisky and soda, exchanged a few words with him, and then came towards George Fraser. Her eyes were alight with excitement, her face had paled.*

*"Something's up," George Fraser thought as he pushed his empty tankard towards her.*

*Gladys picked up the tankard, and while she filled it, she said in a voice scarcely above a whisper, "That's Davie Bentillo. I recognized him in spite of his disguise."*

*George Fraser stiffened. He glanced quickly at the little, red-faced man. Davie Bentillo! What a bit of luck! Every cop in the country was looking for Davie. It could be, although the disguise was superb. He was the same height as Scarletti's ferocious gunman. Yes, it was the same nose and eyes ...Gladys was right!*

*"Nice work, kid," George Fraser said, and his hand crept to his hip pocket to close over the cold butt of his gun.*

*"Be careful, Mr Fraser," Gladys breathed, her face waxen with fear. "He's dangerous."*

Edgar Robinson jogged George's elbow. "Wake up, cock," he said, settling himself comfortably on a stool. "You look like sleeping beauty this morning. Bin on the tiles?"

George Fraser blinked at him, sighed and said, "Morning."

Robinson took off his thick glasses and polished them

with a grimy handkerchief. Without his glasses his eyes looked like small, green gooseberries. "Be a pal and ask me what I'll have," he said, showing his yellow teeth as he beamed at George. "I've bin and left me money at home."

George eyed him without enthusiasm. "Well, what'll it be?"

Robinson put his glasses on again and looked round the bar. "Well, I'd like a double whisky," he said, after a moment's thought, "but seeing as 'ow you're paying, I'll make it a beer."

George signalled to Gladys.

"What's up?" Robinson asked, eyeing George keenly. "Very strong and silent this morning, aren't you? Gotta touch of pox or something?"

"I'm all right," George said shortly. He disliked Edgar Robinson, while admiring his ability as a salesman.

"That's the spirit," Robinson returned, beaming again. "Must have my boys on the top line. The right mental attitude gets the business, you know. If you're worrying about anything, 'ow can you hope to get orders?" He smiled his horsey smile as Gladys joined them. "Hello, my pretty," he went on; " 'pon my soul, she gets more desirable every day. Wouldn't you like a little session with our Gladys in the park, George?"

George looked uncomfortable. Sex embarrassed him, and Robinson was always making him feel awkward by his loose talk in mixed society.

"Oh, shut up," he growled, and without looking at Gladys he muttered, "Give him a mild and bitter, please."

Robinson grinned. "Glad, my girl, I believe we've the privilege of drinking in the company of a virgin. Not being one meself, and knowing from the saucy look in your eye, my pretty, that you'd make no false claims, we knows who we're talking abaht, don't we?"

Gladys giggled, drew another pint of beer and set it before Robinson. She glanced at George's red face, winked at him and said, "Don't you take any notice of him. It's those who talk the most that do the least."

Robinson dug George in the ribs. "She's calling you a dirty old man, George," he cackled. "Maybe you are. What's your particular vice, old boy? 'Ere Glad, don't go away; you might learn something."

"I can't waste my time talking nonsense with you," Gladys returned. "I've got my work to do."

When she had gone to the other end of the bar, Robinson stared at her broad back for a second or so and then winked at George.

"Rather fancy her meself," he said, his small green eyes lighting up. "Think she's a proposition?"

George scowled at him. "Oh, dry up," he snapped. "Can't you get your mind off women for five minutes?"

Robinson gave him a sneering, amused smile. "Funny bloke, aren't you, George?" he said, taking out a crumpled packet of Woodbines. " 'Ere, have a smoke. The trouble with you, me boy, is you're repressed. You're scared of sex, and if you ain't careful, it'll fester inside you, and then anything may happen. Me – I'm as free as the air. It's just a cuppa tea to me. When I want it, I have it, and that way it don't do me any 'arm."

George lit his cigarette, cleared his throat and produced a big envelope from the "poacher's" pocket he had had made inside his coat.

"Now then," he said. "Let's see what I've got to do." He took from the envelope a packet of printed forms and a sheet of paper containing the addresses of the local schools. "I'm planting more forms this afternoon. I've to collect others from Radlet Road school. Ought to get something from them, and this evening I'll make some calls."

Robinson glanced down the list of addresses and grunted. "All right," he said. "Still working Wembley? Where are you going next?"

"Alperton, Harlesden and Sudbury," George returned. "I've got it all doped out. There's a good bunch of council houses in all those districts, and they haven't been worked for some time now."

"I almost forgot," Robinson said, blowing a thin stream of smoke to the ceiling. "I've taken on a new salesman. Thought I'd put him under your wing, George. You can show him the ropes, and he'll be company for you."

"You mean you want me to train him?" George asked eagerly, his big face lighting up.

Robinson nodded. "That's the idea," he said. "He's new to the game, and you know all the tricks by now; so I thought you might as well give me a hand."

"Why, certainly," George said. He was delighted that Robinson should pay him such a compliment. "Yes, I think I can teach him a few tricks. Who is he?"

"Chap named Sydney Brant. Rum kind of a bloke, but he might get some business." Robinson glanced at the clock above the bar. "He ought to be here any minute now. Take him out this afternoon and show him how to plant the forms, will you? And then take him with you when you make your calls tonight. Anyway, I don't have to tell you what to do, do I?"

"You leave it to me," George said, straightening up and feeling important. "Have another beer, Robo," and he signalled to Gladys.

Robinson gave him a sly, amused look. He could see that George was delighted to be given some responsibility. That suited Robinson, as he was getting tired of showing new men how to get orders. If George wanted to do it, so much the better. Robinson had long since given up serious canvassing. He relied on his salesmen to get orders, and took from each an overriding commission. Now that George was showing promise as a reliable salesman, Robinson planned to shift the training onto his shoulders, and in time he hoped he would not have to do any of the work at all.

Gladys gave them two more pints, and George, who was hungry, ordered a beef sandwich.

"Want one?" he asked Robinson.

"Not just now," Robinson returned. "It's a bit early for me. I've only just got up."

While George ate his sandwich, the bar began to fill up, and soon the place was crowded.

Suddenly, edging through the crowd at the bar, George noticed a thick-set young fellow with an untidy shock of straw-coloured hair coming towards them.

There was something about this young man that immediately arrested George's attention. He had a livid scar – a burn – on his right cheek. The skin was raw and unsightly. George guessed the burn had only just been freed of its dressing. Then there was a look of starved intensity in his face, and his grey–blue eyes, heartless and bitter, were the most unfriendly George had ever seen.

This young man – he could not have been more than twenty-one or -two – came up to Robinson and stood at his side without saying anything. He was wearing worn grey flannel trousers and a shabby tweed coat. His dark blue shirt was crumpled and his red tie looked like a piece of coloured string.

Robinson said, "Ah! There you are. I was wondering

where you'd got to. This is George Fraser, one of my best salesmen. George, this is Sydney Brant, I was telling you about."

George flushed with pleasure to be called one of Robinson's best salesmen, but when he met Brant's eyes he experienced a strange uneasiness. There was something disconcerting about Brant's blank face, the indifferent way he stood, as if he didn't give a damn for anyone. The raw, puckered wound upset George, who had a slightly squeamish stomach in spite of his fascination for violence and bloodshed.

"How do you do?" he said, looking away. "Robo was just saying he wanted me to show you the ropes. I'll certainly do my best."

Brant stared at him indifferently and said nothing.

"You'll find old George knows all the tricks," Robinson said breezily.

Why couldn't the fellow say something? George thought. He glanced down at his tankard, swished the beer round in it and looked up abruptly at Brant.

"Robo says he wants you and me to work together," he said. "We – we might do some work this afternoon."

Brant nodded. His eyes shifted to Robinson and then back to George. He still appeared to find the situation called for no comment.

Robinson was not at his ease. He picked his nose and smiled absently at himself in the big mirror behind the bar.

"You couldn't do better than work with George," he said, addressing himself in the mirror. "You'll be surprised when you see old George in action." He patted George's arm. "We'll make a big success out of young Syd, won't we?"

"Don't call me Syd," the young man said in a low, clipped voice. "My name's Brant."

19

Robinson flashed his toothy smile, but his eyes looked startled. "Must be matey," he said, looking into the mirror again. He adjusted his frayed tie. "Can't do business if we aren't matey, can we, George? You call me Robo, I'll call you Syd – right?"

"My name's Brant," the young man repeated and stared through Robinson with bored, cold indifference.

There was an awkward pause, then George said, "Well, have a drink. What'll it be?"

Brant shrugged his thin shoulders. "I don't drink," he returned. "Still, I don't mind a lemonade," and his eyes went to Gladys, who came along the bar at George's signal.

George, seeing her give a quick, alarmed look at Brant, realized that this was the fellow she had been telling him about. Well, she was right. He could understand now what she meant when she had said that he'd given her the creeps. George scratched his head uneasily. He was reluctant to admit it, but the fellow gave him the creeps too.

"A lemonade for Mr Brant," he said, winking at Gladys.

Gladys poured out the lemonade, set it before Brant and, without a word, walked away to the far end of the bar.

Again there was an awkward pause, then Robinson finished his beer, wiped his thick lips on his coat sleeve and slid off the stool.

"Well, I'm off," he announced. "I've got several little jobs to do. I'll leave you in George's capable hands. Don't forget, boys, every door is a door of opportunity. The right mental attitude gets the business. If you haven't the right MA, you can't hope to conquer the other man's mind. You want your prospect to buy the *Child's Self-Educator*. He doesn't want to have anything to do with it because he doesn't know anything about it. It's your job to convince him that the CSE is the best investment he can buy. Get your prospect agreeing with you from the very start of your sales talk. Get inside the house. Never attempt to sell a prospect on his doorstep. Know when to stop talking and when to produce the order form." He beamed at George and went on, "George knows all about it. Follow those rules and you can't go wrong. Good luck and good hunting." His toothy smile faltered a trifle as he felt Brant's sneering eyes searching his face. With a wave of his hand, Robinson pushed his way through the crowd and out into the street.

George stared after him, an admiring look in his eyes. "He knows the business all right," he said enthusiastically. "Believe me, he's one of the best salesmen I've ever met."

Brant sipped his lemonade and grimaced. "You can't have met many," he said, staring past George at the group of men at the end of the bar.

George started. "What do you mean? Why, Robo knows every trick in this game better than any salesman working for the Wide World."

Brant's expressionless eyes shifted from the group of men to George's flushed face.

"He's living on a bunch of suckers who're fools enough to let him get away with it," he said in flat, cold tones, like a judge pronouncing sentence.

George's sense of fair play was outraged. "But it's business. He trains us, so naturally we pay him a small commission. We couldn't sell anything unless he tells us where to go and how to get our contacts. Be fair, old man."

The white, thin face jeered at him. "What do you call a small commission?"

"He told you, didn't he?"

"I know what he told me, but what did he tell you?" Brant jerked a long lock of hair out of his eyes.

George put his tankard down on the bar. He felt it was time this young fellow was taken down a peg or two. "We give Robo ten per cent of what we make. That's fair, isn't it? We get a quid for every order and we pay Robo two bob. Can't call that profiteering, can you?" He studied Brant anxiously. "I mean Robo trains us and arranges our territory. Two bob isn't much, is it?"

Brant again jerked the lock of hair out of his eyes, impatiently, irritably. "What makes you think the Company doesn't pay more than a pound for an order?"

George stared at him. He felt he was on the brink of an unpleasant discovery; something that he didn't want to hear. "What are you hinting at?" he asked uneasily.

"The Company pays thirty bob on every order sent in. That's why your pal Robinson makes you send your orders through him. He not only takes two bob off you, but ten bob as well. I took the trouble to 'phone the Company and ask them what they'd pay me if I sent in my orders direct. They said thirty bob."

George suddenly hated this young man with his straw-coloured hair and his disgusting scar. Why couldn't he have left him in peace? He had trusted Robinson. They had got along fine together. Robinson had been his only companion. Robinson had said that George was his best salesman, and he had given him responsibility. He had always been at hand to smear a paste of flattery on George's bruised ego. George thought of all the past orders he had given him, and he felt a little sick.

"Oh," he said, after a long pause, "so that's how it is, is it?"

Brant finished his lemonade. "Should have thought you'd

found that out for yourself," he said in his soft, clipped voice.

George clenched his fists. "The dirty rat!" he exclaimed, trying to get a vicious look in his eyes. "Why, he'd 've been taken for a ride for that if he'd been in the States."

Brant smiled secretly. "Is that where you come from?"

"Sure," George said, realizing that this was a chance to re-establish himself. "But it's some time ago. I must be slipping. Fancy letting a cheap crook like Robinson pull a fast one on me. If ever Kelly got to hear about it, he'd rib me to death."

The thin, cold face remained expressionless. "Kelly?"

George picked up his tankard and drank. The beer tasted warm and flat. Without looking at Brant, he said, "Yeah – Frank Kelly. I used to work for him in the good old days."

"Kelly?" Brant was still and tense. "You mean, the gangster?"

George nodded. "Sure," he said, feeling an infuriating rush of blood mounting to his face. "Poor old Frank. He certainly had a bad break." He set his tankard down, and in an endeavour to conceal his confusion, he lit a cigarette. "But, of course, that was some time ago."

Brant's thin mouth twisted. "Still, now you know, you're not going to let Robinson get away with this, are you?"

George suddenly saw the trap he had dug for himself. If Brant was to think anything of him, he'd have to go through with it.

"You bet I'm not," he growled, scowling fiercely into his empty tankard.

"Good," Brant said, a veiled, jeering look in his eyes. "That'll save me some trouble. You'd know how to talk to him, wouldn't you?"

"I'll fix him," George threatened, feeling a growing

dismay. "No one's ever pulled a fast one on me without regretting it."

"I'll come with you," Brant said softly. "I'd like to see how you handle him."

George shook his head. "You'd better leave this to me," he said feebly. "I might lose my temper with him. I don't want witnesses."

"I'll come with you all the same." Brant's thin lips tightened. "You don't have to worry about me."

They looked at each other. George felt himself wilt under the baleful look that had jumped into Brant's eyes.

"Okay," he muttered uneasily. "You can come along if you want to."

There was a long pause and then he said, "Well, we'd better do some work. You ready?"

Brant nodded. "Yes." He pushed himself away from the counter. "Tonight'll be interesting," he added, and followed George out of the bar.

# 3

George Fraser had little to say while he and Brant travelled by underground to Wembley. Talking was difficult in the swaying, roaring train, and he wanted time to think over what Brant had told him.

If what Brant had said were true, then Robinson had cheated him out of at least twenty pounds. George considered what he could have done with all that money. Twenty pounds! Why, he could have bought a second-hand car, he thought dismally. He had always wanted a car. He had no idea what he was going to say to Robinson when he saw him that night. If it hadn't been for Brant, he probably wouldn't have had the nerve to raise the matter at all; but now he had to make a show before this unpleasant, disturbing intruder. He would have to make a shot at persuading Robinson to fork up the twenty pounds. He hadn't much hope, as Robinson never seemed to have any money, but it might be worth trying. Of course, Robinson might turn nasty. He might even demand the return of all George's specimen copies of the *Child's Self-Educator* and then tell George to go to blazes. Then what would he do? It'd mean he'd be out of work again, and that thought appalled George.

Well, it was no good worrying, he decided gloomily. After all, Robinson was cheating him, and he couldn't expect to get away with it. He'd tackle him politely and firmly, and hope for the best. It wouldn't do for Brant to think he couldn't handle the situation. Brant seemed now to be regarding him with a little more respect since George had mentioned Frank Kelly. George pulled a face. He hoped Brant wouldn't say anything about that to anyone. He shot a furtive look at the blank, hard face. All he could see was the disagreeable, raw-looking scar and one vacant, glittering eye. Nasty young customer, he thought uneasily. Proper dead-end kid. He wondered if Brant believed him. You couldn't tell where you were with a fellow with such an expressionless face. Anyway Brant hadn't asked any questions, and he seemed to have accepted Kelly after a momentary glimmer of surprise.

The train pulled into Wembley station, and with a sigh of relief George got to his feet. He was glad to have something to do. He didn't want to think about Brant nor what he was going to say to Robinson that night. He forced this disagreeable prospect to the back of his mind and shambled along beside his companion.

"Now, our first job is to call at Radlet Road school," he said, as they walked briskly up the High Road. "I called in there yesterday and planted our circulars. You see, unless we know where the kids live, we can't get any orders. It isn't like selling vacuum cleaners, for instance. With vacuum cleaners it's a straight door-to-door canvass. But in our line we have to know which homes have children and which haven't." He paused while he fished a cigarette from a crumpled carton and offered it to Brant.

"I don't smoke," Brant said shortly. They were the first words he had uttered since leaving the train.

"Oh, all right," George looked at him blankly, and lit up. They moved on, and George said, "Well, we've got to get the names and addresses of all the kids at the various Council schools. It isn't easy, because the teachers don't want to help us. You'd think they'd be glad for the kids to have the books, wouldn't you? But not they." George breathed heavily through his thick nose. "Of course, some of 'em do help, otherwise we'd get nowhere. But the majority are a lazy, suspicious lot. We have to persuade the teacher to pass our forms round the class and get the kids to put their names and addresses on them; then we collect the forms next day and make our calls. It sounds simple, doesn't it, but you wait … you'll see what I mean before long."

All the time he was talking, Brant strode along at his side, his face expressionless and his eyes blank. For all George knew, he hadn't heard a word George had said.

This indifferent attitude annoyed George. All right, he thought, lapsing into a sulky silence, you think it's child's play, but just you wait. You'll find it's not all beer and skittles. You wait until you try to get an order. Be as superior as you like, but with a dial like yours you don't stand a hope. Do you think anyone will want to look at you when you try to talk to them? They'll slam the door in your ugly mug, you see if they don't, and it'll serve you right. Take you down a peg or two, my lad. That's what you want. Be superior if that's how you feel, but you're riding for a fall. You can't say I haven't tried to be friendly, but I'm damned if I'm going to put myself out if you don't meet me half way.

He was glad when they reached the school. Now he could show Brant how successfully he had cultivated the headmaster the day before. They crossed the deserted playground and approached the red-brick school building. In spite of his outward show of confidence, George could never enter a school premises without a feeling of guilt. The LCC had forbidden canvassers to call on Secondary and Council schools, and George always had it at the back of his mind that he would run into a visiting school inspector one of these days and be ordered ignominiously from the school.

He paused at the main entrance, and with an uneasy smile pointed out the notice pinned to the door.

"See that?" he said, anxious that Brant should share his own secret uneasiness. " 'Canvassers and salesmen are not permitted on the school premises.' I told you it wasn't easy, didn't I? It's only when the headmaster's friendly that we can get anywhere."

Brant didn't say anything. He glanced at George with sneering contempt in his eyes.

George pushed open the door and entered the long passage, which smelt of disinfectant, floor polish and stale perspiration. They walked down the passage, past a number of classrooms. They could see through the glass partitions into the small rooms, each containing a number of children at desks. The children spotted them, and heads turned in their direction with the precision of a field of corn moving in a wind.

George shrank from their inquisitive, staring eyes. He hunched his great shoulders and hurried on towards the headmaster's office.

The headmaster looked up from his desk and frowned at them. He was a little man, thin and old. Two or three strands of greying hair had been carefully plastered across the baldness of his head. His large, mild eyes were tired, and his shoulders, under his shabby coat, drooped as if the burden of his responsibilities were too much for him.

"Good afternoon, Mr Pickthorn," George said, with the overpowering heartiness he always assumed when working. "What a magnificent day! Too good to be in, but we've all got our living to make, haven't we?" He stood over the headmaster, large, friendly, anxious to please. "We can't all go gadding about when there's work to be done, can we? Noses to the grindstones, eh?" He lowered his voice and winked. "Not that you and me wouldn't like to be at Lord's today."

It had taken George some time to conquer his shyness when meeting strangers, but now that he was sure of what he was going to say, he was becoming quite a fluent, if automatic talker. He hoped that Brant was being impressed. That'd show him how to talk to prospects. Brant would have to shake up his ideas if he thought he was going to make a successful salesman. People liked to have someone call on them who was cheerful and bright.

Mr Pickthorn smiled vaguely and blinked up at George. "Ah," he said, shaking his head sadly. "Yes, Lord's." Then he glanced at Brant, and the friendly look drained out of his eyes. He glanced hurriedly away, his thin mouth tightening.

There! George thought triumphantly. See what happens when they look at your ugly mug. Go on, be superior. I don't care. At least, they don't look away when I talk to them.

Feeling the changing atmosphere, he went on hurriedly, "I was passing, Mr Pickthorn, so I thought I'd pick up those forms I left yesterday. Are they ready?"

Mr Pickthom fiddled with his pen tray, placing the pens and coloured pencils in their racks with exaggerated care. "No," he said, without looking at either of them. "No, I'm afraid they aren't."

George felt his heartiness, bolstered up by the feeling that Mr Pickthorn liked him, oozing away like air from a leaking balloon.

"Well, never mind," he said, with a fixed smile. "You don't have to tell me how busy you are. I know what you headmasters have to do. Work, work, work, all day long.

Suppose I call back tomorrow? Perhaps you'll find time to get them done tomorrow."

Mr Pickthorn continued to fiddle with his pens and pencils. He did not look up. "I've changed my mind," he said abruptly. "As a matter of fact, Mr Herring, my assistant, drew my attention to it. He's quite right, of course. I wasn't thinking. Of course, the books are good. No doubt about that. I've known the *Child's Self-Educator* for many years, but as Mr Herring pointed out, it's encouraging canvassers, and the Council doesn't approve." He opened a drawer and took out the packet of printed forms that George had left with him the day before. "I'm sorry," he went on, pushing the forms across the desk to George. "Now, if you'll excuse me ..." He gave George a fleeting, embarrassed smile, again glanced at Brant, and then pulled a pile of papers towards him.

"You see?" George said, when they were in the street again. "Now we've got no calls for tonight. The rotten little rat! Couldn't do enough for me yesterday. I spent a whole hour listening to him talk about his blasted garden. As if I cared! He promised me faithfully to distribute those forms. Oh, well, it only goes to prove." He fished out his carton of cigarettes and lit one. "We'll have to do a cold canvass tonight. It means wandering up and down a street looking out for kids, asking them where they live, or spotting toys in the windows or gardens. That's a job I hate! Everyone watches you, and sometimes if you do ask the kids who they are, they get scared and start howling."

Brant shoved his hands in his pockets and stared down at his shoes. His indifferent expression infuriated George

"Well, what do we do?" Brant asked, as if to say, this is your mess, and it's up to you to find a way out.

Choking back his irritation, George took out his list of schools and studied it. "We'd better go over to Sherman

Road school," he said. "It's about half a mile from here. That's the best school in the district. If we don't get our forms in there, we're properly in the soup."

Brant shrugged. "All right," he said, falling in step beside George. "So long as we get something done today."

George shot him an angry glance. "It's all very well to criticize," he snapped, "but if you think you can do better, you'd better try."

"I'll take over if you make another mess of it," Brant returned in his clipped, indifferent voice.

George could scarcely believe his ears. He walked on in silence, fuming with rage. If *he* made a mess of it! Of all the cheek! And *he* was teaching this smug brat – that's all he was – a smug brat! He'd take over, would he? All right, they'd see about that. Perhaps it'd be a good idea to let him make a fool of himself. As if anyone would listen to him, with his scar and his straw hair and his shabby clothes. Then George's caution asserted itself. The kids at Sherman Road were of a better class than in any of the other schools. He couldn't afford to take chances with this school. Every form that was filled up might mean an order.

In the school lobby they found the same depressing notice warning canvassers and salesmen that they were trespassing. Underneath this official notice was another notice written and signed by the headmaster.

*Can you read? Then keep out! No canvassers or salesmen will be seen during school hours. Any attempt to enter school premises without an official permit will be immediately reported to the local authorities.*
*Chas. Eccles.*
*Headmaster.*

George read this notice and experienced a sinking feeling in his stomach. "I've never seen anything like this before," he whispered, furtively looking down the passage that led to the classrooms. "Doesn't look very hopeful, does it?"

Brant shrugged. "You can always tell him you can't read," he said with a sneer. "He might even believe you."

George flushed, and without a word walked down the passage to the headmaster's office. He wished that Robinson was with him. Robo would know what to do. He didn't care a damn whom he tackled or how rude people were to him.

George tapped on the door and waited.

"Come in," roared a voice.

They entered a small, bare room. A big, fleshy man, with a large blond moustache on a round, flat face, frowned at them.

"Who are you? What do you want?" he shouted in a voice made harsh by constant bullying.

George gave him a nervous smile. "Good morning, Mr Eccles," he said, his heartiness wavering. "Forgive me for intruding like this, but I was passing, and I felt that you'd be interested to hear that the new edition of the *Child's Self-Educator* is now ready."

Mr Eccles leaned across his desk, his hard little eyes boring into George. "What?" he shouted. "Selling something? Where's your permit?"

George took an involuntary step back. "Now, please don't misunderstand me, Mr Eccles," he said, trying to control his rising colour. "We're not selling anything. It's just that we thought you'd be interested to hear that the new edition of the *Child's Self-Educator* is – er – ready. It's a magnificent job. Two hundred additional coloured plates, and all the maps have been revised. There's more than two hundred thousand additional words, bringing this wonderful work of reference right up to date."

"Hmm," Mr Eccles grunted. "You people are not supposed to be on the school premises, you know. I haven't the time nor the inclination to talk to salesmen. All right, thank you for calling. Good afternoon," and he picked up his pen and began to write.

Had George been alone, he would have slunk out of the room, but the cold, still, hateful figure of Brant made retreat impossible.

"If you'll excuse me, Mr Eccles," George said, his face now the colour of a beetroot, "there's just one other point I would like to raise with you. You know the CSE, of course. You'll agree with me, I'm sure, that it is a most useful set of books and its reputation in the world of letters is second to none. Any child possessing this magnificent work of reference has an obvious advantage over the unfortunate child who is without it. The task of the teacher is considerably lightened if a child can turn to the CSE and find for itself the answer to those awkward questions that a child is always asking his teacher."

Mr Eccles laid down his pen and pushed back his chair. His movements were deliberate and ominous.

"If I thought you were trying to sell something on these premises," he said with deadly calm, "I would give you in charge."

George shuffled his feet. "I assure you, Mr Eccles," he stammered, "I – I have no intention of selling anything, no intention at all. It's just that I hoped for your co-operation. Unless teachers are prepared to assist us, we are unable to let parents know how invaluable the CSE – and who would deny it? – would be in the home."

Mr Eccles rose to his feet. To George, he seemed to grow

in stature, and broaden like a rubber doll that is being inflated. "You're canvassing," Mr Eccles said in an awful voice, "I thought as much. What is the name of your firm?"

George had visions of a complaint being lodged by the LCC. Although the World-Wide Publishing Company was fully aware of the methods used by their salesmen, officially these methods were not recognized. They were all right, so long as there were no complaints. If there were complaints, then the salesmen were sacked.

George stood staring stupidly at Mr Eccles, his face red, his mouth dry and his eyes protruding. He visualized the arrival of the police and being marched through the streets to the police station.

"Well?" Mr Eccles shouted at him, seeing his confusion and enjoying it. "Who's your firm? I'll get to the bottom of this! I'm going to stop you touts bothering me and my staff. Every day someone calls. If it isn't vacuum cleaners, it's silk stockings. If it isn't silk stockings, it's expensive books that no one can afford to buy. I'm going to put a stop to it!"

From somewhere in the rear, where he had been standing, Brant suddenly appeared in front of George. He walked straight up to Mr Eccles and fixed him with his cold, expressionless eyes.

"There is no need to shout," he said, in his soft, clipped voice. "We've been received at all the other schools in this district with courtesy, Mr Eccles. Surely, we are entitled to your courtesy too."

Mr Eccles glared at Brant, then quite suddenly moved back a step.

"We are men trying to do a job of work," Brant went on, his eyes never moving from Eccles' face. "Just as you are trying to do a job of work. As representatives of the World-

Wide Publishing Company we are entitled to a hearing. The World-Wide Publishing Company has been dealing with the teaching profession for two hundred years. Its reputation for integrity and good work is known and commented upon by the London County Council. The *Child's Self-Educator* is known all over the world."

Mr Eccles sat down slowly. It was as if he had suddenly lost the strength in his legs. "World-Wide Publishing Company," he muttered and wrote on his blotting paper. "All right, I'll remember that."

"I want you to remember it," Brant said. "I'm surprised that a man of your experience does not know who published the *Child's Self-Educator*. Have you a set yourself?"

Mr Eccles looked up. "Who – me? No, I haven't. Now, look here, young man – "

"Then you will be glad to hear that you are going to be presented with a set. That's why we've come to see you."

"Presented with a set?" Mr Eccles repeated, his little eyes opening. "You mean *given* a set?"

"Certainly," Brant said, his hands on the desk. "We're anxious that every teacher should have a set of the CSE, but, for obvious reasons, it is not possible to give so many sets away. It has been decided, however, that the headmaster of the best school of each London borough is to be presented with our de luxe, half-calf edition, free, gratis and for nothing."

If Mr Eccles was surprised by this news, George was utterly flabbergasted.

"Well, 'pon my soul," Mr Eccles exclaimed, a sly smile lighting up his face. "Why didn't you say so before? Sit down, young man. I'm sorry I was so abrupt just now, but if you only knew how I'm pestered all day long, you'd appreciate I've got to do something to protect myself."

Brant drew up a chair and sat down. George, standing by the door, was forgotten.

"I understand, Mr Eccles," Brant went on, after a moment's pause, "that your children's handwriting is of an exceptionally high standard. Mr Pickthorn of Trinity School also boasts of a high standard. We are organizing a harmless competition between schools, and I suggest you might like to co-operate. All we need is a specimen of each of your pupils' handwriting, which will be sent to our head office, and the pupil with the best handwriting will be given a beautifully inscribed certificate and ten shillings. Mr Pickthorn has been happy to help us in this scheme, and we would like your pupils to compete against his. Whatever you decide, of course, will not influence my Company's decision to send you the CSE, which should reach you early next month."

"Pickthorn?" Mr Eccles snorted. "That old muddler! None of his brats can write. He's got no method. Why, in a competition, it'd be a walk over." He frowned down at his blotting pad. "I'd like to do it. 'Pon my word, I would. I'd like to wipe old Pickthorn's eye, but it'll disorganize my day. A thing like that'd need a bit of arranging."

Brant shifted in his chair. "It took less than ten minutes at Radlet's," he said quietly. "All you have to do is to get the children to write their names and addresses on a piece of paper, and we will judge their handwriting from that. It is a simple system, and we shall not need to bother you further, as we shall have the name and address of the prizewinner. Surely, that's not going to upset your school?"

Eccles looked a little blank. "Well, if that's all it is," he said doubtfully. "I suppose I could arrange that. All right, I'll do it. Will you call back sometime tomorrow?"

Brant stared at him with bored eyes. "We have a lot of ground to cover, Mr Eccles. Could we wait? It shouldn't take a few minutes." He paused, and before Mr Eccles could speak, he went on, "By the way, I suppose you would like a bookcase for your set of the CSE? I think I could persuade the Company to part with one. It's a nice piece of furniture, light oak with glass panels."

Mr Eccles got to his feet. "Yes," he said, beaming, "that sounds magnificent. Hmm, yes, by all means." He rubbed his hands together. "Well now, you wait here and I'll get these kids to work. I'll be as quick as I can."

As soon as he left the room, George said, "Have you gone mad? What are you playing at? The Company doesn't give sets away, let alone bookcases. They don't even sell bookcases."

Brant stared at him in a bored, detached way. "He doesn't know that," he said, and his thin mouth sneered.

"Well, he soon will when the books don't turn up," George said, now thoroughly agitated. "He'll report us. Why, he might even tell the police. There'll be a hell of a stink about this. And what's all this about handwriting competitions? I really think you must be out of your mind."

Brant looked out of the window. "Can't you see?" he said with that patient voice that people reserve for tiresome, questioning children. "We're going to get the names and addresses of all the brats in this school. That's what you want, isn't it? You made a mess of it, so I've fixed it. I said I would, didn't I?"

"You'll jolly well pay the ten bob out of your own pocket. I'm not going to throw money away like that," George snapped, flushing angrily.

The cold eyes flickered. "Don't be wet," Brant said. "No

one's going to pay ten bob. Let the brat whistle for it."

"What?" George exclaimed, starting forward. "You're not even going to give a prize after telling all those lies?"

"You dumb, or something?" Brant's face showed a faint curiosity. "Your pal Kelly wouldn't pay 'em a nickel, would he? What's the matter with you – slipping?" He stared at George until George had to look away. "Anyway, why should you worry? We won't be here next month. They don't know our names, and if they complain to the Company, we can deny it. It's their word against ours."

The enormity of such a swindle paralyzed George. He sat down and stared stupidly at Brant.

"It's cheating," he said at last. "I – I don't know what to say."

"Aw, dry up!" Brant said, a vicious snarl in his voice. "The whole business is a racket. The Company doesn't care how you get business so long as you don't tell 'em. They don't pay you a salary and they don't care if you starve. All they're interested in is to get a mug to sell their books. Robinson cheats us out of ten bob on every order we get. Do you think he cares? He doesn't give a damn so long as he gets his rake off. These teachers are only out for what they can get. It's a racket from start to finish." He leaned forward, two faint red spots on his thin cheeks. "It's us or them. If you don't like it, then get the hell out of it and leave me to handle it. I'm out for what I can get, and I'm going to get it. So, shut up!"

George flinched away from the savage anger that faced him, and for a long time the room was silent except for the distant sound of children's voices coming from the classrooms.

# 4

"If it rains," George had said to Brant, looking at the mass of black cloud slowly creeping across the sky, "we shan't be able to work tonight. It's no good calling on people if you're dripping wet. They don't ask you in, and just try selling anything standing on a doorstep with rain running down the back of your neck."

Well, it was raining all right. From his bedroom window George looked down at the deserted street, the pavements black and shiny with rain, and water running in the gutters.

It was a few minutes past six. The little, dingy room was dark and chilly. George had moved the armchair to the window so that he had at least something to look at. It was extraordinary how lonely this room could be. No one seemed to be moving in the house. George supposed that Ella and Mrs Rhodes were in the basement preparing supper. The other boarders seldom came in before seven o'clock: that was the time when George went out. He had the house, as far as he knew, to himself.

He decided that the results of the afternoon's work had been satisfactory. On the mantelpiece was a packet of names and addresses neatly mounted on card and sorted into "walking order". All good calls.

George was rather pleased that it was raining. It would be nice to have an evening off. He had done well the previous evening, and he was three pounds in hand. If he did no further work that week, he would still be all right. At half past six, he decided, he would go over to the King's Arms and spend the evening in his favourite corner. He liked the atmosphere of the pub. He was quite content to remain there until closing time, watching the lively activity, listening to the snatches of conversation and seeing Gladys cope, astonishingly efficient, with the constant demand for drinks. Perhaps he would be lucky tonight and find someone who would talk to him. He would have his supper there, and when closing time came he would have an early night.

After staring out of the window for several minutes, he became bored with the rain-swept, deserted street, and, leaving his armchair, he crossed the room to his dressing-table. Pulling open the bottom drawer, he fumbled beneath his spare shirts and underwear until his hand closed over a cardboard box. He took the box back to the window and sat down, placing the box carefully on his knee.

As he was about to lift the lid of the box, he heard a distinct noise, as if someone were pushing at his door.

An extraordinary expression of guilt and fright crossed his heavy features. Springing quickly to his feet, he thrust the box out of sight under the chair cushion. He stood listening, his head on one side and his eyes half closed. Again the door creaked. Cautiously, noiselessly, he walked to the door and jerked it open. Leo came languidly into the room, glanced up at him with enormous yellow eyes and then leapt up onto the bed.

"Hello, old son," George said, closing the door. "You gave me quite a fright."

He stroked the cat for several minutes. His thick, gentle fingers probed the cat's body, moving caressingly over its head, into the hollow of its shoulder blades, under its chin.

The cat remained still, its eyes closed and its sleek body vibrating as it purred.

The room seemed to George to be suddenly cosy now that he was no longer alone. The rain against the window no longer looked depressing. He was grateful to Leo for coming all the way from the basement to see him, and, bending down, he rubbed his face against the cat's long fur.

Leo rolled on its side, stretched, touched his face lightly with its paw, its claws carefully sheathed. When at last it had settled itself on the bed in a big, furry ball, George returned to his chair. He recovered the cardboard box from under the cushion and sat down again. A glance round the room, a glance out into the darkening street and a moment to listen, assured him that he would not be disturbed. Then he opened the box and took from it a heavy Luger pistol. As his hand closed over the long wooden and metal butt, his face lit up. He laid the box on the floor at his side and examined the pistol as if he had never seen it before. The cat watched him with sleepy, bored eyes.

George's foster father had brought this Luger pistol back from France as a souvenir of the Battle of the Somme. It was in perfect working order, and with it was a box of twenty-five cartridges.

For years George had coveted this pistol. Twice he had been soundly thrashed when caught handling it. But nothing could discourage his desire to own it. As he grew up, the desire increased. As his imagination became more vivid and the rôles he selected for himself to play in his mind-fantasies became more violent, so the desire to possess this exciting weapon became more unbearable.

When he heard that his foster father had been knocked down and killed by a speeding car, George had no feeling of shock, nor of loss. He received the news in silence, thinking that now, at last, the pistol would be his.

He vividly remembered the scene. The fat, red-faced police sergeant who was doing his best to break the news as gently as his clumsy tongue could manage, his foster mother's white, frightened face and his own feeling of pending calamity.

"Dead," the police sergeant had said. "Very painful business, Ma'am. Perhaps you'd come to the 'ospital ..."

George was fourteen at the time. He knew what death meant. He knew that the man who had acted as his father would never again come into the little dark hall, hang up his hat and coat and call, as he always called, "Anyone in?" He would never again say, looking round the door, a frown on his fat, heavy face, "Put that damn pistol down. How many more times do I have to tell you not to touch it?" It meant that the pistol was now without an owner. His foster mother had never taken any interest in it. She probably would never think of it, never ask for it. So, while the police sergeant was still muttering and mumbling, George had slipped from the room and gone directly to the place where the pistol was concealed. He would never forget the ecstatic surge of emotion that had flowed through him as he carried the cardboard box from his foster father's room to his own. For thirteen years the pistol had remained George's most cherished possession.

Every day he found time to take the pistol from its box. He cleaned it, polished its black metal and removed and replaced its magazine. It gave George an immense feeling of superiority to hold this heavy weapon in his hand. He would imagine with satisfaction how those who had been rude to him during his evening's work would react if they were suddenly confronted with this pistol. He pictured Mr

Eccles' reaction if he had produced the Luger, and the horror and fear that would have come to the big, flat face with its ridiculous blond moustache.

George's finger curled round the trigger, and his face became grim.

…*"Get a fistful of cloud," George Fraser snarled, ramming his rod into Eccles' back. "We want those names and we're going to have 'em."*

*Sydney Brant, white-faced, his eyes wide with alarm, crouched against the wall.*

*"Don't shoot him, George," he gasped. "For God's sake, be careful with that gun."*

*"Take it easy, Syd," George Fraser returned with a confident smile. "I've stood enough from this rat." He jabbed Eccles again with the gun. "Come on, are you giving me the names or do I have to ventilate your hide?"*

*"I'll do anything," Eccles quavered. "Don't shoot – I'll do anything you say."*

*"Get on with it, then," George Fraser said impatiently, "and if you try to pull a fast one, I'll blast you!"*

*When the terrified man had left the room, George Fraser wandered to the desk and sat on it, swinging his legs. He winked at Brant, who was gaping at him in open admiration* …

George sighed. That was the way to treat swine like Eccles. He fondled the gun. Brant wouldn't be so keen to sneer and jeer if he thought George would stick this suddenly into his ribs. George had no time for cheap tricks. Look at the way Brant had got those names and addresses. Just a cheap trick. If that was the way he was going to cover the territory, Wembley would be useless for another World-Wide salesman to work. Of course, Brant wouldn't care. He was just a selfish, small-minded trickster. So long as he got what he wanted he didn't think of anyone else.

George pulled the magazine from the gun and turned it over absently between his fingers. Still, there was something about Brant. He was more powerful, more domineering than George. George knew that. But George with the Luger was more than a match for anyone, including Brant.

George picked up the oily rag at the bottom of the box and wiped the gun over carefully. Then he picked up the wooden box of cartridges and slid off the lid. The cartridges were packed in rows of five, tight and shiny. He had never put a cartridge into the magazine. He always made a point of keeping the cartridges away from the pistol. Having cleaned the weapon, he would return it to its cardboard box before taking out each cartridge and polishing the brass cases. He had never wished to fire the gun, and the idea of feeding these small, shiny cartridges into the magazine alarmed him. He had read so much about gun accidents that he was acutely conscious how easily something tragic might happen. In spite of his violent imagination, he would have been horrified if, through his own carelessness, anyone was hurt.

Time was getting on. It still rained, but rain never bothered George. He put the cartridges back in the box, and carried it to its hiding-place among his shirts. Then he went to the cupboard over his washstand and took from it a bottle of milk and an opened tin of sardines.

"Come on, Leo," he called, holding up the tin for the cat to see.

Leo was at his side in a bound, and began twining its great, heavy body round his legs.

George put the tin down on a sheet of newspaper and

filled his soap dish with milk.

"There you are, old son," he said, his face softening with pleasure. "Now I'll go out and get my supper."

Out in the street, the rain was cold on his face and the wind beat against him. As he hurried along, he felt the urge to sing or shout for no reason at all except that driving rain and a boisterous wind gave him a feeling of freedom.

The saloon bar of the King's Arms was almost deserted. It was early yet – not quite a quarter to seven – and only three of the usual *habitués* had braved the weather. George hung up his hat and mack, and went to his favourite corner.

"Hello," Gladys said, smiling. " 'Ere we are again."

"That's right," George said, sitting on a stool and looking at the cold meats, pickles and bowls of salad and beetroot with a hungry eye. "Nasty night, isn't it?"

"Wretched," Gladys agreed. "I've got some nice cold pork if you fancy it, or some beef."

George said he thought he'd try the pork.

"That was the bloke with the scar you were talking about, wasn't it?" he asked as she cut him a liberal helping.

"That's 'im," Gladys said darkly. "I was sorry to see you going off with 'im. Mark my words, 'e's a bad 'un. I know a bad 'un when I see 'im."

"He's working for Robinson," George said, feeling that he should excuse himself. "Can't say I like him myself."

"I should think not indeed," Gladys said firmly. "You watch out. A fellow like that could get you into trouble quicker than wink."

"Oh, I don't know about that," George said a little crossly. Did she take him for a child? "I can look after myself all right."

"I'm glad to hear it," Gladys returned, as if she didn't believe him. She set the plate before him, gave him a roll and butter and a pint of mild and bitter, and then hurried off to serve another customer.

George was quite content to keep in his corner, away from the main bar, and eat his supper, read the evening paper and watch Gladys cope with the bustling activity. The bar was filling up now, and the atmosphere became damp and steamy.

No one paid George any attention. Mr Henry came in and nodded absently to him, but immediately looked away, as if he were nervous that George would wish to join him. Other *habitués* came in. They also nodded to George, but it was a disinterested greeting more from habit than anything else.

His meal finished, George lit a cigarette, pushed his tankard forward so that Gladys, when she had a moment, could see that he wanted it filled, and settled down to the crossword puzzle. The warm, damp atmosphere, the buzz of conversation, the click of billiard balls in the next room, soothed him. It was, he thought, the nicest, most homely atmosphere a man could wish to be in.

At nine-thirty he called for his last pint. One for the road, he told himself. He was pleasantly sleepy, and he looked forward to stretching out in bed. Perhaps Leo would keep him company. Tomorrow still seemed a long way off, and George decided that perhaps, after all, life wasn't so bad.

A hand reached out and touched his arm. George started, and peered at Sydney Brant, at first in blank surprise, then in embarrassed confusion. He felt blood rising to his face, and he nearly upset his beer.

Brant wore no overcoat; his threadbare jacket and worn trousers were black with rain.

"Hello," George said awkwardly. "You gave me quite a

start. What are you doing here?"

Brant leaned up against the counter.

"I'm looking for you," he said. "I thought you'd be here."

"Well, you only just caught me," George said lamely. "I – I was just going to bed."

Brant eyed him contemptuously. Then he looked at Gladys and snapped his fingers impatiently.

"A lemonade," he said, and then turned back to George. "What was your racket?" he asked.

George blinked. "Racket? What racket?"

"You said you worked with Frank Kelly. What did you do?"

George's brain crawled with alarm. This would never do, he told himself, flustered. He wasn't going to admit anything to Brant. It was all very well to tell Ella tall stories, but Brant was quite a different kettle of fish.

"That's my business," he said, looking away. "I don't talk about it."

"Don't be wet," Brant said. "I'm in the game myself."

George was startled: he turned and stared into Brant's hard, grey-blue eyes. He flinched away from what he saw in them.

"What game?" he repeated.

Brant smiled. "I don't talk about that either," he said. "Do you think I'd mess about touting books unless I had to? Would you?"

George had no idea what he was driving at. He said nothing.

"As soon as it's cooled off I'm going back to my racket," Brant said, and he touched the raw, livid scar, his eyes clouding and his face set in grim lines.

So Gladys was right. He was a wrong 'un, George thought,

and, somehow, he felt envious. He knew he shouldn't feel like that, but he had always longed to live dangerously.

For something to say, George blurted out, "That's a nasty scar you've got there. Is it recent?"

An extraordinary change came over Brant's face. It seemed to grow dark and thin. It twisted out of shape so that it was moulded into a mask of terrifying hatred.

He leaned forward and spat on the floor.

"Come on," he said, speaking through stiff white lips. "We're going to see Robinson."

"Not tonight," George returned hastily. "It's raining. Besides, it's too late now. We'll see him tomorrow morning."

With an obvious effort Brant controlled himself. Once more his face became blank and indifferent.

"Do you keep a record of the orders you've taken?" he asked.

"Why, yes," George returned, wondering why he changed the subject so abruptly.

"Got it with you?"

George produced a tattered notebook, and Brant took it from him. He examined the pages covered with George's neat writing and then he glanced up.

"This the lot? I mean from the time you started?"

George nodded blankly.

"Robinson owes you thirty quid. Do you realize that?"

"As much as that?" George was doubtful. "Well, it can't be helped. I shan't get it from him. He never has any money."

"We'll see about that," Brant said, slipping the notebook into his pocket. He finished his lemonade with a grimace, put a shilling on the counter and turned to the door. "Come on," he went on impatiently.

"It's no good tonight," George protested feebly. As he spoke the bar hand began to call, "Time, gents. Time if you please."

He followed Brant out, avoiding Gladys' eyes. It was dark in the street and rain fell heavily.

"I'm going home," he said, water dripping off his long nose. "We'll see Robo tomorrow."

"Come on," Brant said, jerking his words out as if they burned his mouth. "We're going to see him tonight."

"But I don't know where he lives," George returned. "Let's be sensible. We're both getting soaked."

Brant said an ugly word and walked on.

George went with him. He felt there was nothing else to do. Brant seemed to know where to go. He turned down a side street, lined with small, two-storey houses, and after a few minutes he stopped.

"That's it," he said, looking up at one of the houses. "He's got a room there." He pointed to a window on the top floor. Although the blind was drawn, they could see a light was still burning. "Come on," Brant went on, walking up the worn steps. He put his thumb on the bell and kept it there.

George stood at his side, feeling the rain against his face and his heart pounding uneasily.

There was a shuffling sound beyond the door, and a moment later a fat old woman peered inquisitively at them. " 'Ood'yer want?" she demanded, holding a dirty dressing-gown across her ample bosom. "Ringing the bell like that. You'd think the 'ole blooming 'ouse was afire."

Brant advanced a step, his head thrust forward. "We're friends of Robinson," he said, steadily forcing the old woman back into the dark little hall. "He's waiting for us."

" 'Ere, 'alf a mo," the old woman said, trying to block

Brant's progress. "I didn't tell yer to come in, did I? You come back termorrer."

Brant kept moving forward, staring down at the old woman, flustering her. "It's all right," he said. "He's expecting us. Don't worry. We'll go up."

George had followed Brant into the hall, and was aware that rain from his hat and coat was making puddles on the coconut matting that covered the floor.

Brant suddenly side-stepped the old woman and began to mount the stairs. She stood watching him, uneasy, unsure of herself. She stared at George, who hunched his great shoulders, unconsciously making himself look sinister and frightening. He went up the stairs behind Brant.

"The old cow," Brant said, under his breath. "Who does she think she is?"

He walked along the short passage to a door under which they could see a light burning. He paused outside the door and put his ear against the panel. He stood there listening, intent. menacing, and George, standing a few feet behind him, suddenly saw him in an unexpected and frightening light. It was as if he could see evil and danger emanating from him like a thought-form. He was aware, too, that the old woman had come halfway up the stairs and was watching Brant with fear and curiosity.

Brant glanced over his shoulder at George, made a grimace, and jerked his head towards the door. George had no idea what he intended to convey. He had no time to ask, for Brant, turning the handle of the door, pushed it open and walked into the room.

Not wanting to be left in the dimly lit passage under the disconcerting gaze of the old woman, George took a few hesitating steps forward, which brought him to the door.

Brant was standing just inside the doorway, looking

across the large room at Robinson. George peered past Brant, a sheepish, apologetic expression on his face.

Robinson stood before a dressing-table in his trousers and vest. His feet were bare, and the circle of dirt round the ankles embarrassed George, as did the dirty, tattered vest that covered his pigeon chest. He had taken out his false teeth, and his lips were sunk in, giving his mouth an odd, puckered look that reminded George of a dried pippin.

Robinson stood gaping at Brant, terror in his eyes, his blotchy complexion gradually paling as blood drained from his face.

Across the room was a large bed, the head and foot of which were ornamented by brass knobs. A woman lay huddled up in the bed. George could not guess her age. He thought perhaps she was thirty-five to forty. She was big, blowzy and coarse. Her dyed hennaed hair, black at the roots, frizzed round her head like a soiled halo. She wore a pink nightdress which was creased and dirty and through which her great, bulging figure strained to escape.

"Shut the door," Brant said, watching Robinson intently.

Not quite knowing what he was doing, George obeyed. He thrust his trembling hands into his mackintosh pockets and stared down at the worn carpet, fearful of what was going to happen.

The woman in the bed was the first to recover from the shock.

"Who in hell are you?" she demanded in a strident, furious voice. "Get out! Chuck 'em out, Eddie ..."

Robinson, still clutching his trousers, backed away from Brant's baleful eyes.

"Have you fellows gone crazy?" he finally mumbled. He looked round with despairing eagerness, picked up his teeth and slipped them between his trembling jaws. He seemed to draw courage from them, and when he spoke again the quaver had gone from his voice. "You can't come in here like this."

Brant thrust his head forward. "We didn't know you had company," he said softly, "but now we're here, George wants to talk to you, don't you, George?"

"If you don't get out," the woman screamed at them, "I'll call the cops!" She slid out of bed, a mass of jiggling flesh, snatched up her dressing gown and wrapped it round her. "Don't stand there like a wet week," she went on to Robinson. "Get 'em out of here."

Robinson tried to pull himself together. "You'll pay for this, you two," he said, working himself into a rage. "I've a mind to sack you on the spot. You must be drunk. Get out, and I'll see you in the morning."

George, wishing the ground would open and swallow him, groped for the door handle, but Brant's voice froze him.

"Talk to him, George. Tell him what we've come for."

Robinson turned to George. He felt that he could cope with him. "So you started this, did you?" he snarled. "I'm surprised at you! You'll be sorry for this, you see if you aren't. You wait until tomorrow."

George opened and shut his mouth, but no sound came.

The woman, afraid of Brant, swung round on George. "If you don't get out, you big, hulking rat, I'll scratch your eyes out!" she shouted at him.

"Tell this tart to lay off," Brant said in a soft, menacing voice to Robinson, "or you'll both be sorry."

The woman swung round on him with a squeal of rage: then she stepped back, her furious, blood-congested face paling. Robinson also took a step back, catching his breath with a sharp, whistling sound.

Brant was holding an odd-looking weapon in his hand. The harsh light of the unshaded overhead lamp made the blade glitter. The sight turned George's stomach.

"You'd better be careful," Brant said, addressing Robinson and the woman. "We don't want a scene, and you don't want me to get rough, do you?"

The woman sank down on the bed, fear and horror on her fat, flabby face. Robinson was so terrified that he looked as if he were going to have some kind of a fit. His face turned yellow-green, and his legs trembled so much that he had to sit on a chair.

George wasn't in much better state. He expected the woman to scream at any minute and for the police to come rushing in.

Brant seemed to know by instinct that George wasn't going to be much use. He dominated the scene.

"You've been cheating Fraser," he said to Robinson. "I've found out how much you should have paid him." He took the notebook from his pocket. "It's all here. You owe him thirty quid. We've come to collect."

Robinson stared stupidly at him. He opened and shut his mouth like a dying fish, but no sound came from him.

"Hurry up!" Brant said impatiently. "I'm wet, and I want to go to bed. You know you've been cheating, so come on and pay up!"

Robinson gulped. "I – I haven't got it," he said in a voice like the scratching of a slate pencil.

Brant suddenly leaned forward. His hand moved so quickly that George only caught a brief flash of the weapon. Then Robinson started back with a faint squeal. A long scratch now ran down his white, blotchy cheek from which a fine line of blood began to well.

The woman opened her mouth to scream, but the sound died in her throat as Brant looked at her.

"You'll get it too," he said softly, and he edged a little towards her. "Come on," he went on to Robinson. "Do you want any more?"

Robinson, blood on his dirty vest and neck, waved his hand in a frantic, despairing gesture to the dressing-table.

Brant picked up a wallet that was half hidden under a grimy handkerchief. He counted out twenty-two pounds and held them in hand, looking at Robinson.

"Where's the rest?"

"That's all I've got," Robinson sobbed. "I swear that's all I've got."

Brant put the money in his pocket.

"You're through," he said. "From now on we're working this territory. Do you understand? Get out and stay out. If I see you again I'll fix you."

Listening to his words, George experienced a strange feeling that he was witnessing a scene from one of his own fantasies. Those words were the kind of words George Fraser, millionaire gangster, would have said to Al Capone or Charlie Lucky or any of the big shots. Somehow it took the horror from the situation: he half expected the door to open and Ella to come in with a cup of tea, interrupting this vivid, but surely unreal drama.

Brant was pushing him to the door. "Good night," he was saying. "You might be thinking of telling the cops about us, but I shouldn't if I were you. I don't carry this sticker around with me unless I've a job to do. They won't catch me as easily as that: but I'll come after you."

He stood in the doorway looking at Robinson and the woman, then, jerking his head at George, he walked out of the room.

# 5

This is ridiculous, George thought, as he followed Brant down the stairs. He can't get away with this. Who does he think he is? He can't steal my thunder in this way and then calmly walk off as if nothing had happened.

George had enacted the kind of interview they had just had so many times in his mind that Brant's flagrant trespassing on his preserves angered and humiliated him. Of course, he hadn't been particularly bright at the interview. He had to admit that. He had been scared of Robinson and the woman, but that was only because he had felt defenceless. How was he to know that Brant would produce a razor and commit violence? If he had known, he would have brought his gun. Then it would have been quite a different story. With the Luger in his hand, he would not only have dominated Robinson and that ghastly slut of a woman, but he would have also dominated Brant. What an opportunity to have missed! All because Brant hadn't taken him into his confidence. A sullen anger began to rise in him against Brant. It was like Brant to horn in, to push him aside and take all the credit.

Out in the darkness and the rain, George grabbed hold of Brant and jerked him round.

Anger and disappointment and a feeling of shame gave him courage.

"What are you playing at?" he asked roughly. "Why

didn't you tell me what you were going to do? I could have handled it. I know how to handle a job like that – without messing or cutting people."

Brant stared at him: his gaunt, cold face startled. "What are you talking about?" he demanded, shaking off George's hand. "A fat lot of good you were ..."

"So that's what you think?" George said furiously. "Well, it was your fault. I didn't want to go. I told you. If I had known what you were up to, it would have been different."

"How different?" Brant asked. "I've got the money and I've kicked him out of our territory. We're free to do what we like now. What more could you have done?"

George was a little taken aback, but he was so envious and angry that he blurted out, "It would have been different if I'd brought my gun."

"Gun?" Brant repeated. "What gun?"

George had never told anyone about the Luger. It was not the kind of thing you did tell anyone about. He had no licence for it. If the police heard about it, there would be trouble. They would most likely take it from him.

But he told Brant. There was nothing else he could do. It was either that, or loss of face.

"What do you think?" he said gruffly. "I've had a gun for years. Brought it back from the States; only it's not a thing I talk about. The police don't stand for that kind of thing."

"A gun," Brant said, making it sound tremendously important. "So you've got a gun?"

"Had it for years," George repeated, uneasy, yet pleased with the impression he had made. "It saves a lot of talking. I'm not much of a one to talk. I don't need to talk with a gun."

"I didn't know," Brant said, and his hardness and confidence somehow didn't seem to matter any more to George.

"I don't mess around with razors," George went on, his voice sounding strange even to him. "That's small-time stuff."

"You can't get guns here," Brant said mildly, almost apologetically. "But we scared the rat, didn't we?"

"We scared him all right," George returned, losing his ill-temper now that Brant was acknowledging his share in Robinson's defeat. "I'll never forget his face when you produced that sticker," he went on, feeling a generosity that compelled him to give the lion's share of the exploit to Brant.

"Pity you didn't bring the gun," Brant said, equally generous. "He'd've had a heart attack."

George sniggered. Brant, he decided, wasn't such a bad sort after all. "I'll fix him if he tries anything funny," he went on grandly. "What with my gun and your sticker, we've got him where we want him."

"You're a pretty good shot, I suppose?" Brant said, his head down and his yellow hair plastered flat by the rain.

"Me?" George laughed, delighted with Brant's interest. "I was considered to be fair enough. I could split a playing-card edge on at twenty-five yards. Bit out of practice now, of course."

"That's good, isn't it?" Brant said, hunching his shoulders. "I bet you've bumped off a few guys in your day."

George opened his mouth, saw the trap just in time, and walked on without speaking. It would be stimulating to brag that he had been a killer, but not to Brant. It was safe enough to tell Ella. She wouldn't talk, but Brant might.

"What's it like, killing a guy?" Brant asked, after a

moment's pause.

"That's something I don't talk about," George returned, shortly.

Brant glanced at him. "Kelly killed a lot of men, didn't he?"

That was safer ground. "A good few," George said, shrugging his big shoulders carelessly. "It was us or them in those days."

"But you didn't, eh?"

Again George resisted the temptation. "That's something I keep to myself," he said, and after a moment's hesitation, he added gruffly, "Lay off, will you?"

"That's all right," Brant said quickly. "I guess that's something no one would talk about."

"Now you're smart," George returned, surprised at his own audacity.

At the street corner they paused..

"Well, you better take your money," Brant said. There was a note of reluctance in his voice, but he held out the crumpled roll of notes willingly enough.

George hesitated; at the back of his mind, although he was loath to admit it, he knew he would not have had the nerve to have taken the money. He knew that Brant expected him to share it with him, and after a mental tussle, he took the notes, hurriedly counted ten from the roll, and offered them to Brant.

"Here," he said, his face hot with embarrassment, "we'll share on this. After all, you helped get them."

"Fair enough," Brant said, and took the notes, putting them in his pocket.

George was rather taken aback by this cool acceptance of what was rightly his.

"Well, I'll be getting off," Brant said, before George

could recover. "I don't think we'll have any further trouble with Robinson. We'll work the territory and send the orders direct to the Company. If Robinson starts trouble – well, we'll introduce him to your gun."

George nodded. "That's the idea," he said eagerly. "I'll put the wind up him all right."

Before Brant went, he put his hand on George's arm and actually smiled at him. "You're all right, George," he said, pinching George's massive muscles. "You're going to go places."

It took George some time before he could settle to sleep that night. Even the regular, soothing sound of Leo's purring failed to lull him. He felt that Brant no longer regarded him with contempt. He felt somehow that he had impressed Brant – a difficult, almost impossible person to impress. It was risky, of course, to have told Brant about the gun, but he just could not have let him get away with his home-made sticker.

George spent a long time reconstructing the scene with Robinson, only this time it was he who played the leading part. It was he who intimidated Robinson and made him hand over the money, and it was Brant who stood speechless, his grey–blue eyes alight with admiration.

The next evening George met Brant in a pub opposite Wembley underground station. It was quite startling how Brant's attitude towards George had changed. He now seemed to regard George as the leader, and although he still had the same cold, bored expression in his eyes, and the thin hardness about his mouth, he was diffident, almost ingratiating, in his manner. To George's relief, the gun was not mentioned.

"We'd better get to work," George remarked, after

calling for a second pint. "Have another lemonade while I explain things to you."

Brant shook his head. "Not for me," he said, "but don't let that stop you."

"We can manage without Robo all right," George went on, after he had taken a pull from his tankard. "I had a word with Head Office. I told them we preferred to work together, and Robo was willing. They don't care one way or the other so long as they get the orders." He lit a cigarette, and for a moment enjoyed the feeling that he was now the head salesman, instructing a novice. "The first thing you have to do when you're canvassing is to get into the house. It's easy once you know how. For instance, if you knock on the door and say 'Is Mr Jones at home?' the old girl is bound to ask 'Who is it?' If he isn't in, then you have to tell her the whole story, and the old man is tipped off when he does come home. That means he's ready for you when next you call. Don't forget the surprise visit gets the business." George took another pull from his tankard, and then went on, "If, on the other hand, you knock on the door, and when the old girl comes you raise your hat and begin to move away, and at the same time you say, 'I suppose Mr Jones is not in?' then she'll answer nine times out of ten, 'No, he isn't.' You then say, 'I'll look in some other time', and by that time you're halfway to the gate without telling her what you want."

Brant shifted restlessly. "I don't know if all that's so important," he said.

"But it is," George returned. "You try it and see. Robinson worked out all the angles, and they're worth studying. Now, if the old man is at home, your question, 'I suppose Mr Jones isn't in?' gets the answer, 'Oh yes, he is', and as like as not she starts yelling for him. When he turns up, you'll find he'll lean against the doorpost, blocking your entrance and ask what you want. You mustn't tell him until you're inside the house."

Brant had a far-away look in his eyes. He seemed hardly aware of George's droning voice at his elbow.

"You must get inside before you start your sale, so you say, 'I've come to talk to you about Johnny's education.' That usually gets you in," George went on. "If he still won't ask you in, you put it to him straight. 'I wonder if I might come in? I can't very well talk to you on the doorstep.' "

"You've certainly got it wrapped up haven't you?" Brant said. "Well, let's see it work. Come on, I'm sick of this pub."

George consulted his packet of names and addresses. "All right," he said. "Let's try Mr Thomas. He's got two kids: Tommy and Jean. It's important to know the children's names. The old man thinks you're a school inspector if you mention the kids by name, and you're inside before he finds out you're not."

They walked along the wide arterial road, housed on either side by box-like Council dwellings. They were an odd-looking couple, and the women standing in the doorways, the men in their gardens and the children playing in the road, stared curiously at them.

"Here we are," George said, uneasy under the battery of inquisitive eyes. He paused outside a drab little house, pushed open the wooden gate, and together they walked up the path.

George rapped on the door. There was a rush of feet and the door jerked open. Two small children, a boy and a girl, stared up at them with intent, wondering eyes.

"Is your father in?" George asked, smiling down at them.

They did not move nor speak, but continued to gape at them.

Brant said, "Get someone, can't you? Don't stand there gaping at me." His voice snapped viciously, and the two children immediately turned and ran back down the passage.

"Ma ... Ma ... there're two men ..."

George and Brant exchanged glances.

"It's always the same," George said. "Damn kids ..."

A middle-aged, slatternly-looking woman came down the passage, drying her pink, soap-softened hands on a dirty towel.

" 'Oo is it?" she asked, eyeing them suspiciously.

"I suppose Mr Thomas isn't in?" George asked, raising his hat and edging slowly away from the door.

" 'E's in the garden." She raised her voice and shouted "Bert ...'ere ...come 'ere ..."

"That's all right," George said hastily. "We'll go round", and before the woman could protest, he left her and walked round to the back garden.

Mr Thomas was resting after a bout of digging. He stood in the middle of a patch of newly turned ground, his cap at the back of his head, the spade thrust into the soil and the glow of sweat and health on his large, simple face.

He blinked when he saw George and Brant, and paused as he was about to light his pipe, uncertain, uneasy.

"Good evening, Mr Thomas," George said, approaching with a cheerful smile and a wave of his hand. "Getting ready for planting, eh? That soil looks good. By Jove! I envy you this garden."

" 'Evening," Mr Thomas grunted, and took off his cap to scratch his head.

"I wonder if you can spare us a moment?" George went

on. "We've come to have a little chat about Jean and Tommy. I hear they're doing very well at school."

Mr Thomas brightened; embarrassed suspicion left his face. "From the school, are yer?" he said. He looked round the small garden a little helplessly, and then, raising his voice, he bawled, " 'Ere, Emmie! Come 'ere, can't yer?"

Mrs Thomas and the two children joined them.

"These two gents are from the school," Mr Thomas said, wiping his hands on the seat of his trousers. He glared at the children. "Wot 'ave you two bin up to?"

"Oh, it's nothing like that," George put in hastily as the two children looked sheepish. "Your kiddies are a credit to you both. They're doing so well at school I thought you might consider helping them to do even better."

Mr Thomas looked blankly at his wife. "I dunno about that ... " he began, and, getting no support from his wife, he lapsed into silence.

"Perhaps we could go inside for a moment?" George asked, moving towards the house. "I won't keep you long, but it's easier to talk inside than in the garden, isn't it?"

Rather reluctantly, Mr Thomas led the way into the squalid little house. They all crowded into the small front parlour. Mr Thomas dusted two chairs with his cap and pushed them forward, warned his children that if they didn't sit quiet he'd knock their blocks off, and sat down himself. Mrs Thomas stood by the window.

George glanced round the room and cleared his throat. He was not nervous. He knew what he was going to do, he had an interested audience, and the result of what he had to say was his bread and butter. More important still, he wished to impress Brant with his salesmanship.

"Before I come to the point," he began, taking up his position behind the chair and grasping the back of it firmly in both hands, "let me put to you both a very important question. You will both agree with me that education today is the most vital factor in the life of any child?"

Mr Thomas and his wife emphatically agreed that this was so, and Mr Thomas began a rambling account of the lack of education in his time.

George hurriedly interrupted. "Fortunately, Mr Thomas, times have changed. Now, education is so important you can't leave all the work to the school teachers. Many a time your kiddies have asked you questions which you're unable to answer. There're thousands of such questions, and they are very difficult to answer. I've had a lot to do with children, and I know how worrying it is not to be able to satisfy their craving for knowledge."

"That's right," Mr Thomas returned, nodding his head. "Fair terrors these imps are. Always asking questions ..."

"And what questions!" George went on, beaming at the children. "I don't have to remind you of all the conundrums, do I? You know only too well. All the same, these questions should be answered."

Mr Thomas nodded again. He had no idea what all this was about, but he felt that George did appreciate their difficulties and was trying to be helpful.

"Very well, then," George said, getting into his stride. "Children are thirsting for knowledge. Teachers haven't the time to explain everything children want to know. Parents haven't the knowledge. So what happens?" He leaned forward, suddenly looking stern. "Your children, Mr Thomas, are being mentally starved. Make no mistake about that! You would be ashamed to starve their bodies, yet you are openly starving their minds. Knowledge is to the mind what food is to the body."

Mr Thomas began to have doubts about George's good

intentions. He scratched his head and glanced at his wife for support.

George paused until there was a long, awkward silence, and then he flashed on his old heartiness again. "Now, don't let that disturb you," he went on, beaming round on them. "I'm here to put all that right. I have a wonderful work that'll be the silent teacher in your home."

From his hidden poacher's pocket, he produced the specimen of the *Child's Self-Educator*.

"Let me show you."

He laid the book on the table. Mr and Mrs Thomas and the two children crowded round him. He began to turn the pages slowly, making a comment for every page.

"Look at these magnificent pictures. Here, children can slip over to Africa and roam about the jungle in perfect safety. They can see the wild animals, study their habits and learn how they live. The King of Beasts. Isn't that a wonderful picture? Look, Tommy, look at the tiny cubs. They're like ordinary kittens, aren't they? But they'd scratch if you met them in the jungle." He glanced at Mr Thomas. "See how interested the boy is? Every page has been planned to attract children to look further. It's scientific teaching of the highest possible standard." He turned another page. "Now, what have we here? The story of wireless, and, more interesting still, how to construct many various kinds of sets. I'm sure you, Mr Thomas, would be interested in this section. Have you ever thought of making your own wireless? These instructions are simple, and you don't have to have any previous knowledge." He made sure that Mr Thomas was looking at the coloured plates a little wistfully before turning on to another section. "Here's something that's useful to everyone in the home: the Medical section. Your kiddie might scald himself – so many kiddies do – turn to page 155 and you learn how to deal with such an emergency. Your own doctor in your own home! Isn't that something worth having? No waiting, no bills, easy reference – possibly a life saved!" He noted the slow-rising interest, but decided that neither Mr nor Mrs Thomas was as yet quite convinced, so he turned on, delighted with the sound of his own voice, pleased with the set, worn phrases which now automatically came to his lips without the need of thought. "Tommy perhaps has to write an essay on ships: here it is, all ready for him. Tommy will soon be at the top of his class. Jean has a problem in arithmetic: she finds her answer here. You, Mr Thomas, want to know what will best grow in your garden: here is the whole thing ready for you in the Gardening section. A few nights' reading and Mr Thomas' garden is the envy of all his neighbours. Mrs Thomas, although you're no doubt an excellent cook, you can get new ideas from the Cookery section." He stepped back and thumped his large fist on the back of the chair. "It's a great work! A work for every one of you. You will agree with me, I am sure, that it'd be useful to have a set of these magnificent books in your home? Can't you see how they'd help your kiddies get on and assure a sound future for them?"

Mrs Thomas stared at her husband, her eyes bright. "Ain't that a wonderful turn out, Bert?" she said. "I've never seen anything like it. What say, shall we 'ave 'em?"

"Yes, dad," the children chimed in, "let's 'ave 'em. Coo, dad, look at all them pictures ..."

"You shut up," Mr Thomas growled. He scratched his head and fingered the specimen thoughtfully. "I'm not saying they ain't all right, but this sort of thing costs money ..."

"Now let me explain about that," George said, with an expansive smile. "The *Child's Self-Educator* is in four handsome volumes. Although we're making every effort to put this work in all homes at cost price, it still needs a little effort on your part to secure it. Good things don't just fall from Heaven. I wish they did, but they don't. You have to make a small sacrifice for them." He shook his head solemnly. Then, lowering his voice, he said impressively, "It's going to cost you tuppence a day."

"Tuppence a day?" Mr Thomas repeated blankly. "Wot yer mean?"

"Just that," George replied, knowing that he had reached the crucial part of the sale and moving with caution. "Consider what tuppence a day means. A shilling odd a week for your children's future success. Surely that isn't asking too much? We don't collect the money daily or weekly, of course, but monthly: five shillings a month.

"The whole work costs seven pounds, ten shillings. We're not asking you for that amount, we're asking for five shillings a month. The way to look at it is that you're going to pay tuppence a day to help your children and yourselves."

"Seven pahns ten!" Mr Thomas gasped. "Not bloody likely! Not for me, chum. No, I can't afford that." He picked up the specimen and handed it to George. "Thank yer for calling, mister, but it ain't no good."

The two children immediately began an uproar, and Mrs Thomas had to drive them from the room. The small house echoed with their disappointed yells, and George became slightly flustered.

"Now, one moment, Mr Thomas," he began hurriedly, realizing that he had struck the worst kind of prospect – the man who can't afford it. "You've agreed the books are good and ..."

"The books're orl right, but the price ain't," Mr Thomas

said, a stubborn light in his eyes. "It's no use arguing. I can't afford it, so that's that."

George stared at him helplessly, aware that Brant was watching him with a sneering grin.

"Of course you can afford it," George said warmly. "You mean you can't afford to be without it. Tuppence a day! Why, anyone can afford *that*."

"Well, *I* can't, and I don't want a lot of talk," Mr Thomas said irritably. "I've got to get back to my garden."

"Just a moment," Brant said quietly. "I can *prove* you can afford to pay tuppence a day for these books."

Both Mr Thomas and George turned and stared at him. He was eyeing them with a hard, calculating expression in his eyes. Before they could speak he went on, "You're a sporting man, Mr Thomas. I bet you half a dollar you can afford to pay tuppence a day. If I prove to your satisfaction that you wouldn't miss this small sum, will you buy the books?"

"You can't prove it," Mr Thomas said, beginning to grin.

"In that case, you'll get the half dollar," Brant said, putting a half a crown on the table. "Fair enough, isn't it?"

Mr Thomas hesitated, then nodded his head. "Okay, cocky, prove it."

Brant produced a soiled ten-shilling note. "I'll have another bet with you," he said, his lips curling into a smile, but his eyes like granite. "I bet you don't know how much money you have in your trousers' pocket."

Mr Thomas blinked at him. "Wot's that got ter do with it?"

"If you can tell me to the exact penny how much you have in your pocket, I'll give you this ten bob."

"I can do that orl right," Mr Thomas returned, automatically moving his hands to his pockets.

"No ... don't do that. Tell me, without looking, exactly how much you have."

Mr Thomas scratched his head, suddenly embarrassed.

"Well," he said slowly, "I reckon I've got four bob."

Brant leaned forward. "To the exact penny, Mr Thomas. What is it? Four and three or three and ten? Tell me the exact amount and the ten bob's yours."

Mr Thomas scowled. "I dunno," he admitted. "Not to the exact penny. But wot's all this got to do with it?"

"All right," Brant said briskly, putting his ten-shilling note away. "You don't know how much you have in your pocket, do you? So if I put tuppence into your pocket without you knowing it, you wouldn't know you were tuppence to the good? In the same way, if I took tuppence out of your pocket, you wouldn't miss it. It therefore follows that you can afford to pay tuppence a day for these very valuable books."

Mr Thomas gaped for a moment, and then a wide grin spread over his face. "That's smart," he said, admiringly. "I never thought of it that way. Orl right, give us the order form. I'll sign it."

George watched the signing of the order form with mixed feelings. He was angry that Brant had interfered with his sale. He was humiliated that Brant should have come to his rescue so successfully when *he* should have been the one to have shown Brant the dodges. Again it crept into his mind that Brant's success had been a cheap trick. Of course it was a cheap trick. A confidence trick!

But Brant seemed oblivious to George. He took the order form from Mr Thomas, examined it carefully, smiled and folded it. Without looking at George, he put the form casually into his pocket.

There was an awkward pause. George felt blood rising to his face, but this was no time to protest. They both shook hands with Mr Thomas, had a word to say to Mrs Thomas and then walked down the path in silence.

Once out in the road, away from the house, George said, "Look here, old boy, that's my order, you know. I did all the selling, and besides, it was one of my addresses."

Brant smiled. "Don't be a fool," he said, bored and cold, his hard eyes on George's face. "You'd never've landed it: not in a hundred years. What do you think I am – a sucker?" He glanced up and down the road. "Well, I can manage now. I see how it's done. If you ask me, it's a mug's game. All that talking for thirty bob." He shrugged indifferently. "I'm not going to waste my time on this job for long."

George shifted his feet; a tiny spark of anger flared up and then went out. "I think we might split it, old boy," he said a little feebly.

"I thought you didn't go in for small-time stuff," Brant returned, jeering at him. "I got you twenty-two quid last night, and now you're haggling over fifteen bob." He began to move away. "I'll be seeing you. While we're on the ground, we may as well do some work. So long, George."

"But wait a minute ..." George began.

Brant shoved his hands deep into his pockets. "So long," he repeated, and slouched away, his head down, the long straw-colour lock of hair falling forward, hiding his scar.

# 6

It was Saturday afternoon, and George was alone in his room, alone also in the big, dingy house. The other boarders had gone away for the weekend. George had watched them go from his window. They looked, he thought, a little odd and somehow theatrical out of their drab city clothes: the plus fours, the flannel suits, the summer frocks gave them a festive air, not in keeping with George's depressed mood. Ella also had gone off immediately after lunch. It was her half day, and George, peering round the curtain, had watched her hurry to the bus stop. A half an hour or so later Mr and Mrs Rhodes had strolled towards the local cinema. He was now alone in the house, which seemed still and oppressive to him.

Saturday afternoon depressed George: he had nothing to do, nowhere to go, and he usually sat in his armchair by the window with a book and Leo for company.

George found himself this afternoon more restless than usual. His book did not interest him, and he felt the loneliness of the big house weighing down on him. He had Brant on his mind, too. Brant, in two days, had become a star salesman. He had obtained six orders for the *Child's Self-Educator*: nine pounds in his first week! George had only managed to scrape up two orders that week, and he was vaguely resentful of Brant's success. He was sure that Brant was using a series of cheap tricks to obtain his orders.

George tried to convince himself that he would rather not get an order unless the sale was a fair one, but he could not help envying Brant's success – tricks or no tricks.

George found the King's Arms lonely without Robinson for company. Brant seldom came to the pub. Although he was still friendly – if you could call his odd, cold manner friendly – he kept to himself, and George saw him to talk to only when they journeyed out to Wembley together. Even then Brant scarcely said a word.

George put his book down. He stared across at Leo, who blinked, stretched lazily and ducked his head at him.

It was strange how an animal could take the edge off loneliness, George thought. Without Leo, he would have gone out and wandered aimlessly about the streets.

He got up and crossed to the bed. For some minutes he stroked the cat's fur and talked to it, pleased with its ecstatic response. He rolled it gently onto its back, and the cat, its eyes half closed, encircled his hand with its front paws, its claws carefully sheathed. While he fondled Leo, George brooded about their relations. Leo was important to him: how empty his life would be without the cat! It came as a revelation that he was entirely alone, that no one bothered with him, and he had no friend he could trust. A wave of lonely emotion swept through him, and his eyes watered. He didn't care, he told himself, picking Leo up and holding the cat in his arms, its face against his face, its whiskers tickling his nose. He could get on all right alone so long as he kept his health and had Leo for company. All the same, it was a pretty dreary outlook. As he was beginning to pity himself, he heard the telephone ringing downstairs. The bell startled him. Somehow, it sounded creepy, coming up from the deserted basement. He put Leo down and went to the door. It wasn't much use going all the way downstairs. By the time he was down the bell would have stopped ringing. He opened his door and glanced along the dimly lit passage. The bell was ringing insistently – a muffled, nagging note that disturbed him.

He shrugged his shoulders uneasily. Let it ring, he decided. It was certainly not for him. No one had ever bothered to ask for his telephone number. It was probably for one of the boarders, or for Mr Rhodes. But he could not bring himself to shut the door. He had a guilty feeling that he ought to answer the telephone and see who was calling. Then, as he had almost made up his mind to go down, the bell ceased to ring.

He closed the door and went back to his armchair, but a moment later he was on his feet once more as the bell began to ring again.

This time he did not hesitate; he lumbered out of the room, along the passage and down the stairs. It seemed a long way down, and the bell nagged him. He descended the basement stairs with a rush, snatched up the receiver and said "Hello?" in a breathless voice.

"You've taken your time, haven't you?" a flat, metallic voice said in his ear.

"Who's that? Who do you want?"

"It's Brant," the voice said impatiently, as if he ought to have known. "I thought you'd be in. Look, George, I want you to do me a favour."

"Brant? Why, hello … I didn't expect you …"

"Never mind that. Have you anything to do this afternoon?"

"Me?" Of course George had nothing to do. He never had on Saturday afternoons; but how did Brant know? Anyway, he wasn't going to admit it: at the same time, he didn't intend to miss anything. He spoke with caution.

"Well, I don't know. I was reading …"

"You can read any time, can't you?" Brant's voice jeered at him. "I wouldn't ask you, only it's important. I want someone to go to Joe's and leave a message."

"Joe's?"

"It's a club in Mortimer Street, not far from you. They're not on the blower, otherwise I'd've rung 'em."

"Mortimer Street – that's near Paddington Station, isn't it?"

Brant grunted. "I've taken the key of my flat by mistake, and I'll be back late. It's my sister. She doesn't know, and she won't be able to get in. Will you leave a message for her at Joe's?"

"I didn't know you had a sister."

There was a moment's silence, then Brant said, "Well, I have. We share a flat, see? I should've left the key under the mat. She'll have to amuse herself as best she can until I get back. But I want her to know, otherwise she'll kick the door down. Will you do it, George? Just tell the barman I've taken the key and won't be back until after two. He'll tell Cora."

George thought for a moment. He felt a rising excitement. "Why, if you like … I'll tell her myself. I mean I'll wait for her and tell her."

"You don't have to do that. I don't know when she'll go to Joe's. All I know is she'll be there some time tonight."

George had no idea why he should feel so excited and elated. Brant's sister! Not five minutes ago he didn't know that Brant had a sister, and now he was getting het-up about her, as if she were someone exciting, someone who'd be interested in him. It was extraordinary.

"Of course, I'll do it," he said. "You leave it to me, old boy. I'll tell 'em. You don't think I ought to wait and explain it to her myself? They might forget to tell her …"

"They'll tell her," Brant said, his voice a ghostly murmur in George's ear. "You don't have to worry about that."

"All right," George said happily. "You leave it to me. You won't be back until after two, is that it?"

"Something like that. Well, thanks. If you do see her … she's dark, doesn't wear a hat and has a red bone bangle. You can't mistake her. The bangle's about three inches wide."

"Well, maybe I will see her …"

A faint, sneering laugh came over the wire.

"What was that?" George asked, not believing that Brant had laughed.

"Nothing. I've got to get off. So long, George."

"Goodbye," George said, and the line went dead.

George ran up the three flights of stairs to his bedroom. His violent entrance startled Leo, who sat up with pricked ears and wide eyes. George didn't even notice the cat. He stood before the long mirror, and saw, not without satisfaction, that his face was flushed and his eyes bright. This was going to be exciting, he told himself. Organized properly, he would be able to extend the excitement until bedtime. He glanced at his watch. It was still early: a few minutes to three. He must make himself smart. Perhaps a shave. He ran his fingers over his chin. Yes, he could do with a shave. Then a clean shirt, his best suit.

He took a towel and shaving outfit to the bathroom. The geyser lit with a little plop, and while he waited for the water to heat up he stood looking out of the window, across the grey roofs and, beyond, at the blue sky and the sunshine.

Cora! An exciting name. She wouldn't be like Brant. He was sure of that. She was dark, didn't wear a hat and had a red bone bangle: an exciting description! George took off his collar and tie, and filled the basin with hot water. He would spot her all right, he assured himself. Even if he didn't speak to her, it would be interesting to look at her. But, of course, he was going to speak to her. Alone in the steamy little bathroom, George felt very confident. He forgot that he was shy with women. Somehow, Brant's sister would be different. He was quite sure of that. It was odd how stupid he had been about women in the past. He stared at himself in the mirror. There was no sense in working himself into a fright because of what had happened years ago. He had been fifteen then, and big for his age. That always seemed to be the trouble. He was always too big for his age. School masters expected too much from him. During the war, when he was fourteen, people expected him to be in the army. Even at fifteen he had been backward and, of course, innocent. He had been in the park by himself when the woman began talking to him. She was an impressive-looking woman, rich, well dressed, refined. She said she was lonely, and George had felt sorry for her. He was lonely himself. They stood talking beside the duck pond; at least, she did the talking, while George listened politely. He was really more interested in watching the herons; but she was lonely, so he listened. She talked about people being nice to each other, about being lonely and what a fine, strong fellow he was. It was talk that George could understand. So when she suggested he might come to her house because it was chilly standing by the pond, he was flattered, and he did not see anything wrong in going with her.

He thought it odd that she should take him straight up to her bedroom. He had never seen such a beautiful room. But before he could appreciate it, the refined lady seemed to take leave of her senses. George never quite knew how he got out of the house. It was like a nightmare, and he dreamed for many years about running down long passages and opening and shutting many doors with someone screaming names after him as he ran.

That experience kept cropping up at the back of his mind when he had anything to do with women. He never quite got over it. It made him shy and suspicious of women. Of course, sometimes he needed a woman, but his need was not as strong as his nervousness, so he never did anything about it. Once or twice, when he had been a little tight, he had ventured as far as Maddox Street. But the waiting women he found there seemed so unlike any other women he had seen that he had abruptly turned back and caught a bus home.

Now, in the solitude of the bathroom, he only felt the excitement and not the fright that women raised in him.

It was after four o'clock before he left the house. In high spirits he walked briskly down the street. It was a grand afternoon, and he found a secret pleasure in mingling with the crowds moving along the Edgware Road. He was now one of the crowd; he had somewhere to go, someone to meet. It gave him a feeling of security and confidence. He must do this more often, he told himself. It was absurd to bury himself away in his bedroom as he had been doing.

Mortimer Street consisted of a row of small shops, three or four hawkers' barrows and a public house. George had to walk the length of the street before he discovered Joe's Club. It was over a second-hand bookshop. The open door revealed a flight of uncarpeted stairs that rose steeply into darkness, and through the doorway came the smell of stale scent, spirits and tobacco smoke.

He hesitated for several minutes before climbing the stairs. Finally he went up, his hand on the rickety banister, his feet treading cautiously, the stairs creaking under his weight.

There was a dimly lit passage at the top of the stairs, and at the end of the passage there was a door on which was a dirty card with "Joe's Club" printed in uneven, illiterate letters.

George turned the door knob and pushed open the door. He found himself in a long, narrow room, which, he guessed, must stretch the width of the two shops below. At the far end of the room was a bar. Rows of bottles stood on shelves within reach of the bartender's hands. All round the room stood tables on which chairs were stacked, their legs pointing to the dirty, grey-white ceiling. Opposite the bar, at the other end of the room, was a dais containing a piano, three battered music stands and a drummer's outfit. The walls of the room were covered with large reproductions of nudes from *La Vie Parisienne* and *Esquire*. A public telephone box stood just inside the door.

"The joint's closed," a man's voice said at his elbow.

George jumped. He looked round, took a step back and stared at the little man who had come silently into the room. His flat, broad face was unpleasant; his complexion was shiny white, the texture of a slug's body. Reddish hair like steel wool grew far back on his head and gave him a great deal of domed white forehead. His small, bitter, green eyes probed at George inquisitively.

"Besides, you're not a member," the little man went on. His voice seemed to come from the back of his throat, like that of a ventriloquist. His bloodless lips hung open, but did not move as he spoke.

"Yes," George said. "I know." He fingered his tie uneasily. "I really came to leave a message …"

"Why should I bother with messages?" the little man asked curtly. "Do you think I've got nothing better to do?"

That settled it, George thought, delighted. He would have to wait for Brant's sister. You couldn't rely on this nasty little specimen to pass on any message.

"All right," he said, shrugging. "Perhaps you can tell me when Miss Brant will be here? I'll tell her myself."

"Who?" asked the little man. "Miss Brant? Never 'eard of 'er."

"Never mind," George said firmly. "It doesn't matter. I'll come back later."

The green eyes probed his face.

"Do you mean Cora?"

George was startled. "Yes," he said. "Miss Cora Brant."

A sly, sneering smile came into the green eyes.

"Gawd Almighty! We're putting on side, ain't we?" the little man said. "Okay, palsy, leave your message. I'll take care of it."

George's growing dislike for the little man suddenly turned to suspicion. He looked a real bad lot: a shady character: a gangster. He could have been anything – a racing tout with a razor, a pimp with a knife.

Abruptly he turned to the door. "I'll see her," he said shortly. "Don't you bother."

He went downstairs. The little man watched him all the way down. As he reached the street door, the little man called after him, "Now wait. Don't be so 'asty," but George did not stop. He walked rapidly away, his face hot and red.

At the end of the street he paused and tried to make up his mind what he was to do. Obviously the club wouldn't open until the evening. But what time in the evening? He'd have to find that out. He crossed the road and entered a shabby little tobacconist's. He bought a packet of Player's, and as he was waiting for his change he asked, "When does

Joe's Club open?"

The old woman who had served him shook her head. "You want to keep away from that place," she said. "No good's ever come out of it."

George opened the packet of cigarettes and lit one. "Oh?" he said, feeling a stab of excitement. "What do you know about it?"

"Enough," the old woman answered shortly, and put the odd coppers on the counter.

George lowered his voice, "I'm interested," he said. "Perhaps you can help me."

"A den of thieves," the old woman said, her thin, yellow face creasing in disgust. "The police ought to 'ave closed it down long ago. I wish I was the mother of some of those little sluts 'oo go there: I'd warm their backsides for 'em!"

"I'm supposed to meet someone there," George said, looking at her a little helplessly. "I don't want to get mixed up in anything. Who's the little bloke with the red hair?"

"You'll get mixed up all right," the old woman said contemptuously. "You keep away from that 'ole."

"Thanks for the tip," George returned, smiling at her. "But who is the little bloke with the red hair?"

"That's Little Ernie; everyone knows 'im and his women."

"What time does the Club open?" George asked again.

"Seven, and take my advice, keep clear of the place. They might take you for a copper, like I nearly did." The old woman smiled secretly. "It ain't healthy being taken for a copper in Joe's Club."

George raised his hat and went out into the sunshine. Dark with a red bone bangle; a den of thieves; Little Ernie and his women. What a wonderful Saturday afternoon!

He caught a bus at the corner of the street and travelled

to Hyde Park. There he lost himself in the crowds, listening to the speakers, walking along the Serpentine, sitting on the grass. He didn't mind waiting, because the evening was so full of promise. This was the world that fascinated him: the world he had read about and dreamed about.

At half past six he walked back to Mortimer Street. It had a forlorn, deserted appearance now that the hawkers' barrows had gone and the shops were shut. He went into the public house which was opposite Joe's Club and ordered a pint of bitter. He took his glass to the window, where he could see the club entrance. From the window he had an uninterrupted view of the street. He lit a cigarette and waited.

It was a long wait, but he did not mind. The street was full of interest. After seven o'clock a couple of stout, flashily dressed Jews came along, paused outside the Club, talked for a minute or so and then entered. Almost immediately a blonde woman wearing fox furs came down the street with a coarse, elderly man who was talking excitedly, gesticulating with his hands, an ugly look of rage on his badly shaven face. The woman walked along indifferently. She swayed her hips, and George recognized her for what she was. They, too, disappeared up the stairs to Joe's Club. A little later three young girls – the eldest could not have been more than seventeen – all blonde, all wearing cheap, tight little frocks, all talking in high-pitched, nasal voices, disappeared, giggling and yapping, through the shabby doorway.

George ordered another pint and continued to watch. From what he had seen, Joe's Club seemed to attract the most odd type of man and woman from the shadowy night life of London. They were out of place in the sunlit street, like slugs you reveal when you turn over a log that has been lying in thick grass for a long time. Sunshine was not for them. Dark streets, dimly-lit pavements, tobacco-laden air, the clink of glasses, the sound of liquor running from a bottle – that was their background. They were the "wide" boys and girls of London – the prostitutes, the thieves, the pimps, the touts, the pickpockets, the cat burglars, the hangers-on, the playboys and the good-time girls all moving in a steady stream, like a river of rottenness, into Joe's Club.

As George watched them, summed them up, recognized them, he began to think about Brant's sister. Would she turn out to be a brassy, hard little piece like these other girls who had gone up the stairs to Joe's Club? He hated that type of girl. He had no personality to cope with them. He knew what kind of man they liked. He had listened to them in the park often enough. They and their boyfriends: young men with spotty complexions, padded shoulders, snappy felt hats and cigarettes dangling from their loose mouths. Wise cracking: every remark had a double meaning. The girls would scream with shrill laughter, vying with each other in appreciation. You were not wanted if you couldn't make them laugh; if you didn't know all the off-coloured jokes. Would Cora be like that?

George didn't think so. He felt certain that she would mean something to him when they met. He didn't know what their relations would be, but he was sure that meeting her was the most important thing in his life. The longer he waited the more excited he became.

Then as he was about to call for another pint, as the hands of the clock above the bar shifted to eight o'clock, he saw her. She was around twenty and dark. She had on a pale blue sweater and dark slacks and she didn't wear a hat. There was a three-inch-wide red bangle on her wrist. But even without these clues he was quite sure he would have known her. It was as if the finger of destiny had pointed her out to him.

He crossed the bar in two strides, jerked open the door and stepped into the street. He crossed the street, removing his hat, as Cora reached the club door. She stopped when she saw him and stared at him. Her eyes were slate-grey, and had almost no expression when they looked at him.

"Are you Miss Brant?" he asked, colour flooding his face. He tried, unsuccessfully, not to look at her breasts. She was flaunting her figure; with every move of her slim body, her breasts jiggled under the soft wool covering. She ought to wear something, he thought.

"Yes," she said.

"I'm George Fraser," he went on, aware that his heart was thumping wildly. "I don't know if Syd ever mentioned me. He asked me to tell you that he'd be late. He's taken the key …"

Her eyes travelled over him. He had never experienced such intense scrutiny. He felt that she was even peering into his pockets.

"Of course," she said, "I know all about you. But come into the club. We don't have to stand out here, do we?"

Without waiting for his reply, she turned abruptly and walked out of the sunshine and the clean-smelling air into the darkness of the building.

Following her, a helpless victim to the raven hair and slim, jaunty hips that preceded him up the stairs, George went towards his doom.

# 7

George knew the exact moment when he fell in love with Cora Brant. It happened suddenly, and, to him, as dramatically as a blow in the face. He found it was extraordinary that he could fall in love with Cora in this way. It wasn't George's idea of love at all. He had always imagined that two people fell in love only after they had probed each other's minds, learned each other's habits and outlook and come to know each other so well that the obvious thing for them to do was to live together. That was George's idea of falling in love. He often thought about marriage, and how he would behave when the right girl came along. He had assured himself over and over again that he wouldn't do anything hasty. He had always imagined a leisurely, satisfying courtship that would give him an opportunity of offering his affection slowly, but with increasing warmth, until the girl he had chosen gladly accepted him.

But when it happened with this unexpected, extraordinary suddenness he was dismayed to find that he had no control over the situation nor over his feelings. At one moment Cora was just someone – admittedly exciting and unusual – to talk to and to look at and with whom he hoped to alleviate an hour of lonely boredom; at the next she was someone he was physically and mentally aware of in a most overpowering way. For some unexplained reason he was tremendously moved, wanting to cry: an absurd emotion, which, again, he had never experienced before, and which made him feel tremendously happy and light-headed.

He had only a hazy recollection of what had happened in the club. The room had been thick with tobacco smoke, noisy with jive and strident voices. But he had eyes only for Cora Brant. The people around him and the noise were incidental: a background out of focus. He had been so excited that he still was unable to remember what she had said to him. He had only been aware of her presence and his own triumph, and he nursed this triumph with secret and delighted pleasure.

He had bought drinks, and he had been startled that she tackled a pint of beer. The large glass seemed grotesque in her thin, white hand: a claw. He had absently noticed that her nails were scarlet, and her knuckles were a little grubby. And when he looked more closely at her, he realized she was not immaculate in the accepted sense of the word. She was slatternly: her black hair was lustreless, her pale blue sweater was no longer fresh, and there was face powder on her slacks.

But George was not critical. Any woman was a novelty to him, and a girl like Cora Brant was far more than a novelty – she was an exciting experience. Because of the noise of the music and the voices around them, they hadn't said much to each other. George had been content to admire her. He had, of course, explained about Sydney. To make himself heard, he had to lean across the table and shout at her. He found that embarrassing: it was like carrying on an intimate conversation in a crowded tube train. Cora had listened, her eyes on his face, her perfume in his nostrils. She had nodded and shrugged her shoulders, waving to the band as if to say it was no use talking at present.

"We'll go somewhere quieter in a little while," she had said, and had turned to watch the band.

After that it would not have mattered to George if she had not spoken again during the whole evening. She had actually said that they were going to be together, and he relaxed, rather astonished, but so grateful that he could have wept.

Then later, when the band had left the dais for a short interval, she looked at him and raised her eyebrows.

"Shall we go?" she said, pushing back her chair.

Obediently George followed her down the stairs to the street. The sudden decision to leave, the complete indifference to his own plans, and her take-it-for-granted attitude that he wanted to go with her reminded him of Sydney Brant. That was how he behaved. Both of them knew what they wanted. They led: others followed.

Neither of them spoke as they walked along the pavement together. Cora's small head, level with George's shoulder, moved along smoothly before him, as if she were being drawn along on wheels. She left behind her the faintest smell of sandalwood.

The evening light was beginning to fade. Storm clouds crept across the sky. The air in the streets had become stale, like the breath of a sick man, and sudden gusts of hot wind sent dust and scraps of paper swirling around the feet of the crowd moving sullenly along the hot pavements.

At the corner of Orchard and Oxford Streets, Cora paused. She glanced along the street towards Marble Arch: a street thronged with people all making a leisurely way to the Park.

"I'm hungry," she said. "Let's get something to eat."

"That's an idea," George said eagerly, conscious of Robinson's eleven pounds in his wallet. "Where would you like to go? The Dorchester?" He was quite willing to spend his last penny on her if it would help to create a good impression. He had never been to the Dorchester, but he had heard about it. It was the smartest place he could think of that was close at hand.

"The what?" she asked, staring at him blankly. "Do you mean the Dorchester Hotel?"

He felt himself flushing. "Yes," he said. "Why not?"

"What, in those clothes?" she asked, eyeing him up and down. "My dear man! They wouldn't let you past the door."

He looked at his worn shoes, his face burning. If she had struck him with a whip she couldn't have succeeded in hurting him more.

"And what about me?" she went on, apparently unaware that she had so completely crushed him. "The Dorchester in these rags?"

"I – I'm sorry," George said, not looking at her. "I just wanted to give you a good time. I – I didn't think it mattered what you wore."

"Well, it does," she said coldly.

There was a long, awkward pause. George was too flustered to suggest anywhere else. She'll go in a moment, he thought feverishly. I'm sure she'll go. Why am I standing like this, doing nothing? I can't expect her to suggest anything – it's my place to make the arrangements.

But the more he tried to think where he could take her, the more panic-stricken he became.

She was eyeing him curiously now. He could feel her eyes on his face.

"Perhaps you have something else to do …" she said suddenly.

"Me? Of course not," George said, over eager and almost

shouting. "I – I've got nowhere to go. I just don't go anywhere, that's all. I – I don't know where you'd like to go. Perhaps you'll suggest something."

"Where do you live?"

Astonished, George told her.

"Let's go to your place," she said. "I'm tired of the heat and the crowds."

George could scarcely believe his ears.

"My place?" he repeated blankly. "Oh, you wouldn't like that. I mean it's only a room. It – it isn't much. It's not very comfortable."

"It's somewhere to sit, isn't it?" she said, staring a little impatiently at him. "Or can't you take women there?"

He hadn't the faintest idea. It was something he had never contemplated doing. He had visions of Mrs Rhodes' disapproving face, and he flinched away from the thought. Then he remembered once seeing one of the other boarders bring a lady visitor to his room. Of course, the visitor hadn't been like Cora; but if one boarder could do it, why couldn't he? Besides, if they went at once, Mrs Rhodes would be in the basement having supper. She wouldn't even see him.

"Oh, that's all right," he said eagerly. "Nothing like that. We can go if you would like to. It's only the room isn't much ..."

She was beginning to move towards Edgware Road. Now that that was settled, she seemed to have lost interest in him. She walked on as if he wasn't with her.

George tagged along behind. Of course he was excited. To have a girl like Cora in his room! He thought at least she would want to dance, or go to the pictures, or do something extravagant.

She suddenly stopped outside a snack bar.

"Let's take something in with us," she said, looking at the appetizing show in the window. Without waiting for him to agree, she entered the shop.

"Two chicken sandwiches, two cheese sandwiches and two apples," she said to the white-coated attendant behind the counter.

George planked down a ten-shilling note while the attendant packed the sandwiches and apples in a cardboard container.

"How much?" Cora asked, ignoring George's money.

"That'll be two and six, miss," the attendant said, looking first at her and then at George.

"Here you are," George said, pushing the note towards the attendant.

Cora put down one shilling and threepence. "That's my share," she said shortly, and picked up the cardboard container.

"I say!" George protested. "This is my show." And he tried to give her back her money.

"Keep it," she said, turning towards the door. "I always pay for myself."

"You can't do that …" George said feebly, but she was already moving away, and by now had left the shop.

"The sort of girl I'd like to go out with," the attendant said wistfully. "Most of 'em take the linings from your pockets."

George, his face burning, snatched up his change and ran after Cora.

When he caught up with her, he said, "You really must let me pay …"

"Now shut up!" Cora said. "I never accept anything from any man. I'm independent, and if I'm going to see you again, the sooner you understand that the better."

If she was going to see him again! George stared at her

hopefully. Did that mean …? He blinked. It must mean that. People just didn't say things like that if they didn't intend seeing you again.

"Well, if you really want to …" he said, not quite sure how he should react to such an ultimatum.

"I do!" she returned emphatically. "Now come on, don't stand there blocking the way."

"We'll want some beer," George said, falling in step beside her. "I suppose you want to pay for your bottle, too?" He said it half jokingly, and then looked at her quickly to see if he had caused offence.

She glanced at him.

"I'm certainly going to pay for my own beer," she said. "Does that amuse you?"

And as he looked down at her, arrogant, small but durable, it happened. He found himself suddenly, utterly and completely in love with her. It was an overpowering feeling that stupefied him, made him water at the eyes, made him weak in the legs.

They looked at each other. Whether she saw the change in him, he wasn't sure. He felt she must be able to read his thoughts. She couldn't fail to see how completely crazy he was about her. If she did, she made no sign, but went on, her head a little higher, her chest arched.

They bought two bottles of beer at the off-licence at the corner of George's street. Then they went on to the boarding-house.

"I'm afraid it isn't much," George muttered apologetically as he opened the front door. "But if you think you'll like it …" His voice died away as he glanced uneasily round the hall.

There was no one about. The sound of dishes clattering in the basement reassured him.

Cora went straight upstairs. She wasn't a fool, George

thought. She knows I'm nervous about her being here. She's going straight up. There's no nonsense about her.

He eyed her slim hips as she went on ahead of him. She was beautiful. There was absolutely no doubt about it. Most women looked awful in trousers. They stuck out and they wobbled, but not Cora. She was hard, slim, neat.

So he was in love with her. And he was lucky, too. Not many men would be as fortunate as he. She wasn't going to run him into any expense. He knew what girls were like. Spend – spend – spend, all the time. They didn't think you loved them unless you continually spent money on them. But Cora wasn't like that. She was independent. "If I'm going to see you again ..." It was the most wonderful evening of his life!

"Just one more flight," he said, as she glanced back over her shoulder. "And you turn to the right when you get to the top."

She stopped on the landing.

"In here," he said, passing her and opening the door.

He stood aside to let her in.

"It's not much," he said again, seeing the room suddenly in a new light. It did somehow seem small and sordid. The wallpaper seemed more faded and the furniture shabbier. He wished that he had a bright, well-furnished room to offer her.

He saw Leo curled up on the bed.

"That's my cat ..." he began.

Then Leo opened its eyes, took one scared look at Cora and was gone, streaking through the open doorway, sending a mat flying. They heard it rushing madly down the stairs.

George sighed. That hadn't happened for months.

"He's awfully scared of strangers," he said, apologetically, and closed the door. "I had quite a time with him at first, but we're great friends now. Do you like cats?"

"Cats?" She seemed far away. "They're all right, I suppose." She put the cardboard container on his dressing-table and moved further into the room.

George took off his hat and hung it in the cupboard. Now that he was alone with her in this little room he felt shy, uneasy. The bed seemed horribly conspicuous. In fact, the bed embarrassed him: the room seemed all bed.

"Do sit down," he said, fussing around her. "I'll get some glasses. I've got one here, and there's another in the bathroom. I'm afraid they're only tooth glasses, but it doesn't matter does it?"

Without waiting for her to reply, he left the room and hurried to the bathroom on the next floor. He was glad to be away from her for a moment. In fact, he would have been pleased if she had suddenly changed her mind about spending the evening with him. He was finding her a little overpowering. The experience of falling in love with her like this was a bit shattering. He needed quiet to think about it.

He was nervous of her too. There was something cynical and cold and cross about her. He felt that if he said the wrong thing she would be unkind to him. He wanted to avoid that at all costs. So far, apart from the *faux pas* about the Dorchester – that had been a dumb, brainless suggestion – he had managed fairly well up to now. But he was losing his nerve. It was like walking a tight-rope. He had had one narrow escape, and now, out on the rope with a sheer drop below, he was rapidly getting into a panic. What was he to talk about? How could he hope to amuse her for the next hour or so? If only she had asked to be taken to a movie! How simple that would have been! All he would have had to do was to buy the tickets – and anyway, she would probably have insisted on paying for herself – and the film would have taken care of the rest of the evening.

He mustn't keep her waiting, he thought, as he took the glass from the metal holder. He hurried back, hesitated outside the door and then went in.

She was sitting on the bed, her hands on her knees, her legs crossed.

"There we are," George said, with false heartiness. "Let's have a drink. I'm hungry, too, aren't you?"

"A bit," she said, looking at him as she might look at some strange animal at the Zoo.

"Have the armchair," George went on, busying himself with the drinks. "It's jolly comfortable, although it looks a bit of a mess."

"It's all right," she said. "I like beds."

He felt his face burn. He was angry with himself for being self-conscious about the bed, also conscious of the double meaning. He was sure she didn't mean it in that way. It was just his mind.

"Well, so long as you're comfortable," he said, handing her a glass of beer. "I'll unpack the sandwiches."

He kept his back turned to her so that she should not see the furious blush on his face. It took him a minute or so to recover, and when he turned, she was lying on her side, propped up by her arm, one trousered leg hanging over the side of the bed, the other stretched out.

"Take my shoes off," she said. "Or I'll make the cover dirty."

He did so, with clumsy, trembling fingers. But he enjoyed doing it, and he put the shoes on the floor under the bed, feeling an absurd tenderness towards them.

Although the window was wide open, it was hot in the little room. The storm clouds had now blotted out the sun, and it was dark.

"Shall I put the light on?" he asked. "I think we're going to have some rain."

"All right. I wish you'd sit down. You're too big for this room, anyway."

He put the sandwiches on a piece of paper within reach of her hand, turned on the light, and sat down by the window. He was secretly delighted to hear her refer to his size. George was proud of his height and strength.

"Why don't you do something better than selling those silly books?" she asked abruptly.

"It suits me for the moment," George returned, startled by this unexpected reproach; and feeling he ought to offer a better explanation, added, "It gives me a lot of free time to make plans."

"There's no money in it, is there?" Cora went on.

"Well, your brother made nine pounds this week," George said, munching with enjoyment.

"As much as that?" There was a sharp note in her voice.

George studied her. The blue smudges under her eyes, her whitish-grey complexion, her thin, scarlet mouth fascinated him.

"Oh yes. It isn't bad, is it?"

She sipped her beer.

"He never tells me anything," she said in a cold, tight voice. 'We haven't had any money for ages. I don't know how we live. Nine pounds! And he's gone off for the evening." Her hand closed into a small, cruel fist.

"Of course, he mayn't be so lucky next week," George went on hurriedly, alarmed that he might have said something wrong. "You can never tell. There's a lot of luck in the game, you know."

"I could kill him!" she said viciously. "Look at me! I've been in this stinking outfit for months. That's all I've got!"

"You look marvellous," George said, and meant it. "It suits you."

"You're all alike," she returned. "Do you really think a girl ought to live in a get-up like this?" Her lips twisted. "I haven't another rag to my name."

Pity stirred in him. "I say – I'm awfully sorry …"

She finished her sandwich, her eyes brooding and bitter.

"So long as Sydney gets what he wants," she said after a pause, "he doesn't care a damn about me. He doesn't care what I'll do tonight." She suddenly shrugged. "Well, never mind. It's early to worry about that now." She pushed a wave of hair back from her cheek and then rubbed her temple with one finger. "Tell me about Frank Kelly."

"Who?" George flinched away from her.

She bit her knuckle and looked at him over her hand.

"Sydney told me. You and Frank Kelly. At first I didn't believe it, but now I've seen you …"

George emptied his glass and got up to refill it. There was a glint in her slate-grey eyes that could have meant anything: curiosity, admiration, desire …

"Seen me? I don't understand."

"You don't have to pretend with me. I'm sick of men without spine. At least, you're a man."

George slopped a little of the beer on the carpet. A surge of emotion crawled up his back.

"What do you mean?" he asked, putting the glass on the mantelpiece. He tried to control the huskiness in his voice without success.

"You've lived dangerously. You've killed men, haven't you? That means something to me."

George faced her. There was nothing in her eyes now. They

were like drawn curtains. He stared at her, suddenly afraid.

"Who told you?"

"I don't have to be told. I'm not a fool. I know men. When Sydney told me about you, I thought you were one of those ghastly little miscarriages who boast about what they have done: who lie, cheat, and brag because they haven't the guts to live like men. But Sydney told me I was wrong. Even then I wouldn't believe him. He told me you had a gun, and I said you were lying."

George found perspiration was running down his face. He took out his handkerchief and mopped himself. He realized that if he wanted her admiration – and he wanted that more than anything else in the world – he could not admit that he had been lying to Brant. He was caught in his own trap; but, oddly enough, he didn't care. What possible harm could it do if he did pretend that he was a big-shot gangster? She wouldn't tell the police about him. And just suppose she did? He could always say that he had been pulling her leg, and he could prove that he had never been out of the country. All right, if she thought he had lived dangerously, if she thought he had killed men, and if, knowing that, she admired him, he would give her the opportunity to admire him even more.

"I don't talk about that side of my life," he said, picking up his glass. "It only sounds like bragging; but if you really want to know ... well, I suppose I've had as exciting a life as most men."

"Men are such liars," she said calmly, leaning down to put her glass on the floor. "I still think you could be lying ..."

George bit his lip. What was she up to now?

"Show me your gun," she said. "I'll believe you if you really have a gun."

He hesitated. Some instinct warned him not to show her

the gun. He had never shown it to anyone. It was his secret. He had never intended sharing it with anyone.

She was watching him now, her eyes cold and cynical.

"Bluffing?" she asked, in a contemptuous, amused tone.

He went to his drawer and took out the cardboard box.

"You mustn't tell anyone," he said, putting the box on the bed.

She pushed his hand away and took off the lid. She had the gun now. It was odd, but it looked right in her hands. It looked as right in her hands as a scalpel looks right in the hands of a surgeon. She sat up and examined the gun. Her face was expressionless, but there was an intent concentration in her eyes that worried him.

"Is it loaded?" she asked, at last.

"Oh no," George said. "Now let me put it away. I don't know why you should be interested in it."

"Show me how to load it," she urged. "Where are the cartridges?"

Without waiting for him to show her, she slid off the bed, went to the drawer and found the little wooden box.

"No," he said, surprised at his own firmness. "You leave those alone. Put them back."

She was looking at the shiny brass cylinders.

"Why?"

"I don't want any accidents. Please put them back."

She shrugged impatiently; but she put the box back and sat on the bed again. She picked up the Luger and pressed the trigger.

"Why doesn't it work?" she asked, frowning.

"It's stiff," George said. "You have to pull very hard."

She tried again, but she still couldn't pull back the trigger.

"Here, I'll show you," George said, taking the gun from

her. "Like this."

He exerted his great strength, and the hammer snapped down.

"It wants adjusting really, only I haven't bothered. I'll never use it here. At one time it had a hair-trigger, it would fire at the slightest touch; but it's a little out of order now."

"How do you adjust it?" she asked, taking the gun from him and curling her slim finger round the trigger. By holding the gun in both hands and pressing very hard, she managed to raise the hammer an inch or so. "Phew; it is stiff! How do you adjust it?"

George sat on the bed by her side and explained the trigger mechanism to her.

"It's simple; only I prefer to keep the trigger stiff, just in case of accidents."

"You're scared of accidents, aren't you?" There was a mocking note in her voice. "Even when the gun isn't loaded, you're scared."

"It's better to be safe than sorry," he returned, and took the Luger from her. His hand touched hers, and for one brief moment he felt a flame shoot through him: a burning desire to take her in his arms.

He got up at once and put the gun away.

"Now perhaps you believe me," he said, with an embarrassed laugh.

"I believe you," she returned, stretching out on the bed. "Give me an apple, will you?"

He gave her an apple, and took the other himself. He went back to the window, feeling that it was too disturbing to be so close to her.

"I say!" he said, looking into the street. "It's beginning to rain."

"Oh, hell!" She raised her head. "Hard?"

"I'm afraid so." He leaned out of the window, feeling the rain on his face. "It looks as if it's set in for the night. I can lend you my mack, of course, but I'm afraid you'll get wet."

As she didn't say anything, he glanced over his shoulder. She was lying flat on her back, staring up at the ceiling.

"This bed's comfortable," she said, as if speaking to herself. "I think I'll spend the night here. It doesn't seem much sense going out in the rain, especially as Sydney won't be back until late. Besides, I'm tired."

George realized that his breath was whistling through his nostrils. He felt his blood moving through his veins: it was a most odd sensation.

"You'll sleep here – ?"

She seemed to become aware of him.

"Would you mind?"

"You mean – sleep in my bed?"

"Where else do you suggest … on the floor?"

"Well, no. I didn't mean that. I don't know what they'd say …" He floundered; excited, frightened and acutely conscious of wanting her in an overpowering way.

"Oh, I'd go early," she said indifferently. "They needn't know unless you tell them."

"No … I suppose not."

This was fantastic, he thought. She's offering to sleep with me, and I'm behaving like an idiot. He was suddenly stricken by tremendous shyness. This wasn't the way he had imagined it at all. In his imagination he had slept with many lovely women, but it was only after a long and arduous courtship. That really was the most exciting thing about love. Now that the was being so cold-blooded about it, he felt frightened, although his desire was at fever heat.

"Then you don't mind?" she said impatiently. "Make up your mind. Can I stay?"

He moved slowly towards the bed.

"Of course," he said, standing over her. "I – I'd love you to, Cora."

This was the first time he had used her name. It gave him great pleasure. Cora! It was a lovely name.

She looked up at him and yawned.

"And you don't mind sleeping in the chair?"

He stood very still.

"The chair?"

"Perhaps you've got another bed somewhere," she said, and then, seeing the expression on his face, she sat up abruptly. "Oh, God!" she went on. "Did you think you were going to sleep with me?"

George could only stare at her, dumb, embarrassed misery in his eyes.

She swung her legs off the bed.

"I'm going," she said. "I was forgetting you don't know me very well."

George shook his head.

"No, don't. It was my fault. Please stay. The chair's all right."

He crossed to the window and stood looking out, trying to recover from the shock and disappointment.

Of course she was right. He was glad in a way that she hadn't meant it. Only it was such an odd way of putting it. He couldn't be blamed for misunderstanding. She was really quite fantastic. What confidence she had in herself!

And how like Sydney! Taking his bed, making him sleep in a chair, no thought for his comfort. Had she managed to guess that he was easily scared, that he was timid and uneasy with women? Was that the reason why she was pushing him out of his bed – because she knew very well he wouldn't have the nerve to force his attention on her? He didn't think so. How could any girl be sure of that?

She was standing at his side.

"I'll go if you want me to," she said. "You mustn't let me impose on you. I'm selfish. If you don't want to sleep in the chair, turn me out."

As if he would.

"Of course not," he said eagerly. "I'm awfully pleased to have you here. I mean that. I'm sorry I was so stupid. I'm really ashamed of myself …"

She looked at him. Was that odd expression contempt? He looked again, but her eyes had become expressionless.

"All my friends know about me," she said. "I'd forgotten that you don't. Still, you don't want me, do you? You must have dozens of women."

"But I haven't …"

"I don't sleep with men," she went on, ignoring his interruption. "It's part of my independence. I'm very independent. I never take and I never give."

He didn't say anything. What was there to say?

"You'll probably think I'm lying, but I'm not. My bed life is very exclusive. I hate being mauled. It's inconvenient sometimes. I suppose I shouldn't be so damned poor if I wasn't so damned fussy."

George flinched.

There didn't seem to be anything further to say about the subject. They stood side by side looking out of the window at the street lights, the rain and the wet pavements. They remained like that for a long time.

# 8

George was asleep when Ella brought him his morning tea. He raised his head as she drew the curtains, and blinked round the room.

" 'Ave you been using scent, Mr George?" she asked, her shiny little face tilted up as she sniffed the air. "It's ever so nice."

Scent? What did she mean? George gaped at her.

"No," he said, yawning. "Of course not." Then he remembered Cora, and a guilty flush rose to his face.

Ella was watching him.

"Well, I am surprised at you, Mr George," she said, her eyes wide. " 'Oo was she?"

It was no use lying to Ella. She could see his embarrassment too clearly.

"Oh, a friend," George returned, sinking back on the pillow. "She only looked in for a moment last night. I must say her perfume was pretty strong."

Ella wasn't so easily fooled.

"Well, I never!" she ejaculated. "Fancy you bringing a young lady ..."

"Now, look, Ella," George said a little shortly. "I want to rest. I didn't sleep very well. Be a good girl and run away."

"All right, Mr George," Ella returned. "But I'm surprised at you all the same."

George closed his eyes, and after a moment's hesitation Ella went away. George knew that he hadn't heard the last of it, but at the moment he didn't care.

As soon as she had gone he slipped out of bed and opened the door for Leo. He still felt stiff, and his neck ached after the night in the armchair, but he didn't mind. It had been a wonderful evening and a wonderful night.

He got back into bed and drank his tea.

It really seemed like a dream. Looking round the small, sordid room, he could scarcely believe that Cora had been there. He could smell her perfume on the pillow. Her hair had rested there. It had been all very exciting and marvellous, and he was mad about her.

Just then Leo stalked into the room.

"Come on, old boy," George called, snapping his fingers.

But the cat was suspicious, sniffing the air and looking at George with big, uneasy eyes. Obviously it didn't like the smell of Cora's perfume.

"Puss! Puss!" George called. "Come on. Up you come."

Silently Leo turned and slid out of the room. George called, but the cat had gone.

A little distressed, he settled down once more. Well, if Leo wanted to be stupid, then he would have to go his own way, George thought. There were other things to think about besides Leo. He had been longing for the time when he could think back on last night and savour all its excitements, brood over what Cora had said, and dwell on Cora herself.

It had been a wonderful night, in spite of the bad beginning. George hadn't talked so much in his life. It was extraordinary how easy it was to talk to Cora. She led him on. Not that she said much herself, but she knew how to listen. And he had thought that he wouldn't have been able to amuse her! Even now he found it difficult to believe that he had been such a success.

She had wanted to know about his life in the States. That was after she had got into bed. Her getting into bed was exciting. She hadn't been a scrap self-conscious. It was he who had been embarrassed.

"What can I sleep in?" she had asked, "Or do I have to sleep in my skin?"

He had given her a pair of his pyjamas. Of course, they had been ridiculously big, but she didn't seem to mind.

"And now I want to spend a penny," she had said, and he couldn't help going as red as a beetroot. He had to show her where the bathroom was, and he had to hang about outside in case someone spotted her coming out. Although he was shy about it, he secretly enjoyed the intimacy between them.

Then he stayed outside the door until she was in bed. He thought she looked absolutely smashing in bed. She had rolled up the sleeves of the pyjamas, and somehow they seemed to fit her quite well. There she lay, her hair like spilt ink on the pillow, the sheet adjusted above her breasts, and her red nailed hands folded on her tummy.

George had sat by the window with his overcoat over his legs and his feet up on a chair. They finished the beer and had talked. She had asked him to tell her about his adventures in the States. George was too happy to be cautious. So he began to talk. Everything he had read about the gang wars of America was marshalled and trotted out as his own adventures. Never had he been so inspired. He had described how he had been one of the first to arrive at the little cabin in the hills where Ma Barker and her son had made their last stand.

"I'll never forget that day," he said, looking out of the window as he tried to remember what he had read of Ma Barker's death. "We arrived early one morning. There was a ground mist, and we got right up to the cabin without being seen. I was with a bunch of G-men, and they were jittery. I didn't blame them, because hell was likely to break loose any minute.

"I'd had some experience working on both sides of the fence, and I had been in some pretty tough spots. If Fred Barker hadn't played me a dirty trick, I wouldn't have been hunting him with the Feds. At that time I was out for excitement, and I didn't care which side I was on, so long as I got into a scrap.

"The Feds didn't want a battle, but they hadn't the nerve to call on Ma to give up. So I offered to do it. I wanted to show them I had more guts than they.

"I walked to the door of the cabin. I don't mind telling you my knees were knocking.

"I hammered on the door. Ma Barker, a Tommy-gun half hidden behind her back, appeared at the window. I could see her wrinkles, her narrowed eyes and the wattles on her sagging neck.

" 'Come on, Ma,' I said. 'You know me. You're caught, and you might just as well come quietly.'

" 'To hell with you!' she yelled and ducked out of sight.

"Then Fred opened up with a machine-gun. I thought I was a goner. Slugs nipped at my clothes and splattered my shoes with dust. It was a pretty tough moment. One of the Feds started grinding his machine-gun, and that put Fred off. I got under cover with slugs still chasing me.

"We fought it out for over an hour, but they didn't stand a chance. A burst of automatic rifle fire caught Ma as she was peering through the window. When we found Fred, he had fourteen slugs in his carcass."

So he had gone on. He paraded them all before her – Baby-Face Nelson, Frank Nash, Roger Touhy, Jake Fleagle; violence, shooting, racing cars, police sirens. He had never done better.

"And they took me for a ride," he went on, scowling at the ceiling. "Me! They took me in a wood, and they said I was washed up. There were three of them. There was a guy called Wineinger. I can see him now. A pot-bellied little runt, with a scar where someone had bashed him with a bottle. There was Clyde Barrow, thin and mean, with ears like a bat. And Gustave Banghart. They were a dangerous, tough mob, and it didn't look so good. I hadn't anything to lose, so I jumped Wineinger and got his rod. It was the fastest thing I've ever done in my life. I came out of that wood on my feet, and I came out alone."

Oh yes, he had never been better, and she had listened without moving, absorbed, excited. Her intent interest had been a spur to his imagination.

"I'm glad you told me," she had said, when he finally stopped talking. "It was what I expected of you."

Then he had edged the conversation round to Sydney. He wanted to know more about Sydney – what he did, where he lived, how Cora and he got on together.

But she didn't tell him much. She suddenly became guarded. She said she didn't know much about Sydney herself. He didn't tell her things. Look at that nine pounds! He hadn't told her about that. Didn't that show how secretive he was? They never had any money – at least, that was what Sydney always told her. He was supposed to be the breadwinner. She didn't do anything except keep the flat. Yes, they had a flat off Russell Square. George must see it one day. Sydney didn't welcome visitors. He wasn't sociable, but when he was away, George must come.

George had a vague feeling that Cora was frightened of Sydney. "He's very domineering," she said, "and we fight."

But when he pressed her for details, she rather pointedly changed the subject.

"I think I'll go to sleep now," she said, settling further down in the bed. "I was late last night."

George eased himself in his chair. It wasn't a bit comfortable now he was trying to make a bed of it.

"I hope you sleep well," he said. "What time do you want to be called in the morning?"

"Oh, I'll wake up. I always do," she returned.

"I say …" George said, after a moment's silence, "won't Sydney worry where you are?"

"He doesn't worry about me. He doesn't worry about anyone," Cora said. "He's a bit touched, if you must know."

"Oh, I wouldn't say that," George protested.

"Well, I would."

"How did he get that scar?" George asked, at last screwing up courage to ask something that had been worrying him for days. "He's very sensitive about it, isn't he?"

"He had an accident," Cora said shortly.

"I thought it was something like that," George said, still curious. "It was pretty recent, wasn't it?"

Cora didn't say anything.

After a moment's hesitation, George went on, "How did it happen?"

"He's got enemies," Cora said.

George looked up, startled. "Enemies?" he repeated blankly.

"Look here, I want to go to sleep," Cora said sharply. "I

wish you'd turn out the light."

George got up from his chair and crossed the room to the light switch. He paused as he passed her bed. "Comfortable?" he asked, thinking how lovely she looked.

"Yes. Now please put out the light."

George sighed. How much nicer it would have been if she wasn't quite so matter of fact. It was as if she was used to sleeping in strange men's rooms. George didn't want to go to sleep. It was all too exciting. He wanted to sit on her bed and watch her, even if she didn't wish to talk.

But he put out the light and groped his way back to his chair.

"I don't suppose this means anything to you," he blurted out after a long silence.

"Oh, God!" she said impatiently. "Can't you sleep? What means nothing to me?"

"Being here ..." George was glad it was dark. He felt the irritating flush mounting to his face. "I've never had a girl in my room before."

"You're a simple soul, aren't you?" she said. "Are you getting a kick out of this?"

George warmed to her immediately. So she could be kind in a rather patronizing way!

"Of course I am," he said, and encouraged by the darkness, he went on, a little haltingly. "This has been a marvellous evening for me. I don't suppose you realize what it means to me."

"Why not?"

"Well, perhaps you do; but you're not lonely like I am. I spend most of my time on my own. I don't know why, but I just don't seem to make friends. I haven't met anyone I wanted to make my friend – until now." He coughed nervously, alarmed at his own rashness. Well, he had said it now. He almost cringed while waiting for her to reply. Was she going to be kind?

She didn't say anything.

George waited anxiously, and then realized, with a sense of frustration, that she wasn't going to reply.

"I expect you think I'm a bit of a fool," he said, a little bitterly. "I suppose I am really. I suppose most people would think I'm a bit soft being so fond of Leo – he's my cat. It's funny about Leo. I used to think people were a bit soft myself, being fond of animals; but somehow Leo's different." He stared into the darkness, trying to see her. "It's when you're lonely, you know. Animals seem to understand. They don't demand anything from you. If you don't feel like talking, they just sit with you. If you want to go out, they don't mind. Leo's jolly good company, but of course it isn't the same as having someone you can really talk to. Is it?"

She still didn't reply.

He waited a moment and repeated a little louder, "Is it?"

"Is what?" she asked sleepily.

"Oh, nothing; you're nearly asleep, aren't you? I'm sorry. But it's not often I get anyone to talk to."

"That's pretty obvious," she said tartly, turning on her side. "You'd talk a donkey's hind leg off."

But he couldn't let her go to sleep just yet. It was only eleven o'clock, and it seemed such a wicked waste of a marvellous opportunity, just to sleep.

"I say, Cora," he said, lighting a cigarette.

"Hmmm?"

"Shall I see you again after this?"

He could just make out her head lifting off the pillow. "If you're going to smoke I may as well have one, too," she said. "Then I am going to sleep, and if you disturb me again I'll throw you out of the room."

He hurried across the room and gave her a cigarette. The flickering flame of the match lit up her face. She looked up at him, her eyes dark and tired, expressionless.

"You don't mind me calling you Cora, do you?" George went on, bending over her.

"Call me what you like," she said, lying back on the pillow.

The tip of the cigarette glowed red, and he could just see her straight, small Roman nose.

He sat on the edge of the bed. "Shall I see you again after this?" he repeated, because it was something important, something that was preying on his mind. He couldn't bear the thought of not seeing her again.

"I suppose so," she returned indifferently; "only Sydney doesn't like people hanging around."

"Doesn't he?" George was startled. "Why not?"

"You'd better ask him."

"But that needn't mean we won't see each other again, will it?"

"What's the matter with you?" she asked. "Surely a fellow like you has got dozens of girls."

"I haven't," George said, too anxious to keep in character. "I don't like women as a rule. But you're different."

"Am I?" There was a slight note of interest in her voice. "What do you mean?"

George hesitated. What exactly did he mean? He wasn't sure himself. She was beautiful, of course. But was that all that mattered so much to him? He didn't think so. There was something else. There was something strong about her, independent; she was someone he could rely on.

"I think you're wonderful," he said slowly. "You're the

most astonishing person I have ever met."

"Don't be a fool," she said, almost gently. "Of course I'm not."

Encouraged by her tone, George said, "But you are. You're lovely. You're so independent and headstrong. You know your own mind. You – you're interesting."

She lay silent for a long time. George wondered uneasily if he had offended her. Then she said, "You're not falling in love with me, are you?"

George clenched his fists. In love with her? He was mad about her!

"Oh yes," he said. "I'm in love with you. The moment I saw you …"

"Men are fools, aren't they?" she said in a confidential tone, as if she was speaking to another woman. "The men who have said that to me! Hundreds of them!"

"I'm sure of that," George said, sighing. "But it needn't matter to you, need it? I mean a girl like you wouldn't be bothered with anyone like me."

"You're a bit spineless, aren't you?" Cora said, flicking ash on the floor. There was contempt in her voice.

"I suppose I am," George said, crushed. "You see, I'm not used to women. I don't understand them."

"Well, at the rate you're going on, you never will," she returned. "What makes you think I wouldn't be bothered with you?"

George shrugged. "Well, you won't, will you?"

"What does that mean? You won't, will you?"

"What's the good of talking about it? You asked me if I loved you, and I said I did. You don't love me, do you?"

"Of course I don't," she returned, "but that doesn't mean that I couldn't love you, does it?"

George stared at her. "What was that?"

"Don't be so dumb!" There was an impatient note in her voice. "I said that doesn't mean I couldn't love you, does it?"

"Could you?"

"Not if you behave like a stuffed bull. A girl likes a little action now and then."

George could scarcely believe his ears. "Action?" he repeated blankly.

"My God!" she exclaimed, and suddenly laughed. "I don't believe it's possible! You're nothing but a schoolboy! Why don't you grow up?"

He began to tremble. God! He was making a mess of this, he thought desperately. What a stupid fool he was! She was inviting him to make love to her, and all he could do was to sit and tremble!

"What's the matter?" she asked sharply. "Aren't you well?"

"I'm all right," he said, and suddenly reached out for her hand. It felt cool and slim in his burning great paw. "Cora! I say, Cora ..." and he pulled her upright and kissed her clumsily.

She made no move, leaning back against his arm, her face a white blur in the darkness. Her perfume intoxicated him, the touch of her smooth cheek against his lips sent blood pounding in his ears.

"I do love you so," he said, and kissed her throat, holding her against him tightly.

They remained like that for a minute or two, then she pushed him away.

"All right, George," she said, "now back to your chair. That'll do for one night. It seems you can grow up when you want to."

He didn't want to go, and took hold of her hand.

"Be nice to me, Cora," he pleaded. "Let me kiss you again."

"I said that's enough," she said sharply. "Here, put this somewhere," and she gave him her cigarette butt. He took it and crossed the room to the fireplace. His legs felt weak, and he was in a kind of stupor. When he had got rid of the cigarette butt he stood at the foot of the bed, looking into the darkness where she was.

"We will meet again, won't we?" he said, terrified now that this experience was going to slip through his fingers, like all the dreams he had ever had.

"We'll meet," she returned, yawning, "and now I'm going to sleep."

"But what about Sydney? What shall we do about him?"

"He needn't know."

This excited him almost as much as when she had said that she might come to love him. Having a secret between them – a secret from Sydney – seemed to seal the bond of their relationship.

"Are you on the 'phone?"

"Hmm."

"Can I ring you sometimes? We might go out one night."

"All right."

"I'd better make a note of the number," George felt feverishly in his pocket for a pencil.

"It's in the book, Harris & Son, greengrocer. We've got a place above the shop."

"That's wonderful. Harris & Son. That's easy to remember, isn't it?"

"Now for God's sake go to sleep," Cora said. "If you dare say another word I'll really be angry with you!"

"All right," George said, satisfied. "Good night."

"Good night," she returned shortly, and he heard her turn over in the bed.

He groped his way to the chair and settled down. He glanced out of the window. It had stopped raining, and a misty moon floated in the sky. The pavements looked black and shiny in the street lights. In the distance a clock struck the half hour after eleven.

George shut his eyes. He was too excited to sleep. The whole of his cramped, lonely world had suddenly opened up like a gay sunshade. What an evening it had been! His life was going to be very different now. With Cora, he need never be lonely again. Whenever he wanted someone to talk to, he could ring her up. If he hadn't enough money to take her out, he could always have a few words with her on the 'phone. There was a telephone box at the corner of his street. There would be no need to stand in the passage in the basement, for everyone to hear what he had to say to her. Marvellous things, telephone boxes, he thought. Little houses of glass where you could talk to the one you loved, see the people passing, and knowing they could not overhear what you had to say. You need never be lonely if there was a telephone box handy and a girl like Cora at the other end of the line.

He had been a bit of a fool with her. But he had been lucky. Or rather she had been pretty decent about it. "A girl likes a little action now and then." Fancy her saying that! Well, he wouldn't wait for such an invitation again. Not he! He'd take her in his arms and kiss her right off next time they met. What was it she called him ... a stuffed bull? Well, she wouldn't have to call him that again. She *was* marvellous! Simply smashing! And Sydney wasn't to know about it. Queer about Sydney. What did she mean about "enemies"?

What enemies? "He's got enemies," she had said when he had asked how Sydney had got the scar. What an odd thing to say! He looked furtively across the room at the bed. He wanted to ask her to explain. Better not, he thought. She's got a temper all right, and it wouldn't do to provoke her again. No, that was something he would ask her the next time they met. He'd ring her tomorrow, just to show that he hadn't forgotten her ... as if he ever could! Yes, he'd ring her tomorrow.

Eventually he went to sleep, and when he woke at six o'clock the next morning, feeling stiff and cold, she had gone.

# 9

The next four or five days were, to George, exciting, confusing, exasperating and worrying. He had imagined that he would have been able to talk to Cora on the telephone at least once a day, and to see her within forty-eight hours of their first meeting. But it didn't work out like that at all. Cora, it seemed, was as illusive as a will-o'-the-wisp. Take Sunday, for instance. Now, Sunday was a good day for George's work. He usually began his calls immediately after lunch and worked through until dark. He was always sure of finding his prospects at home. He had arranged with Sydney to work this Sunday, and before getting up, he made elaborate plans for talking to Cora.

It was obvious that since the telephone was in the greengrocer's shop, he would have to make certain that Sydney wasn't in the flat when he telephoned. If the greengrocer had to call Cora to the 'phone, Sydney would want to know who was calling. So Sydney had to be out of the way. George found this added complication rather pleasing. It was much more exciting to have to plot and plan to talk to Cora than just to go to the telephone box and ring her in the usual way. The thing to do, he decided, was to 'phone from Wembley when he knew for certain that Sydney was actually working on the job. He knew Wembley pretty well now, and he remembered there was a public call-box at a junction of four streets which they had still to canvass. He would make a canvass or two, and then, when he was sure that Sydney was safely inside a house, he would slip over to the call-box and have a word with Cora.

He liked the idea immensely. Cora would be amused, too. He would give her a running commentary on Sydney's movements. "He's coming out of the house now. By the frown on his face, it doesn't look as if he got an order that time. He's looking up and down the road. I expect he's wondering where I've got to. He can't see me from where he's standing. There he goes now. He's opening another gate. There're three kids in the front garden; they're following him up the path. He's knocked on the door. He's waiting. I wish you could see how he looks at those kids. He'd like to bang their heads together. Hello, that's a bit of luck for him. The old man himself has come to the door. They're talking now. The old boy doesn't look too pleased. I expect his afternoon nap's been disturbed. But trust old Sydney. He keeps plugging away. Yes, I thought so; he's got into the house. The front door's shut now. Well, it looks like another CSE is on its way from the factory …"

Oh yes, Cora would be tickled to death. And then he would tell her how much he loved her and make plans to take her out the following evening.

George was finishing his lunch at the King's Arms when Sydney appeared. The moment he caught sight of the hard, white face with its disfiguring scar, he felt a qualm of uneasiness. Sydney nodded to him and ordered his inevitable lemonade.

"Hello," George said; the beef and pickles he was chewing suddenly tasted of sawdust.

Sydney grunted. He came straight to the point. "Did you see Cora last night?"

George felt his face grow red. "Cora?" He repeated,

wondering in panic whether she had told Sydney that they had met.

"Deaf?" Sydney said rudely, eyeing him. "What's the matter? You're going puce in the face."

George gulped. What a hateful, arrogant brat this Sydney was! he thought furiously. He put his hand to his cheek. "Got an exposed nerve," he muttered, looking away. "It gives me jip sometimes."

Sydney helped himself to a sardine on toast. "Did you see Cora last night?" he repeated.

"I – I left the message," George said. "Didn't she get it?"

"Oh, she got it; but the little bitch stayed out all night."

George flinched. He thought sadly that George Fraser, millionaire gangster, would have knocked Sydney's teeth out for calling her that.

"That's not a nice way to talk about your sister," he protested; "perhaps she stayed with friends. It was a pretty poisonous night, wasn't it?"

"Friends?" Sydney repeated, his blank, hard eyes still probing George's face. "What makes you think she's got friends?"

"How do I know? Hasn't she?"

"No. I haven't any friends either. We don't want friends."

Was Sydney threatening him in a subtle way? George wondered uneasily.

"If I knew who she was sleeping with, I'd mark him for life," Sydney said viciously.

George suddenly felt sick. He remembered the razor blade set in the cork handle and how Sydney had slashed Robinson's face. He remembered particularly the lightning movement that Sydney had made: a movement impossible to avoid.

"Well, I delivered the message," he said, cutting up his beef with exaggerated interest. "That's all you wanted me to do, wasn't it? I don't know anything about anything else."

"Yes, George," Sydney said softly. "That's all I wanted you to do – deliver the message."

"Well, that's what I did," George said shortly.

"She won't stay out again in a hurry," Sydney muttered, half to himself.

Immediately George became alarmed. Had he done anything to her? He suddenly lost his nervousness of Sydney. The thought that this vicious thug might have hurt her enraged him.

"What do you mean?" he asked, turning on Sydney.

"Just that," Sydney returned; "she knows what she'll get the next time she stays out all night."

Perhaps, after all, he had only threatened her, George thought, his unexpected surge of anger dying down. Well, that showed how careful they had to be. This confirmed his belief that Cora was frightened of Sydney. And no wonder. "A bit touched," she had said. Looking at him now, George thought he might really be a bit touched. There was something vicious about those eyes: not only vicious, but fanatical.

He thought it safer to change the subject, and began to talk about their afternoon calls.

He was now most anxious to speak to Cora. He wanted to hear her side of what had happened. If she wanted protection, she only had to ask him. If Sydney really had ill-treated her, he'd make him sorry. Just how he would do this he didn't know, but the details could be worked out later.

Once on the territory, George found it much harder to get to the telephone box than he had imagined. For one thing, all his calls were at the wrong end of the long street. Then Sydney seemed to be doing most of his canvassing in the front gardens. George was so anxious to talk to Cora, so worried that Sydney would spot him sneaking into the telephone box, that he spoilt four calls, where he was pretty sure, if he had been in the right mental attitude, he would have got orders.

This is ridiculous, he thought. I'm throwing away money. I can't go on like this. I'll go to the call-box right now. I won't wait for Sydney to get out of sight. I'll tell him I'm making a date with a friend, or something like that.

He hurried down the street towards the telephone box. As he passed one of the little houses, Sydney appeared at the front door. George kept on, feeling himself growing hot.

"Where you going?" Sydney called.

George glanced over his shoulder. "I've got a 'phone call to make," he said, without stopping. "It won't take me a minute."

He caught a glimpse of Sydney's sneering smile, and then he looked quickly away. Did Sydney suspect who he was going to call? No, he didn't think so, but it couldn't be helped if he did. George just could not wait any longer.

It took him some time to find Harris & Son in the telephone book. There were twenty-seven columns of Harrises to wade through. The telephone box was hot and stuffy, and George kept looking down the street, worried in case Sydney suddenly decided to find out whom he was calling. When eventually he found the number, he was dismayed and exasperated to find that he had no coppers. He decided recklessly to use sixpence, but the sixpence persisted in falling right through the box and coming back to him: it was as if it was endowed with human feelings and resented his extravagant mood. Thoroughly irritated, George left the 'phone box and looked up and down the road. Sydney had disappeared, but a policeman was coming along. George got some coppers off the policeman – coppers from a copper! he thought foolishly – and returned to the telephone box. He dialled the number and waited. *Brr-brr!* ... *Brr-brr!* In a moment or so he would be listening to her cold, tight, exciting voice. What a marvellous invention the telephone was! he thought. They were taking their time about answering. He shifted impatiently. Phew! It was hot in this booth. *Brr-brr!* ... *Brr-brr!* The bell went on and on. No one answered. George stood there, obstinate, sweating, irritated. What were they playing at? he asked himself. Why didn't they answer? Then he remembered. What a fool! Sunday! Of course, the shop would be shut! Oh hell! Now he would have to wait until tomorrow. He hung up and pressed button "B". Coming out into the sunshine, he felt suddenly deflated. Twenty-four hours ... how absolutely sickening! he thought. Why did she have to have a telephone in a shop? That meant he would never be able to talk to her on a Sunday. That meant that from now on Sunday was going to be the worst day of the week, instead of being the best day. It was a day he looked forward to because he had something to do in the afternoon as well as in the evening: it was also the best day for business. Now it would be the day when he was cut off entirely from Cora.

As it happened, it turned out to be the worst day he had had for a long time. People were ruder to him, more people were out, more people wouldn't come to the front door, although he could see them peeping at him through the curtains. When he did get inside, he found he wasn't concentrating, and he did not succeed in getting anyone sufficiently enthusiastic to sign an order form. Those who showed a slight inclination to buy put him off by asking him to call again. "I want to think about it," they said. "I don't want to rush into anything."

Of course, to make matters worse, Sydney got three orders. At the end of the evening, when they decided to go home, Sydney joined him at the corner.

"How many?" he said, looking at George with a jeering expression in his eyes.

George was tempted to lie, but he knew Sydney would demand to see the completed order forms, so he just shrugged and admitted he hadn't had any luck.

"Well, I got three," Sydney said in triumph. "What's the matter with you? Got something on your mind?"

Of course he had something on his mind, but he couldn't tell Sydney about that.

"It's just the luck of the game," he said, envious and disappointed. "I've worked through a lot of dead calls, and I'll get a batch of orders tomorrow."

"You hope," Sydney said, and laughed.

Monday wasn't much better. He was in a fever of excitement all the morning and afternoon. When Sydney and he reached Wembley at four o'clock, and as soon as Sydney was safely out of the way in one of the little houses, George rushed to the telephone box.

" 'Ullo?" said a man's voice in George's ear.

"Could I speak to Miss Brant?" George asked, trying to imagine what the man looked like from the sound of his voice.

" 'Oo?"

"Miss Brant," George repeated, raising his voice.

"Not now, yer can't. I got no one to send."

"But I must speak to Miss Brant," George said firmly.

"Well. I dunno. I can't leave the shop, now can I? It

means going hup the stairs. I ain't good at stairs, either ... not at my age, I ain't. Can't you ring later? The missus'll be back then."

"No, I can't," George said, thoroughly irritated. "I understood that Miss Brant could use your 'phone. I want to speak to her."

"Orl right, orl right," the voice said crossly. "I'll give 'er a yell. 'Ang on, will yer?"

George waited. It was insufferably hot in the telephone box, and he pushed the door open. He could hear voices faintly over the line. Once he heard the voice that had spoken to him shout, "Two pahnds of greens, six pahnds of spuds and a pahnd of onions ..." And he swore under his breath. The old devil wasn't getting Cora at all, he thought savagely. He was serving his rotten customers! But there was nothing else to do but wait. Time was going. He really ought to be on the job. Well, he wasn't going to hang up now he'd got so far. He would have to work a bit longer to make up for losing time like this. Oh, come on! Come on! he thought furiously. Why don't you hurry!

He waited nearly five minutes, then he heard the voice bawl, "Emmie ... Emmie ... someone wants that Brant girl on the blower ..."

"That Brant girl!" How dare a greengrocer talk like that! Well, anyway, it wouldn't be long now. Any second he would be hearing her voice.

"You doing your selling by 'phone?" Sydney asked.

George nearly jumped out of his skin, he whirled round, his face turning crimson, to find Sydney lolling against the telephone booth, watching him with suspicious, calculating eyes.

"I shan't be a minute," George spluttered, not knowing which way to look. "I'll be right out," and he tried to pull the door to, but Sydney had wedged it back with his foot.

"What's all this telephoning about?" Sydney asked. "Yesterday and now today. I thought you were a keen salesman."

"Hello?" Cora said in George's ear.

George looked from Sydney to the telephone mouthpiece. Sweat was running down his face. He didn't know what to do.

"Hello? Who's there?" Cora asked, her voice snappy and impatient.

He daren't speak to her with Sydney listening. Damn the rotter! George thought desperately. Why can't he go away!

" 'Phoning your best girl?" Sydney asked, a sneering grin on his face. "I wish you could see your mug! You look like a pickpocket caught in the act. Well, I won't embarrass you; only time's getting on, you know."

"Hello? Hello? Hello?" Cora was saying.

George waved Sydney away: an imploring, frantic gesture. Shrugging, Sydney slouched off, and as the booth door closed, a sharp click sounded in George's ear. Cora had hung up!

Sydney was still hanging about a few yards away, watching George through the glass panels. It was no good! He didn't dare risk dialling the number again. He was sick with disappointment and frustrated rage. Damn Sydney! Damn the greengrocer! Oh, damn everything!

Tuesday and Wednesday were as bad. Both times when George rang he was told that Cora was out. In desperation, he risked calling her on Thursday morning before he went to the King's Arms, and after some delay Sydney's voice floated over the line. Hurriedly, as if he had trodden on a snake, George hung up. Five days now and he hadn't spoken to her or seen her. And he had thought he was never going to be lonely again! It was worse now: far worse. Before, he didn't have this clamouring for the flesh, wasn't tormented by thoughts of loving Cora, holding her in his arms, feeling her smooth cheek against his lips.

He had to do something! This couldn't go on. His work was suffering. He had only earned thirty bob in five days, while Sydney had made himself seven quid. It infuriated George to hear the way Sydney sneered at seven pounds.

"Chick feed," he said, when George handed him the money order received from Head Office. "It's almost time I slung this job in. Seven nicker for slogging my guts out every evening. In the old days I'd do a job that'd take me an hour or so, and pick up twenty quid as easy as kiss your hand."

"What job?" George asked curiously.

Sydney brooded. "When things cool off a bit," he said at last, "maybe I'll let you in my racket. But right now I've got to keep out of sight," and then, for no apparent reason, he flew into a vicious rage and went off, looking almost murderous.

The more George saw of Sydney the more uneasy he became. The fellow was unbalanced. Perhaps he really was cracked. These sudden vicious tempers, the vicious, fanatical look in his eyes, the mysterious hinting about "his racket" worried George. The thought of Sydney's razor worried George even more.

Well, he certainly wasn't going to mix himself up in Sydney's racket. He knew instinctively that it was crooked. Sydney was the kind of fellow who'd land up in jail. Jail bait, that's what he was!

In spite of his instinctive fear of Sydney, George was determined to speak to Cora the next day, Friday. Even if it meant doing no work at all and staying in a telephone box all the evening, he was going to talk to her! He wanted her to spend Saturday evening with him. He planned to take her to a movie and then to dinner somewhere. He had put away the eleven pounds that Sydney had got from Robinson, ear-marked for this outing. He was determined to stand treat: he wasn't going to have any nonsense from Cora about paying for herself. And what was more, when they met he would kiss her: he'd show her he was a man of action.

To be certain of speaking to Cora, he decided not to work that evening. He told Sydney he wasn't feeling too well. He said he'd drunk some bad beer: it had upset his stomach.

"I think I'll stay at home," he said, avoiding Sydney's probing eyes. "I don't feel like going out on the job tonight."

"Please yourself," Sydney said, shrugging; "it's your loss. You'd better pull up your socks. You've only taken one order this week."

George didn't need to be reminded of this unpleasant fact, but he assured himself that once he had seen Cora he would be able to settle down to work again. Selling books demanded all your attention. How could he concentrate when he was longing so much to hear Cora's voice?

As soon as he was sure that Sydney had taken himself off to Wembley, he left his room and hurried to the call-box at the end of his street. At first the line was engaged, then he dialled a wrong number, then he found he hadn't any more pennies, and he had to go to the newspaper shop across the street to change a shilling. When he got back there was a woman in the box, and she kept him waiting nearly ten minutes. He had ceased to be impatient. He was now obstinately dogged: determined, whatever happened, to speak to Cora. If it took him a hundred years to speak to her, he wouldn't mind, so long as he succeeded.

At last the woman left the call-box, and George took her place. There was a ghastly smell of cheap scent and stale perspiration in the box: it was like an oven, too. But George didn't care. He dialled the greengrocer's number and waited.

" 'Ullo?" asked the irritatingly familiar voice.

They went through the same dreary performance: the greengrocer wanting to know " 'ow I can leave the bloomin' shop?" and George coldly determined that the greengrocer should call Cora to the telephone.

"She's in 'er bawth," the greengrocer said after a wait of nearly a quarter of an hour, and he hung up before George could leave a message.

There were three people waiting outside the telephone box by now. They were all glaring at George, and when he came out one of the women muttered, "And about time, too. Some people think public telephones are private property!"

George didn't care what they said or thought. He walked over to the King's Arms, had a pint, avoided conversation with Gladys – by this time he was almost hysterical with frustrated temper – and returned to the telephone box half an hour later.

Again he had to wait while a man finished his conversation. Watching him through the glass, George guessed he was talking to his girl. There was a fatuous, smug expression on his face, and he talked for a good ten minutes.

When George finally got through to the greengrocer's again, the rough voice nearly snapped his head off.

"Look 'ere," it said violently. "I got better things to do than answer bloomin' telephones like this. I'll 'ave to complain if this goes on much more. You've been ringing hup every day this week!"

127

Complain! That'd mean Sydney would hear about it! He might even guess that it was George making the call. It might give him a clue that it was George who had spent the night with Cora. The memory of the gleaming razor blade became vividly unpleasant.

"But I haven't even spoken to her," George protested. "I can't help it if she's always out, can I?"

" 'Ere, miss, 'ere," the greengrocer suddenly bawled. "This 'ere bloke's on the blower again. Every day 'e's been on ... it's got to stop."

"Hullo," Cora said. "Yes?"

George knew she was in a temper all right, but it was so marvellous to hear her voice – even if it did sound snappy – that he didn't care.

"This is George," he said, aware that he had begun to tremble violently.

"Have you been ringing every day?" she barked at him.

"I'm afraid I have," he returned in studiedly gentle tones, quite sick with fear that she was going to be unkind.

"Well, couldn't you have been a bit brighter?" she demanded. "You've caused a lot of bother as it is."

"I'm terribly sorry," George said, "but I did want to speak to you."

"What do you want?"

In that kind of temper it was quite likely she would refuse to go out with him. But it had to be now or never. Now he had at last caught her. He couldn't just fawn and cringe and go away.

"I – I was wondering ... if you haven't anything to do tomorrow ... I mean, would you like to come out with me? ... that is, if you're not busy or something."

"What do you mean ... or something?" The waspish note was still in her voice.

"Well, you know ... if you're not going out with anyone else."

"Oh, I see."

There was a long pause while he waited for her to add anything to this, but she didn't, so he screwed up his courage, and, knowing that he was inviting a direct snub and refusal, said, "Well, do you think you could?"

She still tried to make him pay for causing a bother on the telephone by appearing to be dense. "Could I ... what?"

"Could you come out with me? I – I thought we might do a movie and have dinner somewhere."

"I can't waste my money on movies," she said shortly.

"But this is my treat. I – I'm inviting you ..."

"Oh."

There was another long pause, then he said, "What would you like to see? There's a good movie at the Empire ... Spencer Tracy."

"I don't think I can go to a movie," she said, a gentler note in her voice. "I'm busy tomorrow."

It was his turn to say "Oh" now.

"I could come to dinner."

He brightened at once.

"Oh, good! That's fine. Where shall we go?"

"I know a place."

"All right. Then when shall we meet?"

"Eight o'clock at the pub opposite Joe's." Now that she had made up her mind to go out with him she was taking charge of the outing. George didn't care. He had won his point about paying for the outing or at least he thought it was going to be all right – and if she wanted to say where they were to meet and where they were to dine, it was all right with him.

"That's fine," he said. "I say, Cora – I'm looking forward …" but the telephone was dead. She had hung up.

Even that didn't detract from his happiness. At last! After all those beastly hours, trying … trying … trying to get her, he had finally succeeded, and she was coming out with him again!

He drew a deep breath and came out into the fresh air, feeling fine.

# 10

Cora, with George tagging along a step behind, turned off the main road into a narrow street, lined on one side by backs of shops, and on the other side by a brick wall, along the top of which bristled pieces of broken glass, set in cement. At the end of this street she turned the corner and walked down an even more sordid street of small, shabby shops. A group of dark-skinned, bare-headed men stood at the corner; they glanced at George, and then concentrated on Cora. They stopped talking and eyed her, their faces expressionless, their eyes hot and intent. Cora went on her way, her small head held high, unaware of their interest.

They came to a double-fronted shop, the big windows hung with yellow muslin curtains. The glass panel of the door was painted green. Gilt letters, "Restaurant", crawled diagonally across the green expanse.

Without pausing, Cora pushed open the door and went in. George followed her.

The room in which they found themselves was long and narrow. Tables lined each side of it, and vast mirrors, fly-blown and yellowing with age, hung from the walls. Red-shaded lamps stood on each table.

A big woman, her hair straggling and untidy, as if someone had upset custard over her head, sat at the cash desk. Behind the bar near the door was a tall, elderly Hebrew in a dirty white coat. Two waiters stood idly at the end of the room. There were only a few people at the tables: bright-eyed women, hatless and bold; dark-skinned men, immaculately dressed, middle-aged and wooden.

Cora sat down at a table with her back to the wall. George, following her, felt the woman in the cash desk examining him closely. Somehow, he didn't quite know why, the atmosphere in this dimly lit, gaudy room made him uneasy.

He was aware, too, that the men at the tables paused in their eating and watched Cora furtively, under lowered eyelids: their eyes on her slim hips and the shameless movement under her woollen sweater.

She was wearing the same outfit, and the red bone bangle, as she had worn when they first met. Their meeting tonight wasn't at all how George had planned it to be. He had arrived at the pub at a few minutes to eight to find Cora already there. She was drinking a whisky and water, and she seemed peevish. Of course, he hadn't kissed her. Even if they had been in the bar on their own, he wouldn't have had the courage, now that he was once more face to face with her. He really marvelled that he had kissed her the other night. That had, of course, only happened because it had been dark.

As soon as Cora saw him she finished her whisky and came to meet him.

"Come on," she said shortly, without even a smile of greeting, "I'm hungry," and she walked right out of the pub without giving him even a second glance, and went off down the street.

George, bewildered and a little hurt, hurried after her. She kept on, a scowl on her face, and George followed her. He decided not to speak to her. He could not think of anything to say, anyway, that wouldn't irritate her, so he kept behind her until they reached this little Soho restaurant.

He had an uneasy presentiment that the evening wasn't going to be a success.

He sat down opposite her, his back to the room. She looked past him at the waiter, a bent, elderly man who came over to them with a bored, tired look in his eyes.

George was about to ask her what she would like, but, still ignoring him, she said to the waiter, "Oysters, grilled steaks, salad and ice-cream. Two bottles of vin rouge: and let's have some service."

The waiter went away without saying anything, but by the way he flicked his soiled napkin, he managed to express his contempt for them.

Two bottles of wine! Oysters! My word! George thought, she knows what she wants all right.

Well, he couldn't just sit there and say nothing. He hadn't said a word since they met in the pub.

"It's lovely to see you again, Cora ..." he began, wondering if he was going to set her off.

She seemed suddenly to realize that he was in the room.

"I'm bad tempered," she said, resting her chin on the back of her hand. "I'll be all right in a moment."

That's better, George thought. As if I didn't know she was in a temper. Well, so long as she admits it, she may get over it soon.

Feeling that he must add something to the meal – Cora ordering everything had rather deflated him – he beckoned a waiter and ordered two large dry martinis.

"Nothing like a cocktail to cheer you up," he said, smiling. "I've been in the dumps myself today."

She didn't say anything. He noticed she was staring across the room at a table in the far corner. There was an intent look of spite in her eyes.

Puzzled, George glanced at the man sitting at the table. He was a slender blond with a complexion like peaches and cream, and big, soft eyes like a deer. He was wearing apple-green trousers, very neat, with pleats at the waist; and his coat was fawn colour.

George turned to Cora. She wasn't looking at the blond man in the corner any longer, but at him. There was that odd expression in her eyes that made George feel like a strange exhibit in a zoo.

The waiter brought the two martinis.

"Here's how," George said. "I've been looking forward to this no end."

She glanced at him, and her lips smiled, but her eyes still remained sulky. They drank. George was surprised at the "kick" the martini had.

"These are jolly good, aren't they?" he went on, still too nervous to begin a real conversation.

"They're all right," she said, and again her eyes strayed to the blond man across the room.

This won't do at all, George thought. Why does she keep looking at that horror over the way? She couldn't be interested in that type, surely? Why, anyone with half an eye could see he was a cissy. Perhaps she was just bored. Anyway, he couldn't let her attention wander like this.

"I've been worrying about you," he said leaning towards her. "Did you get into trouble for staying out all night?"

"Trouble?" Her eyebrows went up. "You talk as if I'm a child. I can stay out all night if I want to."

Baffled, George sipped his martini. Not quite the same idea that Sydney had conveyed. He glanced at her thoughtfully.

"From what Sydney said …"

"Oh, don't listen to him. He's always bragging about how he treats me. I go my way, and he goes his."

George was sure she was lying, but there was no point in

telling her so.

"Well, I worried because I wondered if I should have kept 'phoning. I didn't want to get you into trouble."

"I wish you wouldn't keep 'phoning," she said shortly. "Old Harris doesn't like it."

Before he could say anything further, the waiter brought the oysters. When he had gone, George muttered, "I wanted to speak to you. You said it was all right to 'phone."

"Oh, don't nag!" she said sharply, and forked an oyster into her mouth.

There was no doubt she was in a foul temper. Or was she nervous about something? George studied her. She did look tired and jumpy. There was also an uneasy expression in her eyes.

"What are you staring at?" she demanded, looking up and catching his eyes on her face.

"You," George said simply. He felt an overwhelming love for her suddenly well up inside him. "What's wrong, Cora? Is there anything I can do to help?"

"Wrong, what should be wrong?"

"You look nervous ..."

"Do I?" she suddenly laughed. "I'm in a foul temper, that's all."

He could see the tremendous effort she was making to sound natural. It began to worry him. There was something on her mind: something she was anxious that he should know nothing about.

"I got up late," she went on. "Everything's gone wrong today." She finished her cocktail just as the waiter came with the two bottles of wine. He drew the corks and filled their glasses. "I feel like getting tight tonight," she went on.

George was still not satisfied. "Are you sure there isn't

something else?"

"Of course not!" she said, the waspish note back in her voice. "It's just that it's been a hell of a day, and I'm tired."

"Well, never mind," George said, certain now that there was something on her mind. "The wine will make you feel better."

And he began to talk to her about the only subject he was really competent to talk about – crime in America. He didn't want to talk to her about that. He would much rather have talked of his love for her, and even to confide in her that all his stories of violence and adventure were figments of his imagination, and that he was only a simple type of fellow, but very much in love with her. But she was so unsympathetic and hard and nervous that he knew it would be inviting disaster to be sentimental. So he told her more fictitious stories of his adventures in America. He had been reading a lot lately, and was well primed with material. She seemed to welcome these stories, probably because she didn't wish to talk herself. While he talked, she smoked incessantly. The ashtray was piled high with cigarette butts, smeared with lipstick. She had scarcely touched her meal, but she had drunk a good deal of the sour red wine. When George asked her if she felt all right, as she had made such a poor dinner, she said abruptly that it was too hot to eat. Remembering that the first words she had greeted him with were, "Come on, I'm hungry", George shrugged hopelessly. Her moods defeated him.

But she listened to his tales of crime, sitting still, with her chin in her cupped hands, her eyes expressionless.

George soon became engrossed in his own stories, and when the lights in the restaurant began to go out, he realized with a start of surprise that it was half past eleven and he was a little drunk. The restaurant was empty now, except for the blond man at the table opposite, the Hebrew barman, the fat woman at the desk and the waiter who had looked after them.

"We'd better be going, I suppose," he said regretfully. "I'm afraid I've been doing all the talking again. I hope I haven't bored you."

Cora shook her head. Her face was flushed by the wine, and when she spoke, the sickly smell of the wine was on her breath. "I wanted you to talk," she said. Then she looked again at the blond man at the table across the room. George suddenly realized that all the time he had been talking to her she had been casting glances in this man's direction.

He couldn't resist saying, "Do you know that man?"

She looked through him, her eyes drawn curtains, "That isn't rain, is it?"

George frowned. "I hope not." He glanced over his shoulder. Rain marks showed on the windows. "It is, I'm afraid. Aren't we unlucky? It always rains for us."

"Oh, damn! I hope we can get a cab."

George signalled to the waiter, who brought the bill. It was for twenty-five shillings. Cheap, and jolly good, George thought. We must come here again. Only perhaps she'll be less worried and jumpy next time. He had to admit that the evening hadn't been a success. Cora had behaved – was behaving now – like someone awaiting a major operation. She had not been concentrating, and George was prepared to swear that she couldn't have repeated to him anything of what he had said to her during the whole evening. Her eyes were never still, and she continually moistened her lips with her tongue. She had all the symptoms of acute nervousness.

George waved away the change which the waiter brought him. "Shall we go, or shall we wait a bit?" he asked Cora.

"We're closed now," the waiter said as he moved away.

"Oh, well," George said, pushing back his chair, "I suppose we'd better go, then."

Cora drew a deep breath and got to her feet. George was surprised to see that she swayed unsteadily. It dawned on him that he was feeling comfortably tight. The martinis and the two bottles of wine had found their way to his head. He grinned a little foolishly. They certainly seemed to have found their way to Cora's legs.

"Steady," he said, taking her arm; "careful how you go."

She pushed him away. "Shut up, you fool!" she said in a low, furious whisper. Her eyes blazed, and George was so astounded by her vehemence that he gaped at her. She lurched unsteadily down the aisle between the tables, and he heard her muttering furiously to herself. The sudden change in her mood stupefied him. She had seemed sober enough while she had been at the table, but now she seemed as tight as a tick.

What was she up to now? What was she doing at the blond man's table? George stood watching her, unable to make up his mind to follow her. She had paused, her arms folded across her breasts, facing the blond man, who looked at her with curious, bored eyes.

"Well?" she said loudly. "You'll know me again, won't you?"

The blond man eyed her up and down and looked away, a sneering little smile on his face.

"You heard what I said, you cheap masher," Cora went on, her voice high pitched. "You've been trying to make me all the evening!"

George wanted to sink through the floor. How could she behave like this? Had she suddenly gone mad?

The blond man flicked his cigarette ash on the carpet. He

continued to smile, but he was regarding Cora now with a frozen look in his eyes.

"Run away, little girl," he said, "or I shall get annoyed with you."

"Keep your filthy eyes off me in the future!" Cora suddenly screamed, and, leaning forward, she spat a stream of obscene vituperation at him.

Although George was shocked into a stupefied immobility, he was aware that the woman with the blonde hair, the Hebrew behind the bar and the waiter were standing tense and angry, looking at Cora.

The blond man ceased to smile. "You're drunk," he said. "Get out before I have you thrown out!"

Cora snatched up a glass of wine that the blond man had scarcely touched, and with one swift movement threw the wine in his face.

Somewhere in the building a bell began to ring. George was conscious of the bell more than he was conscious of the stillness of the blonde woman, the Hebrew and the waiter, although they were menacing enough. He was more scared of the bell than he was of the blond man, who sat staring at Cora, wine running down his face into his shirt and coat.

Then a concealed door half way down the room opened, and two men came into the restaurant. They looked like Greeks – hard little men with flat, squashed features, dressed in black, with black cloth caps on their bullet heads.

The blond man said in a drawling voice, "Well, you'll certainly pay for that, you drunken bitch."

George rushed to Cora's side. He was sick with fright, but he wasn't going to let anything happen to her.

"Cora!" he said, taking her arm. "My God! Cora!"

He could feel her trembling, and he realized that she was

as terrified as he was.

"Don't let them do anything to me!" she said wildly, clinging to him. "George! Get me out of here. Don't let them touch me!"

This frantic appeal stiffened George's courage. He pushed her behind him and faced the two Greeks.

"Now, don't get excited," he said, his voice sounding as if he had a pebble in his mouth. "I'm sorry about this ... she didn't know what she was doing ..."

The blond man got to his feet. His face was white now with vicious rage. "Take care of this lout, Nick," he said. "Get the girl away from him."

George thought, desperately, furiously, They won't have her! They'll have to kill me first. If I'd only got my gun! He put his hand behind him and pushed Cora against the wall; he stood in front of her, crouching a little, his left fist extended, his right slightly across his body. Vaguely he remembered seeing James Cagney stand like this, protecting his girl. Cagney had faced a room full of thugs and he'd licked the lot! George eyed the two hard little men, who kept just out of his reach, like two terriers waiting for an opening to jump in. The blond man was still behind his table: he was wiping his face with a napkin.

"You'd better be careful," George said. "I don't want to hurt anyone!"

The blond man suddenly laughed. "Fix the fat fool," he said sharply. "Go for him!"

The Greek called Nick edged closer, and George swung wildly at him. His great fist smashed into empty air, as the Greek shifted his head.

Cora screamed and clutched at George, hampering him.

Then suddenly long, thin blades flashed in the shaded light. The sight of the glittering steel shocked George's courage into a frozen ball of terror.

Something flashed, and pain seared him.

They'll kill me! he thought, and like a wounded, terrified bull, he lashed out frantically.

A red curtain of terror hung before George's eyes. He heard Cora scream. Then he found himself on the floor, a rattling, groaning noise in his ears, and he realized that he was making the noise himself.

A solid weight dropped on his shoulders, pushing him flat on the dusty, smelly carpet. Nick knelt on his back.

"Don't move," the Greek said. "She'll be back in a little while."

George lay still.

Then a sound came from somewhere in the building – a violent scream, which was immediately stifled, as if by a ruthless hand. Every nerve in George's body stiffened.

"Still!" Nick said, breathing garlic and wine fumes in George's face.

Slowly and cautiously George raised his head and looked round the room. The woman at the cash desk, the Hebrew behind the bar and the waiter were all staring at him.

George thought he heard another muffled scream, but he could not be sure. He looked at the others, but they showed no sign that they had heard anything. The woman at the cash desk curled a straggling lock of dyed hair round her fat finger. Her eyes were stony, blank.

What were they doing to Cora? George made a convulsive movement.

"Still!" the Greek warned, pressing a sharp knee into George's back.

The silence in the room and in the building terrified George. Minutes ticked by slowly. It seemed to him that he had been lying on the dirty, evil-smelling carpet for hours.

Then suddenly the Greek got up. "Right," he said, and kicked George hard in the ribs. "Get up, you."

Somehow George crawled to his feet. Without quite knowing what he was doing, he took out his handkerchief and wrapped it round his bleeding left hand. He swayed unsteadily as the other Greek appeared, pushing Cora through the concealed doorway.

Then somehow they were in the street together, in the darkness and the rain.

George stood gulping in the hot, damp air, unnerved, his limbs trembling.

"What happened?" he said. "What did they do to you?"

Cora, her arms tightly crossed, doubled herself up. Her long wave of hair fell forward, concealing her face. She stood like that for several minutes, and the rain poured down on her.

"Can't I do anything?" George said, forgetting about his own wounds, frightened to touch her, terrified by her behaviour. Her ragged, laboured breathing made a dreadful sound in the rain and the darkness.

She began to walk up and down the street, still doubled up, still holding onto herself.

"Cora! Tell me!" he said, following her. "What is it?"

They were near a street lamp now, and she suddenly straightened. Her hair was plastered to her head by the rain. She looked wild. A hissing sound came from her lips, and he could see she was grinding her teeth.

"They crammed a pillow over my face," she gasped, "and then they flogged me with a cane!" She drew her saliva into a ball of fury and spat into the darkness. "They did that to *me*! I'll make them pay! I'll make *him* pay, too! The treacherous swine! *He* knew what they'd do! I'll kill them all for this! All of them!" And she began to cry with rage and pain, wriggling her body and stamping her feet.

George stood in the rain, helpless, watching her with dismayed, bewildered pity, the handkerchief round his hand growing soggy with blood.

Suddenly she grabbed his arm, her fingers biting into his muscles. "Don't look at me," she panted, standing first on one leg and then on the other. She contorted her body, arched her back, straightened and bent double again. "Damn you!" She broke away from him and went down the street, only to stop a yard or so farther on. She held her head between her hands and began to walk round in small circles. Then she came back to him and gripped his arm again. He could feel the fever in her, burning through his coat sleeve.

"Take me home," she cried, pulling at him. "For God's sake, take me home. I'm hurt! I'm on fire! Don't stand there doing nothing, you stupid, stupid fool! Take me home!"

# 11

George never quite knew how they reached the little flat above the greengrocer's shop. He vaguely remembered stopping a taxi, but had no recollection of the actual drive. He remembered the long, painful climb up some stairs, and Cora hammering wildly on a door. He remembered, too, hearing Sydney shout, "All right, all right. I'm coming! Stop banging on that bloody door."

Then he had a dim recollection of Sydney, in a dirty white dressing-gown, staring at him in blank astonishment.

He took a step forward, and his knees gave under him. He fell heavily. Before he blacked out he heard Cora scream: "You swine! You said he wouldn't touch me! Oh, I hate you! I hate you!" and then he lost consciousness.

He had no idea how long he remained unconscious. He must have drifted into a heavy sleep before coming round. But when he opened his eyes it was morning and he was lying on the floor, a pillow under his head and a blanket over him. He sat up slowly and looked round, not quite remembering where he was.

He was aware of pain, and found his hand had been expertly bandaged and sticking plaster covered the cuts on his face. He pushed the blanket aside and stood up. He didn't feel too bad. A little weak, perhaps, but otherwise not bad. He looked round the room with blank astonishment. It was a perfect pigsty of a room. The mantelpiece was thick with dust. The fireplace was full of cigarette ash and butts. A table, pushed against the wall, was piled with old newspapers, unwashed crockery and empty bottles. A dish containing some evil-smelling meat was under an armchair. On all the flat surfaces of the furniture were sticky circles made by wet tumblers. Two bluebottles buzzed angrily against the dirty windows.

"Hello," Sydney said quietly. "How's the bold warrior?"

George blinked at him. Sydney was standing in the doorway, dressed in the dirty white dressing-gown, his lean, hard face cold and expressionless.

"I must have fainted," George said, moving over to an armchair and sitting down. He examined his hand uneasily. "Did you do this?"

Sydney grunted. "Don't worry about that," he said casually. "I shoved a few stitches in it. It'll be all right."

"Stitches? You put stitches in it?"

"Why not? In my racket you get used to razor-cuts. Did you see what they did to Cora?"

"They beat her ... didn't they?" George went cold.

"They certainly did. Nice mob. They'll pay for this, George."

George held his head in his hands. "I don't understand," he said. "Why did she do it? She threw wine in his face."

"Never mind why she did it," Sydney said. "You're in love with her, aren't you?"

"Yes," George said, no longer caring what Sydney would say or do.

"That's fine," Sydney said, his eyes glowing like live coals. "I'm glad about that. You and me are going to fix Mr bloody Crispin."

"Crispin?"

"The nice looking lad who beat Cora. She told me what happened. She was tight, but that doesn't matter. No one's going to touch her without getting into trouble. I'd handle him myself, only you and me can do it better."

"Do what better?" George asked. He remembered the two Greeks and their razors, and he felt a little sick.

"We'll see him tonight. You and me. He's got a bungalow at a place called Copthorne. It's not far. He'll be down there today. Well, we'll go down, too, and we'll take a cane. It's a lonely place, and we won't be disturbed. We'll see how *he* likes a beating. That's what we'll do."

"Wouldn't it be better to complain to the police?" George asked, in sudden fright. "They're dangerous. Look what they did to me."

"When you were in the States," Sydney said, cold cruelty in his eyes, "did you go to the police?"

George waved his hands nervously. "That was different," he said. "No one went to the cops in those days. It's different now."

"No, it isn't," Sydney said. "This is something personal. We'll be dangerous too. We'll take your gun."

George stiffened. "No, we won't!" he said. "I'm not doing a thing like that. That's how accidents happen."

"Oh yes, you are, George," Sydney said, wandering across the room. "You don't have to load it. Crispin will fall apart just to see the gun. I'm not suggesting you kill him. I don't like murder myself. Feel like getting the gun now?"

Again George was going to refuse, when he suddenly thought of the blond man's sneering smile. He thought of the two Greeks creeping towards him with their razors. With the Luger in his hands, they would have been terrified. A smouldering anger – something he had never before experienced – urged him to seek revenge. Cora's shrieks still rang in his ears.

He got to his feet. "All right," he said, "but I'm not loading the gun."

"I'll come with you," Sydney said. "Come and talk to me while I dress."

George followed him into a tiny bedroom.

"Who is this Crispin?" he asked, leaning against the wall.

"I used to fool around with him," Sydney returned, slipping his blue shirt over his head. "Keep this under your hat. He knocks off cars in a big way. There's bags of money in that game." He glanced quickly at George and went on, "I chucked it after a bit. Got too hot for me. Cora hates the guy. He doesn't know she's my sister. He'll have a surprise when he sees me – and you." He was dressed now. "You'd better have a wash. Those cuts on your face aren't deep, but you look a bit of a mess. Those Greeks know how to use a razor all right."

He took George into the grubby little bathroom. George stared at himself in the mirror. A long strip of plaster ran down the side of his face, and another strip was above his ear. He rinsed his face, getting rid of the blood smears. There was blood, too, on his coat and collar.

"I look a sight," he said, suddenly secretly proud of himself. He looked tough and frightening: a real gangster.

"I'll find you a scarf," Sydney said. "You can change when you get to your place."

"Where's Cora?" George asked, drying his face on a grimy towel.

"Asleep," Sydney said indifferently. "She's got weals on her back as thick as my finger."

George flinched. His anger blazed up.

147

"Let's go," he said.

It was only seven-thirty by the time they reached George's place, off the Edgware Road. The house was silent: no one was up. George took Sydney to his room and closed the door. While Sydney sat on the bed, whistling softly, George changed his shirt, put on another suit and had a hurried shave.

In the familiar surroundings of his room his anger died down. He was now beginning to realize what it meant to live dangerously. He had read so much about it in the past; had constructed scenes in which he had experienced breathless adventures, fought and killed men, and had gloried in it all. But this was different. This was something out of his control. He knew that if in one of his fantasies he were trapped by desperate men, he would not be killed. He would be able to create a situation that would save him at the last moment. But this business was different. If that Greek, Nick, had wanted to kill him, he could have done so. It was just sheer luck that he hadn't cut George's throat.

George suddenly hated the thought of what was going to happen that night. He had been angry, but now, back in his room, the thought of fresh danger gave him a sick, nervous feeling in his stomach. To beat this man Crispin was primitive justice, but it was bound to lead to trouble. If they did succeed in catching Crispin alone, did Sydney really think that Crispin wouldn't get his own back on them later?

As he rinsed his razor, he considered whether he should refuse to go with them, but immediately saw the impossibility of this. If he wished to keep Cora's regard – and there was no question about that – he would have to go through with it. All he had to do was to threaten Crispin with the gun. Well, that was all right. He could do that. There would be no danger in that, as the gun wasn't loaded. He was confident that Crispin would obey him if he had the gun in his hand. It was an ugly-looking weapon. It would scare him stiff. Besides, Sydney would be there.

"Getting cold feet?" Sydney asked in a sneering voice.

George started. He had forgotten that Sydney was in the room. He had been so busy with his thoughts that Sydney had gone completely out of his mind. He turned.

"Of course not," he said. "I've been in tighter spots ..." and then he stopped.

Sydney was holding the Luger carelessly in his hand.

"Where did you get that from?" George said, suddenly angry. "I'll trouble you not to go to my drawers without asking me."

Sydney smiled. "Keep your wool on," he said, examining the Luger with interest. "I only wanted to satisfy my curiosity."

"Well, give it here, then," George demanded, crossing the room. "I suppose Cora told you where I kept it." He decided that he would hide the gun in another place in the future.

"She did," Sydney returned, his finger curling round the trigger. "What's the matter with it? Is it jammed?"

"No," George said shortly. "It's stiff, that's all. The trigger wants adjusting. Here, let me have it."

Sydney pulled at the trigger, and with an effort managed to snap down the hammer.

"With an action like that," he said, tossing the Luger on the bed, "you don't have to worry about accidents."

"That's why I keep it that way," George said, picking up the gun and slipping out the magazine. He made sure there was no cartridge in the breech, grunted, and shoved the gun in his hip pocket. It felt bulky and heavy, but it gave him a secret thrill to have it against his hip.

"Well, are you ready?" Sydney asked, getting up.

George nodded.

"Let's go, then," Sydney said, and they left the room and began to walk downstairs.

George suddenly remembered Leo.

"Just a tick," he said. "I've got to feed my cat."

"Forget it," Sydney said shortly. "There are other things to think about besides cats."

George ignored Sydney's impatience, ran back to his room, put a saucer of milk and the remains of the sardines on the floor where Leo could find it, and then hurried after Sydney, who was waiting for him in the street.

"Go back and keep Cora company," Sydney said. "I've got things to do." He looked at George with a jeering grin. "She thinks you're quite a hero."

George went a dull red. "Does she?" he asked eagerly. "Well, I don't know about that. I couldn't do much against those razors." He nursed his aching hand. "If it had been a fair fight ..."

"I know, I know," Sydney said, moving away. "You tell her about it. I've got things to do."

George was delighted that Sydney wasn't returning to the flat. He hurried to Russell Square, eager to be alone with Cora. He passed a chemist's shop, and remembering what Sydney had said about the weals on Cora's back, he retraced his steps, went in and asked for a bottle of witch-hazel.

It was after nine o'clock when he entered the little flat. Cora was in the bathroom. She shouted through the door that she wouldn't be long, and he wandered into the sitting-room.

He put the Luger on the mantelpiece, and after looking round the room, he decided that he might as well tidy up a bit. The decision gave him some pleasure. He had nothing to do, and he liked messing in a house.

He went back to the bathroom and told Cora through the panels of the door what he intended to do.

"Come in," she shouted. "I can't hear you."

He opened the door and looked into the tiny, steam-filled room. Cora was lying in the bath; only the back of her head and white shoulders were visible from where he stood. She glanced over her shoulder. A damp cigarette hung from her mouth.

"What is it?" she asked, a little sharply.

"How – how are you, Cora?"

"I'm all right," she returned. "God! You look a sight."

George grinned happily. "I know," he said. "It's my hand that's bad. These are only scratches."

"You've got guts," she said. "I didn't think you had it in you."

It was worth the pain and the terror to hear that.

"This'll take the smarting away," George said, putting the bottle of witch-hazel on the wooden bath surround. "You just rub it in ..."

She regarded the bottle, reached out a wet hand and picked it up. She read the label, frowning.

"Thank you, George. You're thoughtful. Now run away and tidy up, as you put it. I won't be long."

George worked happily until Cora joined him. She was wearing Sydney's dirty white dressing-gown.

"You are a busy little bee, aren't you?" she jeered, looking round the room, her eyebrows making question marks.

He had put the old newspapers and empty beer bottles in one corner. He had wiped off all the sticky circles on the furniture and cleared up the mess in the fireplace. The dirty dishes he had taken into the kitchen. Already the room looked cleaner and brighter.

George grinned sheepishly. "I like doing this," he said. "I'd like a place of my own."

She sat in the armchair, lowering herself cautiously and with a little grimace. She lit a cigarette. "You're a bit of a dope, aren't you?" There was an unexpected note of kindness in her voice that George hadn't heard before. He looked at her quickly, but she was regarding him with far-away, bored eyes, as if she were only half aware of his presence.

"I say, Cora ..." he began, and then hesitated.

She glanced up sharply. "If you're going to talk about last night, you'd better skip it. I'm in no mood to go over that business now."

George scratched his head, embarrassed. "Well, all right," he said; "but hang it all, Cora, I think you ought to explain. I mean I – well, look at me. And then, you've been hurt too. I think I ought to be told. What I mean to say is – "

"Oh, shut up!" Cora said, shifting her body in the chair. "We'll talk about that later. Suppose I was tight? No one's going to leer at me all the evening without a come-back. And no one's getting tough with me without damn well paying for it! Now, shut up, George!"

Baffled, George's gaze wandered round the room. Then he had an idea. "Where are your clothes, Cora?"

"In the bedroom. Why?"

"I'll wash them for you. They'd look quite smart. I'm a bit of a dab at that kind of thing."

She lifted her shoulders helplessly, closed her eyes and didn't say anything.

He went into the bedroom and collected the sweater and slacks. He found an unopened packet of Lux in the kitchen and he shut himself in the bathroom.

When he had hung the garments out of the back window

to dry in the sun, he returned to the sitting-room. She was still there, a cigarette dangling from her lips, her eyes brooding.

"I've got some hot water ready," he said. "I'd like to wash your hair."

She giggled suddenly, explosively. "You're crazy," she said.

George shook his head. "No, I'm not," he said stubbornly. "I want you to look nice."

She studied him for a long moment. "You really are in love with me, aren't you, George?"

"Of course. You didn't doubt that, did you?"

She got to her feet and crossed over to him.

"All right: wash my hair if you want to."

They went into the tiny bathroom together, and Cora sat on a stool before the wash-basin.

"Have you ever washed any other girl's head?" she asked, watching George with a thoughtful expression in her eyes.

George wrapped a bath towel round her shoulders. "No," he said. "I've never wanted to before."

"So there were other girls?"

He hesitated. "Well, no, there were no other girls," he said. "You see, until you came along ..."

"I think you're a bit potty," she said, holding her head down. "Aren't you, George? Just a little potty?"

He poured water over her hair, then the shampoo. His hands felt her hard little skull. The water turned a muddy brown.

"Dirty slut, aren't I?" Cora said, with a sudden embarrassed laugh. "Does it put you off?"

"Keep still," George said. "I've nearly finished." He experienced an overwhelming feeling of love and pity for her: a feeling that he imagined a mother must have for her child. "There. Now you can sit up. Come into the other room and sit in the sun. It'll dry quickly in the sun."

When Cora was sitting by the window, George turned his attention to the room.

"Maybe I could sell these newspapers for you," he said.

"You're the giddy limit," Cora returned, laughing. "Try if you want to. I've been too lazy to bother with them. There's a sheeney across the way who buys junk. He keeps open on Sundays."

George nodded. "I'll try him. There's such a lot of rubbish here. You can hardly move for falling over it. And the bottles, too. Can I clear them all out?"

"Go ahead, if it amuses you," she said, regarding him with a puzzled expression in her eyes.

It took George a long time to shift the rubbish, but it pleased him to do so. He made four journeys to the junk shop, and finally, hot and a little exhausted, he presented her with five shillings.

"There!" he said. "A clear flat and five bob. It's funny, isn't it, that even rubbish is worth money?"

She nodded. "You're an awful dope, George," she said. "Why don't you think big? Look at the effort you've just made to get five bob. With that effort you could have made five pounds."

He thought about this seriously. "I don't think so," he said at last. "You see, no one can make five pounds quickly unless he has specialized knowledge. Even if it's only backing a horse, you have to know the right horse to back. You can't make money unless you've been properly trained." He shrugged uneasily. "Perhaps that's why I've never had any real money."

She flicked the cigarette butt into the empty fireplace. "If I liked to go on the streets," she said, "I could earn a hundred pounds a week. I don't have to have specialized knowledge to do that."

"Why don't you?" George asked, interested to hear what she would say.

She smiled secretly. "Because it's too easy."

"I wonder."

"All right. Because I'm too proud. I've got other ideas."

"I don't understand how you two live. Does Sydney keep you?"

"You're curious, aren't you?"

George nodded. "I suppose I am. Well, perhaps I shouldn't ask."

"We get along. We've been getting along like this for a hell of a time ... getting nowhere."

George stood over her. "You can't go on like this, Cora," he said. "I can't go on the way I'm going on now much longer. Couldn't we get together? You and me might do well if we stuck together."

"Think so?" she said, looking out of the window. "Well, there're things to do first. I've got other things on my mind ... important things," and her hands closed into tight little fists.

She's thinking about tonight, George decided uneasily. In his burst of activity he had forgotten about Crispin and the two Greeks. Instantly his old fears returned.

"I say, Cora," he said, moving over to the fireplace, "shouldn't we leave bad alone? I mean there might be more trouble." He glanced in the mirror at the plaster strips on his face. "They're a pretty rough crowd."

"If you expect us to stick together," Cora said slowly, "you'll have to show a little more guts. I don't like men without spine." She stood up and, turning her back, she pulled her dressing-gown aside. "Take a look, George."

He had one momentary glimpse of the red and black marks on her white flesh before she jerked the dressing-gown into place: a sight that sickened him, angered him and embarrassed him.

She faced him, her eyes probing and cold. "Well?"

"Oh, Cora," he said, going to her. He put his arms round her, but she was hard and resisting. She pushed him away.

"Not now, George," she said impatiently. "All that can come when this business is over." She glanced up at him. "If you really care for me, you're not going to let Crispin get away with this. You've talked a lot about what you did in the States. I want to see what you can do here. When I've seen that, I could be very nice to you." Her eyes came alive for a moment. "Very nice to you," she repeated.

This was too important to George for any misunderstanding. He clutched her hands.

"I'll do anything for you, Cora," he said, looking wildly into her eyes for her assurance. "If I do that, you will be nice to me? You will be really nice?" He wanted to say, "You're promising to give yourself to me?" but he hadn't the courage to come out with it as bluntly as that.

She seemed to know what was in his mind, because she gave him an unmistakable look of promise.

"You won't be disappointed, George," she said. "I don't like men messing me about, but you're different. You'll get your reward."

Later, they went out for a snack. George wanted to take the gun, but Cora wouldn't let him. "Leave it there," she said, a little sharply. "It won't run away."

He walked a step behind her, and glanced from time to time at her with secret pride. The pale blue sweater had shrunk a trifle, but it looked bright. The slacks had a knife-edge crease which he had put in with great care, using an old-fashioned flat-iron he had found in the kitchen. Her hair was sleek and glossy. She had taken pains to put her lipstick on neatly. He thought she looked lovely.

Although she did not complain, she walked stiffly, but she held her head high, and she had lost none of her arrogance.

They went to the pub at the corner of the street and leaned up against the bar. They ordered pints of bitter and sausage rolls.

"This is fun, isn't it?" George said, in seventh heaven.

She flicked a flake of pastry from her mouth and grimaced. "Think so?" she said, biting into the sausage roll again.

"I suppose it's nothing to you," he said, hurt; "only I've been lonely for a long time. Having a girl like you for company means a lot to me."

She raised the beer glass and drank, gazing at him with thoughtful eyes over the top of it. She put the glass down and drew a deep breath.

"You're a sentimental fool, aren't you?"

He looked to see if she were jeering at him, but she was serious in an unexpectedly kind way.

"I suppose I am." He brooded, looking down at his shoes. "But there's nothing wrong in that. I know people sneer at sentimentality, but they're usually pretty unhappy themselves."

She wasn't listening to him. Her attention was centred on a short man who had just come in. George followed her gaze. He recognized the man. It was Little Ernie.

Little Ernie joined them. "My word!" he said, staring at George, "has she been making love to you?"

George didn't say anything.

"For Gawd's sake," Little Ernie went on to Cora, "what's 'appened to the bloke? Saw 'im a week ago, and 'e was as lovely as an oil painting. Look at 'im now."

"Dry up, Ernie," Cora said. "He's been in the wars."

"I'll say 'e 'as," Little Ernie said, undisguised admiration in his eyes. "Well, well. What'll you 'ave?" He rubbed a dirty finger under his nose and then wiped his finger on his trouser leg.

"We've got drinks, thank you," George said, a little stiffly. He didn't like this man. He didn't like the way he was eyeing Cora, a lewd look in his small green eyes.

Little Ernie rapped on the bar with a coin. "Hurry up," he shouted. "I ain't got all day. Gimme a double Scotch." He turned to Cora. "Sure you won't 'ave one?"

"All right," she said, leaning her back against the counter. She propped herself on her elbows and thrust her chest at him. "Give George one, too. You're lousy with money, aren't you?" '

Little Ernie winked. "I get by," he said, and raising his voice he shouted, "Make it three doubles, Clara, and out of the boss' bottle!" He looked at Cora again, then he glanced at George. "Fine gel, ain't she?" he said. "What a dairy! You could make pounds outta 'er if you knew 'ow to 'andle 'er."

"Shut your dirty trap," Cora said, her eyes bright with suppressed laughter. "George's not like you." She reached round and picked up her glass. "How's Eva? Still buying your suits?"

Little Ernie's cruel face darkened. "You don't 'ave to shout all over the shop, do you?" he said, glancing uneasily over his shoulder. "Old Crockett was down the street not five minutes ago. She's all right. She's a good girl. Work! Gawd love me, I've never known a girl to work like it!"

Cora sneered. "That's her trouble, Ernie. She does like it."

George was listening to this conversation and not understanding a word of it. He wished Little Ernie would go away. He was so repulsive that he embarrassed George.

"Believe she does," Little Ernie agreed thoughtfully. "You're a smart gel, Cora. Pity you don't get wise. I could fix you up in no time. Think of it! A flat of your own, 'undred smackers a week, and a dawg if you wanted one."

The barmaid planked down the three double whiskies, and Little Ernie parted with a pound.

"Gimme twenty Players and keep the change, ducks," he said. He turned back to Cora. "Well, I suppose you know what's good for you," he went on. "Only if you ever change your mind, give us a ring." He picked up his whisky. "Well, 'ere's to better days." He drank half the whisky, sighed and rested his small foot on the brass rail. "What 'ave you been doing to yourself?" he said, eyeing Cora. "You look orl right; a proper knockout."

"My new valet," Cora said, nodding at George. "He washed my pretty clothes and gave me a shampoo."

Little Ernie stared at George blankly.

George turned scarlet under the bitter, green eyes.

"Well, well," Little Ernie said. "Fancy that." He picked his nose and moved restlessly. "Hmm, well, well." He seemed at a loss for words.

"He's not a cissy," Cora said, glancing at George as if he were a stranger. "He's a tough guy, and when I say tough, I mean tough. He was Frank Kelly's gunman."

Little Ernie put down his glass. "Is that so?" He stared at George with interest.

George wished that Cora hadn't brought that up again. He shuffled his feet and fiddled with his tie. "Have another Scotch?" he said, in a desperate attempt to be at his ease.

" 'Ave one yourself," Little Ernie said. "It's on me." He snapped his fingers at the barmaid. "Same again, Clara, and don't drown 'em." He looked at Cora questioningly, but she only gave him back a jeering smile. "Kelly's gunman, eh? Hmm, what are you doing over 'ere?"

"Mind your own business," Cora snapped, before George could think of anything to say. "He's one of us now."

The green eyes narrowed. "Is that so?"

"That's right. Three thugs once took him in a wood. They had ideas about him. He walked out on his feet and alone," Cora said, her eyes, cold and hard, on George's bewildered face. "But he's modest. He doesn't talk about it." She fished a crumpled packet of cigarettes from her hip pocket. "He's quite a guy."

Little Ernie lit her cigarette and then produced two cigars. He offered one to George, who took it, not because he wanted it, but because he was so embarrassed that he wasn't quite certain what he was doing.

"Seems a quiet type of bloke, doesn't he?" Little Ernie went on regarding George.

"He's quiet all right," Cora returned. "Aren't you, George?"

George mumbled something. He didn't know what all this was about, but he did feel a sense of pride at the respectful way Little Ernie was regarding him.

"Syd said you'd be here. I thought he was joining us. What's he up to?" Little Ernie asked suddenly.

"He's busy," Cora said.

Little Ernie handed round the whiskies again. "Oh, well," he said, "I expect 'e is, but 'e said 'e'd be 'ere. Seen Crispin lately?" he went on casually, after a pause: too casually.

George started, slopping his whisky. He felt Little Ernie's eyes on him.

Cora nodded. Her expression didn't change. There was a jeering, confident expression in her eyes that obviously impressed Little Ernie.

"I saw him last night: so did George."

Little Ernie glanced at the sticking plaster and at George's bandaged hand and whistled. "Impulsive bloke, our Crispin," he said. "Shouldn't be surprised if 'e didn't get 'imself into a spot of trouble one of these days."

Cora smiled again, her face frozen. "Neither should I."

The two eyed each other. George, watching them uneasily, had a feeling that a drama was being enacted before his eyes, yet he could not understand what it was all about.

"Funny stories one 'ears," Little Ernie went on, watching Cora like a hawk. "Gawd knows who puts 'em in circulation. I did 'ear you and Crispin 'ad a little fun together last night."

Cora sipped her whisky. Her eyebrows lifted.

"I had a little fun," she said quietly. "Crispin's share is on ice at the moment, isn't it, George?"

George grunted. He had no idea why she was talking like this. To him it seemed dangerous. If they were going to get their own back on Crispin, why tell this sordid little man about it? Suppose he warned Crispin?

"Well, well." Little Ernie studied George, who was scowling down at the floor. He thought George looked a pretty tough *hombre*.

"He put me over a table and flogged me with a cane," Cora said calmly. "It hurt like hell ... it still hurts like hell."

Little Ernie's eyes bulged. "Gawd!" he exclaimed. " 'E must 'ave been barmy to do a thing like that to you."

Cora nodded. "George thinks so, too. In fact, George got quite annoyed about it. The Greeks had to cool him with razors. Now, of course, George is really mad. Aren't you, George!"

"Yes," George said uncomfortably.

He tried to show how angry he was by scowling at little Ernie and tightening his mouth. He had no idea how menacing he looked. He never took into account his great bulk, nor the fact that when he frowned his big, fleshy face was misleadingly hard and coarse. The strips of plaster also added to the effect. It was impressive enough to make Little Ernie whistle again.

"Well, for crying out loud," he said, "what's going to 'appen?"

Cora's eyes went blank. "You want to know a lot, don't you?" she said, stretching out her leg and looking at her shoe that George had cleaned so industriously. "It mightn't be healthy to know too much, Ernie."

He nodded. His eyes, quick as a ferret's, showed he was startled. "That's right," he said. "I don't want to know. I don't want to know anything about you three. 'Ave another drink?"

Cora shook her head. "You're not staying, are you, Ernie? Because we've got things to talk about."

"Who, me? No, I'm not staying. I've got to get along. You know me, Cora, always on the move. Well, so long." He grinned at George. "So long, palsy. Glad to 'ave met you," and he left them.

George finished his beer. The whiskies and the beer gave him rather a pleasant floating feeling. He knew he was just a little tight.

"You told him a lot, didn't you?" he said, looking at Cora questioningly.

"Ernie's all right," she said shortly. "He hates Crispin as much as we do. Besides, it's as well to let them know we're a mob now, not just a boy and a girl."

This continual hinting worried George. What did she mean when she kept saying he was one of them? Now she was talking about a mob.

"I may be a bit dense," he said slowly, "but I wish you'd explain. What mob? What do you mean by mob?"

She regarded him steadily. He again experienced the disconcerting feeling that she was looking inside his skull, even inside his pockets.

"I shan't be a moment," she said, fishing out her little purse from her pocket. "I want to spend a penny."

He understood then that these hints did mean something, but she had no intention of telling him.

He watched her walk across the room, jaunty and arrogant, to the door marked "Ladies".

# 12

It was a good film, and George gave it all his attention. The atmosphere of the cinema soothed him. The darkness, the bright screen, the drama which he could watch as an interested onlooker gave him a feeling that he had escaped into another, more pleasant world. He knew, at the back of his mind, that outside in the hot sunshine his world waited impatiently for his return; but for the next two hours here was escape.

He had been disappointed that Cora had wished to see a movie. The whiskies had made him amorous, and as soon as they left the pub he began a clumsy manoeuvre to persuade Cora to return to the flat.

He was careful, of course, not to let her know what he had in mind, but his eyes, his flushed face and his incoherent speech gave him away. Not that she let on that she had spotted his little game; she didn't. She said she felt like a movie, and although he had protested, and even said that it would be nicer if they went back to the flat together, imploring her with his eyes, she remained adamant.

He was hurt and angry that she could be so hard. What was the sense in wasting the afternoon in a cinema, when they could have been together alone and undisturbed in the flat?

He had sulked, and was determined that when she asked him which of the three cinemas they should choose, he would pointedly show his indifference.

But she didn't ask him. She walked down the street a step ahead of him, passed the first cinema and went straight to the box office of the second one, a few hundred yards farther down the road.

"Get circle seats," she said abruptly, and went on towards the stairs. He got the tickets and followed her, seething with frustration and disappointment. And when she pushed one and sixpence into his hand, he snatched the money from her and pocketed it without a word.

But once he had settled down in his seat, the magic of the darkness, the music and the drama on the screen overcame his ill temper.

It was a good picture: the kind of picture he liked. There were beautiful women, tough, well-dressed men, and music. There were long sequences of dimly lit streets and shadowy figures, guns in hand, moving silently from doorway to doorway. There were gun battles in the dark. There was a bedroom scene that titillated his desire for Cora, so that he fumbled for her hand and held it moistly, until she impatiently withdrew it.

As the drama progressed, he became so engrossed that he even forgot Cora was with him, and when the film came to an end he was sorry.

Moving down the stairs, a little dazed by the bright sunlight, he realized that he was a few hours closer to pending danger. Perhaps, after all, he could persuade them not to go; but his courage failed when he saw the cold, distant expression on Cora's face.

She, too, seemed to realize that time was running out. He could tell that she was uneasy. There was a subtle tension about her which hinted at taut nerves. When he made a comment about the film, she did not seem to hear him. She walked on, moving through the crowds almost as if she were sleepwalking.

It was six o'clock, and George wanted a cup of tea. He suggested they might have one, but she paid no attention. She kept on inexorably, alone in a crowd of people, deep in her secret thoughts.

He felt she was going to a definite place, and as he followed her, he had a premonition of danger. It was so acute that he stopped and caught at her arm.

"Where are we going?" he asked sharply. "Why are you so quiet? Is there something wrong?"

They stood in the middle of the pavement. The crowd broke up, passed them and joined up again. They received angry glances.

"Come on," she said with equal sharpness. "It's only round the corner."

She went on. His uneasiness growing, George followed her.

In a few minutes they were in a quiet side street, and this time it was Cora who stopped.

"There's a shop down there," she said, pointing and looking at him with a curious intentness. "Go and buy a whip. A horsewhip will do. Something you can hide under your coat." She thrust a pound note into his hand.

In spite of the sun and the hot pavement, George suddenly went cold. His instinct warned him to have nothing to do with this. It was as if he were being asked to cross a piece of ground which he knew was not solid and into which he was certain he would sink, and then suffocate.

"It's Sunday," he said, drawing away from her. "You can't buy anything today."

"Why do you think I came here?" she said impatiently. "They are all Jews down here. They closed yesterday."

His mind darted like a startled mouse for a way of

escape.

"I'm not buying it," he said obstinately. "If you want it, you'll have to get it yourself. I'm not having anything to do with it. I – I don't believe in that sort of thing."

She looked at his set, obstinate face and she suddenly smiled. "You're quite right, George," she said softly; "it's stupid to wait. When two people are in love …" She pushed the pound note again into his hand. "Get the whip and let's go back. We've still time before he returns."

George stared at her, seeing in her eyes a fainting desire: an unmistakable invitation of receptive, expectant femininity.

"Cora!" he said, his fingers clutching the pound note, "you mean – now? You really mean *now*?"

"I said I'd be nice to you, didn't I? Well, why should we wait? … Only you'll have to hurry."

He went down the street with an unsteady, shambling gait, a feverish, incoherent puppet, without a will, without regard to danger, without a thought for anything except what she was offering him.

He blundered into the shop she had indicated. Saddles, rolls of leather, horse blankets, dog collars, trunks, bags and whips overflowed on the counter, the floor and the shelves behind the counter.

An elderly man with a great hooked nose came out of an office at the back of the shop. He looked curiously at George.

"Good afternoon," he said. "Is there something I can show you?"

George looked round the shop, his eyes bloodshot and wild. He saw a whip, a riding switch, whalebone bound in red leather, with an ivory handle. He picked it up with a shudder.

"I'll have it," he said, thrusting it at the Jew, and threw

down the pound note.

The Jew shook his head. "I think it's a little more than a pound," he said, picking up the whip with long, caressing fingers. He turned the price ticket and glanced at it. "It's a fine piece of workmanship." He smiled. "It's fifty-five shillings."

George gulped. "Give me something for a pound, something like this, only for a pound."

"Certainly." The Jew did not move, but continued to touch the riding switch with caressing fingers. "I should like to point out, sir, that it would be more economical to buy a better whip while you are about it. Now, this is something that will last a lifetime. It is beautifully made and impossible to wear out. The extra money will be saved over and over again."

What was the matter with this fool? George thought, feverishly. Didn't he know he was wasting precious time?

"I don't want it," he said violently. "Give me what I want, and for God's sake stop talking!"

He was not aware of the sudden alarm that jumped into the Jew's eyes, nor his curious stare at George's congested face.

George was only aware of the passing time, and when the Jew offered him another whip, saying in a grieved voice that it was a guinea, George threw down a shilling on top of the pound note, snatched up the whip without looking at it, and rushed from the shop.

Cora was waiting at the corner, serene and arrogant. Her hands were thrust deep into her pockets and her eyes watchful.

"I've got it," George said thickly, falling into step beside her. "Let's go back."

She allowed herself to be hurried through the streets. They did not speak. George was only conscious of a pounding in his ears and a suffocating desire for her. He almost pushed her up the stairs to the flat, and when she had to search through her pockets and purse for the key, he stood trembling, in an agony of suspense.

Finally she opened the door and they entered the flat. He threw the whip into the armchair and caught hold of her.

"Hello, George," Sydney said from the door.

George didn't look round. His arms dropped to his sides, and he stood staring down at Cora with glazed eyes. The hateful sound of Sydney's voice crushed him.

Sydney wandered into the room and regarded him sharply.

"I say, what a state you're in!" he said in his sneering voice.

George turned away. He caught a cold, jeering look from Cora that sent a stab into his heart. He was sick with disappointment and frustration.

"What have you been up to, Cora?" Sydney went on, flopping into the armchair. "What's this?" he continued, picking up the whip. "Oh, something for Crispin, eh? That's wonderful." A quick, cautious note crept into his voice. "Did George buy it?"

"He bought it," Cora said, wandering across the room and opening a cupboard. "He didn't want to at first, but I persuaded him; didn't I, George?" She took from the cupboard a bottle of whisky and two glasses.

George sat down limply and wiped his face and hands on his handkerchief. He didn't say anything. He had a feeling that they had, between them, tricked him in some way. He felt that ever since Sydney had telephoned him, asking him to take the message to Joe's Club, a series of carefully planned manoeuvres had taken place to trap him.

Cora came over to him with a glass half full of whisky.

"Have a drink, George," she said, putting the glass in his

hand. "You look as if you needed it."

Then she sat on his lap and slipped an arm round his neck. His suspicions were immediately lulled, and in their place came an overwhelming tenderness and love for her. She rested her head against his shoulder and gently swung her legs. She, too, had a stiff whisky in her hand.

Sydney was eyeing them with thoughtful interest.

"It seems I came back a bit too early," he said, settling more comfortably in his armchair.

"You did," Cora returned, tormenting George by rubbing her face against his. "George and I had made plans, hadn't we, George?"

He gripped her tightly, but didn't say anything. His hand trembled so that he slopped a little whisky on her slacks.

"Careful, George," she said, and suddenly laughed. "You know, our George is quite a lad," she went on to Sydney. "I believe he'd make one of the world's greatest lovers."

"Never mind about George," Sydney said. "We've got other things to think about."

Cora slipped off George's lap. She crossed the room and picked up the whip.

George, feeling suddenly deflated, watched her. She swished the whip once or twice, her face spiteful. Then she laughed.

"I'll bet he'll yell the place down," she said.

"It's all fixed," Sydney said. "He'll be alone. I've got a car. We leave at eight-thirty. It'll take us about an hour. By that time it'll be getting dark."

Cora raised her glass. "To our new member," she said, looking at George, and she tilted her head and emptied her glass.

George felt hot. Whisky burned in his stomach. He was a little light-headed, but uneasy, nervous.

The past hour had been difficult. As the hands of the

clock crept forward, all of them showed signs of strain. Even Sydney, for all his sneering coldness, began to fidget and look at the clock.

Cora drank steadily. She showed no sign that the whisky was affecting her, except that her face became paler and her eyes brightened.

When, at last, Sydney got to his feet, there was an immediate tightening of the tension. George looked from one to the other.

"Perhaps we ought not to go …" he began, facing them.

They stood side by side, brother and sister, their eyes cold and cautious, oddly alike. They stared at him as if he were a stranger.

"Don't talk wet," Sydney said.

"Go on," Cora said. "We're coming."

Sydney shrugged and moved to the door. He opened it and began to walk down the stairs.

Cora went to George.

"You're coming back here tonight," she said, putting her hand on his arm. "I don't cheat. I meant what I said, only I didn't think Sydney would be back so soon." Her eyes were inviting. Then she added, "I'll be nice to you tonight – promise."

After that it didn't seem to matter. When he turned to pick up the gun, she was before him. She took it up very carefully by the barrel.

"I'm your gun moll," she said, her mouth smiling. "I want to carry it." She slipped it into a leather bag she had slung from her shoulder. Then she went up to him. "Kiss me," she said.

They left the flat a few minutes before eight-thirty. It was a sultry night; the sky was cloudless, but there was the smell of rain in the air.

They joined Sydney in the street a few moments later. There was a smear of lipstick on George's mouth and he seemed bemused.

None of them spoke. Cora walked stiffly because of the whip she had thrust down the leg of her slacks. George was between the two of them, and it seemed to him that they were his jailers.

They turned down an alley and into a little courtyard. A dark green Ford coupé was standing round the corner, out of sight from the mouth of the alley.

Sydney unlocked the door and slid under the wheel. Cora got in at the back.

"Come on," she said to George, who was hesitating.

He got into the car beside her and slammed the door.

"I didn't know you had a car," he said blankly.

"He thinks this is our car," Cora called to Sydney.

Sydney laughed. It had a mirthless sound. He started the engine and drove the car slowly down the alley.

"Well, isn't it your car?" George asked.

"We borrowed it," Sydney said. "Now shut up. I want to think."

They drove out of London in silence. As Big Ben, coming over a wireless set, struck nine, they passed through Wimbledon. Later they got on to the Reigate road.

George sat hunched up, alone and lost. He thought of his room in the dull boarding-house and Leo. That part of his life seemed remote now: he wasn't even sure that it had ever happened. But Cora – he could feel her thigh against his – was real enough, so was the back of Sydney's head, and the swift passage of the car through the darkening streets: all frighteningly real.

He lost count of time. He didn't want to think about it. He felt that the car was taking him towards a destiny from which there was no escape.

Sydney leaned forward and switched on the headlights.

"We turn off just about here," he said shortly: there was a nervous hesitation in his voice.

They peered through the windows. They were over-anxious, as if it were the most important thing in the world not to miss the turning.

They saw it at last, and they both exclaimed.

"All right," Sydney said, braking sharply. "I'm not blind."

They turned into a country lane and stopped. The headlights made the grass banks and hedges on either side of the lane look startlingly fresh and green.

"It's just at the end of the lane," Sydney said, cutting the engine. "We'll leave the car here."

He twisted round in his seat so that he could look at them. The white moonlight lighted his face. It frightened George. The ghastly scar burned red, and there was a look of animal viciousness and hatred in Sydney's eyes.

"We'll go in together," Sydney went on. His voice trembled in a breathless kind of way. "If he shows fight, give George the gun. Now listen, George, this is important. Go up to him and ram the gun in his stomach. Do you understand? Wind him. Look tough. You don't have to say anything; I'll do the talking. When Cora gives you the gun, walk up to him and slam it in his guts. That'll take the starch out of the rat. You wait: it'll do you good to see the way he'll curl up. Then we'll go for him."

George licked his dry lips. "Listen, just a minute..."

Cora put her hand on his knee. Her touch sent the blood pounding in his head. Words of caution died in his mouth.

"What is it?" Sydney asked.

"Nothing," Cora said. "He's fine, aren't you, George?"

"Well, don't mess about," Sydney said. "This is serious.

Now come on; let's get it over."

He got out of the car.

"We're coming," Cora said.

As Sydney moved away down the lane she fell against George, her hands pulling his head down to her open mouth. A suffocating desire engulfed him. They remained like that for some time, their mouths crushed together, and then Cora pushed him away and slid out of the car.

"Come," she said.

As if hypnotized, George followed her. His heart hammered against his ribs and blood sang in his ears. He couldn't think about Crispin. He couldn't think of anything.

Cora held his arm. She was pulling him along. He couldn't see, and his feet stumbled. Sweat dripped down his face. The air had gone dead. There was no movement in the trees; no wind, only a hot stillness that oppressed him. In the distance, thunder rumbled. A line of black clouds began to edge above the horizon.

"Quiet," she said softly, and he could feel her trembling.

Sydney moved towards them out of the darkness.

"It's all right," he whispered. "He's there, and alone."

He went on ahead. Cora followed, seemingly able to see in the dark. She steered George through a gateway and up an overgrown path. Then suddenly they came on a small bungalow. One window was open, and light streamed from it into the garden.

The three of them stopped abruptly. Thunder crashed not far away, startling George, so that he clutched Cora's arm. Her muscles felt hard under his hand, as if she were keyed up, her nerves at breaking point.

They edged forward so that they could look into the room. Crispin, in a blue and white flowered dressing-gown, was sitting at a table. A cigarette dangled from his lips; he was writing on a pad of notepaper. A lawyer's briefcase lay half open at his elbow. It appeared to be bulging with pound notes.

George shivered. The sight of all that money frightened him even more than the thought of bursting in and assaulting this strange-looking man. He glanced at Sydney. He could just make out his features in the light from the window. He was hissing between his teeth, a frightening look of pent-up hatred in his eyes.

A spear thrust of blue-white lightning split the sky, was followed in a few seconds by a tremendous clap of thunder. George ducked instinctively. A drop of ice-cold water fell on his hot face. It began to rain.

Cora jerked at his arm. Sydney was already creeping towards the front door. In a kind of dream, George followed him. As before, when they had burst into Robinson's room, he suddenly felt extraordinarily at ease. This was, of course, just another of his fantasies. George Fraser, millionaire gangster, was again on the job. It couldn't really be happening to poor old George, the lonely, cat-loving book tout. Not this: this was too fantastic. It would be all right. In a few minutes Leo would come in and jump up on his bed. Ella would come in with his tea. There was no need to get alarmed, or for his heart to pound like this. He might just as well enjoy this fantasy. What the devil was this little runt of a Sydney doing, leading the way? George Fraser always led the way. It was too late now. Sydney had opened the front door. They were all in the room now, looking at Crispin.

This was exciting! Crispin was behaving just as George imagined he would behave. He had turned green with terror.

George flexed his great muscles and scowled at him.

"Hello, Crispin," Sydney said.

Crispin put a hand on the leather briefcase. He didn't move his body and he didn't say anything.

"Get up, Crispin," Sydney said. "I've had to wait a long time to get even with you. We have you now where we want you."

Slowly Crispin rose to his feet; even then he couldn't find his voice.

"I've brought a whip," Cora said, polite as a tailor at a fitting. She pulled the whip from her trouser leg and laid it on the table.

"We'll start with that," Sydney said.

Cora zipped open her bag casually and took out the Luger.

A faint click sounded through the room. It was immediately lost in a clap of thunder.

"Here, George," she said, and pushed the gun into his hand.

George looked at Crispin. Crispin looked at him and then at the gun. His face seemed to fall to pieces. He began to back slowly away.

Oddly enough, the heavy Luger felt good in George's hands. He felt extraordinarily elated to see the terror in Crispin's face.

Crispin, white, his mouth working, backed against the wall. He looked lonely.

George bore down on him.

"Don't ..." Crispin said, and squirmed against the wall like a beetle pinned alive to a board.

"Get your hands up," George said, and rammed the gun hard into Crispin's chest.

A zigzag of brilliant lightning streaked through the window. Thunder sounded like a trunk being moved in an attic. Above the crash of the thunder came another sound – a sharp crack, like the breaking of dry wood magnified many times. A wisp of smoke rose in the air: it smelt of gunpowder.

In that moment of sound George felt the gun in his hand kick like a live thing, and it jumped out of his hand onto the floor. He became conscious of two things: a tight, deep-throated scream from Cora, and a curious red mess on the wall where Crispin had been standing.

Slowly, his eyes travelled from the red stain down the wall, past the sideboard, to the floor. Crispin lay huddled up, as if the bones in his legs had been broken. There was a red stain on the front of his white and blue dressing-gown.

A voice came to George, as if someone were shouting in a tunnel. He heard the voice, but the words meant nothing to him.

It's all right, he said to himself. This has happened to you hundreds of times before. All you've got to do is to hang on and wait. You'll wake up in a moment.

Someone was shaking him. A strident voice was shrieking at him.

"You fool! You fool! You stupid, bloody fool!"

Something hard hit him in the face, and he shivered. Something inside his head exploded into fire and darkness, and just before the darkness he felt a sharp flash of nausea. He staggered, clutched at nothing, recovered his balance and groped with blind fingers.

The shock left him after a while.

Cora was speaking again. She was speaking softly.

"You did it," she was saying. "We don't touch murder. That's something we don't stand for. We didn't tell you to shoot him. We only wanted you to frighten him."

He could see her eyes, slate-grey, hard, frightened. Her

face was misty. He looked at Sydney. He wavered before George like weeds in a fast-moving river.

Then – *snap*! – everything became sharp and clear. Cora and Sydney seemed to spring to life, sharp-etched, like a film that has been suddenly correctly focused.

He stared down at Crispin, caught his breath and shied away.

"No!" he said huskily. "The gun wasn't loaded! I didn't do it! I didn't do it!"

They watched him, cold, pitiless and accusing.

"It's your mess," Sydney said, his voice flat and metallic. "Keep away from us. We don't want you. We don't touch murder."

George wasn't listening to him. He was looking at Cora. She wouldn't desert him: "I don't cheat," she had said. "I'll be very nice to you tonight – promise." She'd promised, hadn't she? She couldn't desert him now. She must know that this had nothing to do with him.

He went to her.

"Cora!" he said. "I didn't do it! You know I didn't. The gun wasn't loaded. I can prove it. The cartridges are at home. There's twenty-five of them. That's all I had. They haven't been touched! Don't you understand? They haven't been touched!"

Her mouth curled in loathing.

"You stupid, creeping fool!" she cried. "I hate you! Look what you've done! Don't ever dare come near me again!" And she struck him across the face with her clenched fist.

Then they went out and left him.

He stood looking at Crispin; he was numbed with horror. Slowly he bent and picked up the Luger. It smelt strongly of gunpowder. He examined it. The safety catch had been moved. He pressed it down. There came a faint click. His memory moved, groped, floundered. There had been the same clicking sound when Cora had given him the gun. He remembered now. Had she deliberately released the safety catch? He didn't think it likely. He didn't know. His finger curled round the trigger. The hammer instantly snapped down. He snapped the hammer down three times before it dawned on him that someone had fixed the trigger mechanism so that the gun would fire at the slightest touch. Even then he was too terrified to think much of the discovery.

Rain beat in through the open window, and the curtains ballooned into the room as waves of hot air disturbed them. Thunder crackled.

George stood still, listening. He heard a motor-car start up. It seemed to be moving at a great speed, and its sound quickly died away.

He found himself looking at the table and noting with stupefied fascination that the briefcase full of money was no longer there.

# 13

George opened his eyes. The room was shadowy, but comfortingly familiar. The faint dawn light edged round the blind. It was early.

Although his body ached, and there was a feeling of lassitude in his limbs, his brain was clear and awake. He raised his head and glanced at his wristwatch. It was half past five. He lay back again and stared up at the ceiling, his mind crawling with alarm. He must avoid panic. He must relax and go over the whole business carefully and calmly. If he thought enough about it, got it into its right perspective, there must be a way out. The trouble was that he wasn't very good at thinking, nor was he very good at keeping calm, nor, of course, had he killed a man before.

He sat up in bed and deliberately turned the pillow, patted it and lay down again. By this simple act – something that anyone would do – he hoped that he would recapture a feeling of security. He adjusted the sheet under his chin and moved his legs. The bed felt warm and comfortable. The little black cloud of panic that had begun to edge over his brain receded. It would be all right, he told himself, if he kept calm.

He closed his eyes, and immediately Crispin's crumpled body in the bloodstained dressing-gown swam into his mind. He started up, his fists gripping the sheet. This wouldn't do, he thought, and forced himself to lie down again.

It took some time before he could trust himself to think. But he knew that he could not for long avoid facing the facts. He had killed a man. Now he must make plans. He had no idea what plans he had to make, but he couldn't lie in bed for the rest of his days. He had to decide what he was going to do. The easiest way, of course, would be to go to the police and tell them everything. That would shift the responsibility from him to them. They couldn't do anything to him. It had been an accident. He could prove that it had been an accident. The cartridge must have been in the breech for a long time. George frowned. No, that couldn't be right, because he had pulled the trigger many times, liking the sound of the sharp snap of the hammer. If the cartridge had been in the breech it would have been fired long ago. Then how did the cartridge get into the breech? He had twenty-five cartridges, but he had never put one of them into the magazine. He had been most careful about that. He was so sure about this that he began to consider whether it was his gun that had fired the fatal shot. Perhaps someone lurking outside had fired through the open window. Then he remembered how the gun had smelt of gunpowder, and his mind again began to crawl with alarm.

Someone must have put a cartridge into the gun. That could be the only explanation. Someone had also fixed the trigger mechanism. He would tell the police. It wasn't his business to say who did it. All he had to do was to show them the box of cartridges, and they could see at a glance that none of them was missing. Surely that would prove his innocence?

He looked at the dressing-table across the room and then got out of bed. He opened the drawer and took out the small wooden box of cartridges; then he got back into bed

181

again, holding the box tightly in his hand. He mustn't lose this box, he told himself. His life depended on it. That seemed an exaggerated statement to make, but it was true. His life did depend on it.

He'd go to the police and explain. He would open the box and show them the tight-fitting cartridges. He took the lid off the box. One cartridge was missing. He looked at the empty space for a long time and then he put the box very carefully on the table by his bed.

He lay back on his pillow and began to weep, weak with hysterical fear. He had known all along that a cartridge would be missing. It was all part of this ghastly nightmare: this web that was inexorably creeping round him, but he had tried to make himself believe that there was still a loophole of escape.

It was some time before he began to think again. Now his brain moved in quick darts, snatching at anything that could sustain hope.

He didn't arrive at any conclusion, and he knew he wouldn't arrive at any conclusion until he had controlled the panic that was gripping his heart and his mind.

Somehow one of the cartridges that belonged to him had got into the gun. How? Who did it?

His mind darted to Sydney.

Sydney ... Well, yes, he could have taken a cartridge from the box when he had sneaked the Luger from George's drawer while George had been shaving. It was just the sort of sly thing that Sydney would do. Then, while Cora and he had been at the movies, Sydney could have fixed the trigger mechanism and put the cartridge in the breech. Cora knew, of course. It was obvious. That was why she had insisted that George should leave the gun on the mantelpiece when they went to the movies. It was there for Sydney, who was waiting for them to go. It also explained why Cora had insisted on carrying the gun when they set off for Copthorne.

"I'm your gun moll," she had said, and she had kissed him. He thought of Judas, and remembered how shocked he had been when, as a child, he had read of the betrayal. The same sense of shock returned.

Well, he was getting on. He now knew how the cartridge had been put in the gun and how the trigger mechanism had been fixed. Cora had put the finishing touch to the trap. Just before she had given him the gun she had deliberately slipped back the safety catch. He remembered distinctly hearing the soft little click as the catch snapped back. It was almost as if she and Sydney had planned the murder of Crispin.

His mind shied away from this idea. He remembered Cora's look of loathing.

"We don't touch murder. That's something we don't stand for. We didn't tell you to shoot him. We only wanted you to frighten him."

Then why had they fixed the gun like that?

George rubbed his sweating face with his hand. There was something wrong. He had had a feeling all along that there was something wrong, but he had been so besotted with Cora that he had not heeded his own uneasiness.

Begin at the beginning, he said to himself. The telephone booth at Joe's. That started it.

"It's a club in Mortimer Street, not far from you. They're not on the blower, otherwise I'd've rung 'em," Sydney had said.

*But they had been on the blower.* He had seen for himself the telephone booth in the Club.

Sydney must have known that. But if he hadn't lied about the telephone, there would have been no reason for George to go to Joe's and leave a message for Cora. And that would have meant that he would never have met her, never have fallen in love with her, never have been a besotted fool and never have allowed himself to be persuaded to commit murder.

The more he thought about it, the plainer it became. The story about the key and Cora not being able to get into the flat had been part of the plot. It was so simple that it had never crossed his mind that he was walking into a trap.

What devils these two were! The trouble they had taken to trap him into murder. He remembered the briefcase full of money. There must have been five or six hundred pounds in that case. That was the motive, of course! They had trapped him into killing Crispin so that they could steal the money! He sat up in bed, his eyes wild. Then the scene in the restaurant had been part of the plot. Cora had deliberately staged that business to fool him into believing they had no other motive in visiting Crispin but for revenge. And they had fooled him. Was it possible that she had allowed herself to be flogged like that just to fool him? There was no doubt that she had been flogged. He had heard her shrieks and had seen the marks. The red, bruised, broken skin was something you couldn't fake. Had she really accepted such a beating in order to provide a false motive just to fool him?

He floundered in a pit of doubt, turning the facts over in his mind. Then he remembered something she had said to Sydney when they had returned to the flat, just before he had fainted, "You said he wouldn't touch me!" He remembered, too, how nervous she had been, and that after she had thrown the wine in Crispin's face she had begged him not to let Crispin touch her. It looked as if Sydney had also double-crossed Cora. He had trapped *her* into picking a fight with Crispin, assuring her that she would come to no harm.

The more George thought about it, the calmer he became. It was an utterly fantastic story, but he felt confident that if he kept his head and explained everything very carefully, and in its proper sequence, the police would believe him.

The face of Little Ernie suddenly swam into his mind, blotting out the vision of hope he had so carefully constructed.

Cora had practically told Little Ernie that George was going to get even with Crispin.

"I had a little fun," she had said. "Crispin's share is on ice at the moment, isn't it, George?"

And Little Ernie had looked uneasy. He would remember the conversation, and when he heard about Crispin's death, he would go to the police.

George began to sweat again. What would the police say after they had listened to Little Ernie? And then he thought of the whip. What had happened to the whip? Cora had been diabolically clever in the way she had persuaded him to buy the whip. So much for her promises. Well, he would know another time – if there was another time. If the police found the whip, they would trace it to him. The old Jew would remember him. He had been so anxious to get Cora back to the flat that he had behaved like a madman. He put his hand to the strips of plaster on his face. The Jew would remember those strips. How easy it would be for the police to spot him! The Jew would give the police a full description of him. It would tally with the description that Little Ernie would give them. No one had seen Cora. She had kept away from the shop. The whip had been left in the bungalow. It was an obvious clue. He hadn't even removed the price ticket. It wouldn't take them more than a few hours to trace it, and then his description would be in the newspapers.

He lay back in bed, his throat dry and his heart pounding.

He felt he could explain everything except the whip. It proved that he was planning revenge. Without the whip it would be Little Ernie's word against his.

What a fool he had been! Why hadn't he taken the whip with him? Why had he run out of the bungalow and pounded down the lane without making sure that he had left no fingerprints or anything that could incriminate him?

He stumbled out of bed and stood trembling on the cold linoleum. This wouldn't do, he thought, wringing his hands, and he crushed down his fear. It was twenty minutes to seven. Ella would be in with his tea in a little while. He mustn't let her suspect that there was anything wrong. She must find him as she always found him, sleepy and in bed. When she had gone he would get dressed and take a train to Three Bridges, which was the nearest station to Copthorne. It wasn't likely that anyone would discover Crispin's body for some time. With luck, no one ever went to the bungalow except Crispin. He would have to be very careful, of course. He thought of the *Child's Self-Educator*. He could pretend that he thought there was a child in the bungalow, and he would go up to the door and ring the bell. If no one answered, he would break in and get the whip.

He became calm again. It was all right so long as you kept your head and used your brain. Once he had the whip he could go to the police and explain everything, but it wouldn't be safe until he had it.

A soft scratching at the door startled him; then his face softened. He opened the door and let Leo in. He got back into bed, and the cat jumped up and settled down close to him. It began to purr.

George stroked its long hair. "You're all I've got, Leo," he said softly. "There's no one else, and even you can't help me."

The regular, contented noise the cat made soothed him. Very gently, he stroked the top of its head, and it stretched out a paw and touched his face, as if understanding that he was alone, in need of affection and sympathy.

Later, Ella came in. She put down the cup of tea and walked across the room to pull up the blind.

When she saw his face, she gave a little scream. "Why, Mr George," she said in horror. "What have you done to your poor face?"

"I got into a razor fight," George said after a moment's hesitation. "That's why I stayed out last night. They're only scratches, Ella. Don't look so frightened."

She continued to gape at him. "A razor fight?" she repeated. "Oh, Mr George!"

Just to see the admiration and awe in her eyes was like a tonic to George's crushed, frightened ego.

"It's nothing," he said carelessly. "I've been in tighter jams before. Mark you, I did have an anxious moment, but I taught the fellow a lesson."

"How did it happen?" Ella asked. "Who was he?"

"Be a good girl and don't ask questions," George returned, suddenly cautious. "Promise me you won't tell anyone. The fellow got hurt, and I don't want to get into trouble. Mind you, he started it, but I did give him a terrific hiding. Now don't ask any more questions, and if anyone asks if I was in last night, will you say I was?"

Ella, her eyes like marbles, promised.

"You're a good sort, Ella," George said. "I think I'll go out and get something for my head. It aches like mad. The chemist will be open by the time I get dressed."

Obviously Ella wanted to hear more details, but George seemed so ill and worried that she felt a sudden pity for him.

"Shall I put on your bath, Mr George?" she asked.

"No, I won't wait," he said quickly. "I want to fix this head."

As soon as she had gone, he got up and had a quick, uncertain shave. It was difficult, with the plaster in the way, but he managed somehow. He dressed and gave Leo some milk.

"I'll have to get you some food tonight, old chap," he said, rubbing the cat's head. "I've been pretty busy, but I'll bring you something nice tonight."

He picked up his book specimens, slipped them into his pocket, and was ready to go.

He reached Victoria Station a few minutes past eight-thirty. There was a local train that stopped at Three Bridges, due out at eight-forty. He had just time to buy a paper and his ticket before the train left.

He got a corner seat facing the engine, lit a cigarette, and glanced quickly at the other two occupants of the carriage. They did not even glance at him as they settled in their corners.

He searched the newspaper for any hint that Crispin's body had been found, but he found nothing to alarm him. A tiny paragraph tucked away at the back of the paper gave him pause. A green Ford coupé had been stolen from outside a doctor's house the previous afternoon and so far had not been traced.

So the car had been stolen. Was there no end to the wickedness of these two? They were so callous and calm about everything. Why, driving down to Copthorne, they might easily have been arrested for being in possession of a stolen car, and the loaded gun would have been found. George gritted his teeth. They would all have gone to prison.

He folded the newspaper and put it in his pocket. As he did so, he wondered what Sydney and Cora were doing at this precise moment. They were probably in bed and asleep, secure in mind that they had safely fastened the murder on to him. Or perhaps they had decided to pack up and leave London. With all that money they could go anywhere. Whatever happened to him, George thought grimly, they wouldn't get away with this. If they were still at the flat, he would go and see them. He would have it out with them: threaten them with the police.

The train began to slow down, and finally pulled into Three Bridges station. He began the long walk to Copthorne. It was a perfect summer morning, the sun was not too hot, the country looked fresh and green.

One or two cars passed him, but he was nervous of asking for a lift. He didn't want anyone to remember him. He had been careful to put on a pair of flannel slacks, a sports shirt and an old tweed jacket. He looked like a City clerk on holiday.

Eventually he arrived at the turning that led to the bungalow. He paused at the top of the lane, listening and watching. Nothing aroused his suspicions. Taking out his book specimens and holding them in his hand, he walked down the lane. As he approached the bungalow he became nervous and on edge. It was lonely in this country lane. The bungalow seemed to be the only building within sight. The only sounds that came to him were the rustling of leaves in the wind and the twittering of the birds. It was not an atmosphere that should have created fear, but by the time he had reached the wooden gate that led to the bungalow he was terrified.

He paused outside the gate and looked up and down the

lane, screwing up his courage to go on.

Suppose the police were waiting for him? Suppose this silent, overgrown garden concealed a trap?

He struggled with his fears. He had to get the whip. It was worth any risk. He would be all right if he kept his head and showed them his book specimens. He would say that he had wanted a day in the country and was canvassing to make his expenses. That was a straightforward story. They would believe him. It wasn't as if he looked like a murderer.

He drew a deep breath and pushed open the gate. It squeaked sharply, setting his teeth on edge. Again he had a powerful urge to turn back, but he forced himself on.

Cautiously, he moved up the overgrown path. In the shelter of the trees and high hedges, the garden was silent and close. The scent of clover and wallflowers was heavy in the still air.

He reached the bungalow and rapped on the door. Sweat ran down his face as he stood in the hot, sheltered porch, listening, his nerves slowly tightening.

And as he stood there, a thought crept into his mind that drove the blood from his heart. Suppose Crispin answered the door? Suppose he got up from the floor and opened the door and stood before George with blood on his dressing-gown?

George backed away, his mouth open in an idiotic grimace of terror. He couldn't even run away. He stood paralyzed, waiting. Nothing happened.

He fought down the panic that had seized him, conquered it and returned to the door. He rapped again.

There was no one in the bungalow except Crispin: and Crispin was dead.

George put an unsteady hand on the door-latch, lifted it and pushed upon the door. He braced himself and peered into the room. Then breath whistled between his clenched teeth, and blackness dropped like a curtain before his eyes. He clung to the doorpost and waited. Evil-tasting bile rose in his mouth; he wanted to be sick.

Except for the furniture, the room was empty.

George's heart began slowly to pump blood back to his brain. It was some minutes before he could move again. Then he stepped into the room and stared with unbelieving eyes at the carpet where Crispin had fallen. There was no sign of murder in the room. Fearfully, George looked for the red mess on the wall. That was not there either.

Was he going out of his mind? Had all the fantasies of violence that he had created in the past brought him to this? Were Sydney, Cora, Crispin and all the other nightmare people mere figments of a deranged imagination? Was it possible that the murder had happened only in his mind?

He looked wildly round the room, and then he stiffened.

*On the sideboard lay the whip.*

There was no question about it. It was there, leather and whalebone, and the little white price ticket on the handle.

He edged forward and picked it up. He stood for several minutes gazing at it, aware that it was the symbol of his sanity.

Then, in the hush of the lonely room, above the drone of the bees and the rustle of the hollyhocks against the window, he heard voices.

Still grasping the whip, he stepped to the door and listened. A man was speaking some way off in the garden behind the bungalow.

Moving silently, in blind panic, George slipped out of the house, crossed the path and sank down on his knees under the overhanging hedge. He found a dry ditch that ran along the side of the garden, and cautiously lowered himself into it. He adjusted the leaves of the hedge so that they formed a screen over him.

He found that he had a good view of the bungalow, and he was confident that he could not be seen. He waited, his hand gripping the whip, his heart fluttering against his side. He heard the sound of feet moving through the long grass. Then round the corner of the bungalow came four people: the Hebrew barman, the two Greeks and the woman with the blonde, untidy hair.

They looked odd and somehow sinister against the background of the peace and fertility of the garden.

The Hebrew wore a double-breasted, navy-blue suit, shiny at the elbows and knees; on his head was a bowler hat. The woman had on a shapeless cotton dress; its pattern of flowers had faded with constant washing. Her thick legs were bare, and blue-black veins crawled up the backs of her calves. Her feet were squeezed into a pair of high-heeled court shoes. The two Greeks were in their black suits and cloth caps. They carried spades on their shoulders, and their boots were heavy with yellow clay.

A cigarette dangled from the blonde woman's lips. Her fat, loose face was expressionless, but the Hebrew was weeping. He did not make a fuss about his grief. Tears welled out of his eyes and ran down the wrinkles in his leathery skin. He made no attempt to wipe them away.

The woman looked at the bungalow, her eyes bleak. "Was he expecting anyone?" she asked.

The Hebrew lifted his shoulders in despair. "I know nothing," he said. "He didn't confide in me. I told him it was dangerous to have a lonely place like this. I told him many times."

The woman sat down abruptly on the grass. She was only a few yards from where George was hiding. She plucked a long piece of coarse grass and began to chew it.

"Sit down. The sun will do you good."

The Hebrew and the two Greeks sat down near her. They looked self-conscious, worried. The Hebrew still wept.

"The way you go on!" the woman said impatiently. "I'm his mother. Shouldn't I be the one to weep?"

The Hebrew took out a handkerchief and wiped his eyes. "You're hard, Emily," he said. "What a burial to give a son!"

The woman, Emily, snapped her thick fingers. "He wouldn't mind. He didn't believe in God. Is that what's worrying you?" She brooded, tearing the blade of grass with her sharp teeth. "What did you expect me to do? Leave him there for the police to find? They would be crawling over us like flies on bad meat in no time. Haven't they done enough harm?"

When he didn't say anything, she went on. "Who do you think did it?"

"Vengeance is mine, saith the Lord," the Hebrew said, pulling at his long, straggly moustache.

"You don't fool me," Emily said. "I know what you're thinking, don't I, Max?"

"Do you?"

The two Greeks had lit cigarettes. They were not listening to this conversation. They lolled back on their elbows, their dark faces raised to the sun, their eyes closed.

But Max listened. He sat bolt upright, his long, thin legs crossed like a working tailor, his bowler hat very straight on his pear-shaped head.

"We don't have to worry about the police," Emily went on. "He wouldn't have liked it. We can find out who did it, and we can settle the score, can't we?"

Max looked across the garden. "There's the money," he

said. "He should never have brought it here. Seven hundred pounds!"

"Stop worrying about the money," Emily said sharply. "Is that what you're crying about?"

"The gun worries me," Max said, not listening to her. "A razor, yes, but a gun! ... It's someone we don't know."

"Well, we can find out, can't we?" Emily persisted. "Does the whip mean anything?"

"It must do. It's new. Crispin wouldn't buy a thing like that."

There was a long pause. A bee droned across the hot garden and lighted on a hollyhock.

"Who was that girl? The one Crispin thrashed?" Emily said, plucking another blade of grass and chewing it.

"I was thinking about her, too," Max said. "The whip might tie up with her. Do you mean that?"

"It could do. And the big man. Who was he?"

Max shook his head. "I don't know. I've never seen either before. There was something odd about the way that girl behaved. She wasn't drunk. She was faking."

"Crispin was a fool to have touched her. She might have complained to the police."

"Why didn't she?"

"Yes, why?"

There was another long pause while they brooded.

"Maybe they came down here for revenge; found the money and killed Crispin to steal it," Emily said at last.

"How could they know Crispin had this place? No one knew that he came here."

"Sydney Brant knew," Emily said thoughtfully.

"Brant? He hasn't been around for months. Besides, after Crispin burnt him, he was too scared to come near the place. This is nothing to do with him; but the girl and the big man … maybe, I don't know …"

"Well, we can't waste time. We must settle this business. Whoever did it will have to pay."

"They'll pay all right." Max's harsh voice floated on the still air, and George shivered. These people, so calculating, so ordinary to look at, plotting revenge in the hot sunshine, had a nightmare quality that made his flesh creep. "We'll have to find out about the big man. We'll have to find out where the whip came from. Once we know that, it'll be easy!"

Emily brooded. "Well, trace it. The price ticket will help." She looked across at the Greek, Nick. "Get the whip," she went on. "I want to examine it."

With his blood freezing in his heart, George watched the Greek get up and wander into the bungalow. He was away a few minutes and then he came to the door.

"It is not there," he called.

"The whip," Emily said, snapping her fingers impatiently. "Don't keep me waiting. Bring me the whip."

"It is not there, I tell you," Nick said indifferently.

Emily and Max exchanged glances.

"Find it for the fool," she said.

Max got up and walked stiffly into the bungalow. Nick shrugged. He came back and sat down, a frown of irritation on his flat, ugly face.

"He will not find it," he said sullenly. "It is gone."

Emily said nothing, but her fat hands squeezed into fists.

Max called from the window. There was an urgent note in his voice. "Emily!"

The woman got up and stared at the gesticulating figure at the window.

"I told you," Nick said. "It is gone," and he lolled back on his elbows and closed his eyes.

# 14

A week went by. As each day gave way to night, and night gave way to another day, George's fears receded. He was not, after all, going to be hunted by the police. The murder was to remain a secret shared only by Cora, Sydney and himself, and Emily, Max and the two Greeks. The vast police organization, trained and equipped to track down a murderer, was not going to swing into action against him. He had read so often about police methods, and knew that once the hunt was on, the fugitive seldom escaped. It was the thought of this efficiency and the vast man-hunting machine that had frightened him.

As long as no one discovered Crispin's body, he would be safe. He had only to keep away from Russell Square and the Soho district to avoid being discovered by Emily and her mob. How could they possibly find him, unless he was stupid enough to visit their territory? They had no organization to trace him. They did not have thousands of uniformed, highly trained men to keep a constant watch for him. They could not circulate his photograph or his description in every newspaper in the country. How, then, could they hope to find him – so long as he was careful?

Although, as the days went by, he began to settle down to his ordinary routine life, the murder continued to prey on his mind. He no longer thought in terms of violence, nor did he read his American pulp magazines. The pictures of the bruised faces of the gangsters after the third degree, the bloodstained, bullet-riddled corpses, the gang battles, which before had thrilled him, now made him feel sick. He had been purged of violence. He had seen a man die violently, and now he had no further interest in reading about murder.

He had bad dreams, too. Continuous nightmares, that began as soon as he fell asleep, drained his vitality. One dream constantly recurred. It was a dream of terrible intensity. He dreamed that Cora came into his room, and he thought she leaned over him with the fainting desire in her eyes that inflamed his blood. And as he reached out to seize her, she seemed to waver before his eyes and slowly transform into the tall, elegant figure of Crispin – Crispin in all his horror: the twisted grimace of terror and blood welling thickly from a great hole in his chest.

George found also that he had to make a tremendous effort to go out each evening to work. He had lost his hearty manner with his prospective buyers, and they now seemed suspicious of his strained, white face and his brooding eyes. He had to make twice as many calls, and even then he sold fewer sets of books.

Saturday afternoon found him restless and uneasy. He was sitting alone in his room by the window, and his mind kept dwelling on that fateful, yet marvellous Saturday afternoon when he had first met Cora. It was about this time that Sydney had telephoned. Even now the house was empty except for Leo, who was somewhere in the basement. George thought of Cora, and his body cried out for her. Somehow, the murder now seemed trivial beside the clamouring desire that was torturing him, had been torturing him for the past days. At this moment he did not care how badly she had treated him. If she came into the room now and offered to be nice to him, he would have forgiven her everything.

Thinking of her, remembering her, brooding on that exquisite moment of fear and excitement when she had kissed him so passionately in the stolen car, he began to make excuses for her behaviour. Perhaps it wasn't her fault. Perhaps she had been in the power of her brother, and had been forced to betray George against her will.

Was it possible that she had really loved him all the time, and that Sydney was at the bottom of the whole business?

George got to his feet and began to pace up and down. He must see her again. It was no good torturing himself like this. He must see her, and have it out. She might be longing for him, too, wanting to see him, but afraid of what Sydney would say.

His physical need for her was so overpowering that it swamped all caution and reason. He knew at the back of his mind that she had trapped him into murder, that she was as bad as Sydney, but he wanted her too badly to care.

He didn't believe really that she could ever love him. In his present mood of frustrated desire, he did not mind, just so long as she would be "very nice to him": even just once. If he could only have his moment with her, a brief spell of bliss, he would be content, even if she were a beast to him afterwards.

He sat still, gnawing his underlip. If he wanted her so badly, he'd have to do something about it. He would have to see her. Then why was he hesitating? He would go to her flat now – this very minute. As soon as he had made the decision, a great weight rolled from his mind. The decision was something he had been longing to make for the past few days.

He picked up his hat, and as he crossed the room he looked at himself in the mirror. He stared at his white, drawn face in astonishment. It was as if he had only just become aware of himself, and the change shocked him. He had aged; there were streaks of white in his hair at the temples. He had lost weight, his eyes were feverish and deep set, and the thin red scars from the razor-cuts gave him a look of menace. He continued to stare at himself for some minutes, then left the room, uneasy, worried.

When he reached Southampton Row, he got off the bus and walked towards Russell Square. He glanced at his watch. It was a few minutes after four. He wondered if she would be in. What was he going to say to her? Suppose Sydney came to the door? He became more and more undecided as to what he was going to do. But he kept on, refusing to heed the warning note that was sounding at the back of his mind, determined, if he did nothing else, to look at her flat once again.

He turned the corner of her street. People busied themselves with their weekend shopping. The pavement before the row of small shops was crowded with women, small children and perambulators. He could see the greengrocer's shop over which was her flat. The greengrocer, elderly, bald and fat, was outside the shop. He was shovelling potatoes onto the scales while a tired-looking woman waited, a string bag ready to receive them.

George stood for some time at the corner, unconsciously assuring himself that it would be safe to cross the street.

Finally, he made up his mind and walked towards the greengrocer's shop with mounting excitement. As he drew near, he looked up at the window of her flat. The drab muslin curtain told him nothing. For all he knew, she might be watching him, and the thought sent his blood racing through his veins.

He slowed down as he reached the shop. A smell of potatoes, fruit and onions hung in the air. He glanced at the door that led to her flat, and then he paused. There was a notice stuck on one of the glass panels of the door, and a sudden feeling of dread came to him.

The greengrocer had gone into the shop: there was a momentary lull in trade.

George stepped quickly to the door. He read the sprawling handwriting on the notice:

FURNISHED FLAT TO LET
Two bedrooms, sitting room, kitchen, bath.
42/- weekly.
Apply: Harris & Son. Greengrocer. (Next door.)

So they had gone. They had packed up and bolted. In a way, he wasn't surprised. It was the obvious thing to do. They were making sure that no one would get on to them; that Emily and Max and the two Greeks wouldn't get the money from them.

He wondered how long they had been gone. It crossed his mind that they might have left a clue which would lead him to them.

While he was hesitating, the greengrocer came out and glanced at him inquiringly.

Without stopping to think, George blurted out, "I'm interested in this flat."

"Flat?" the greengrocer repeated. "Yes, it's still in the market. It's a nice little place. 'Ave it meself if it weren't for the stairs. Can't manage the stairs now. Not as young as I was."

"Can I see it?" George asked.

"I'll get the keys."

There was a short delay. Then the old man returned.

"It'll be a month in advance," he said, a bitter, injured note in his voice. "I've 'ad enough of fly-by-nights. If yer want the place, it'll be a month in advance."

"Had trouble with the previous tenants?" George asked, taking the keys.

"Done a flit," the old man said, and spat in the road. "Might 'ave known no good would 'ave come from those two. Wot 'e did for a living I never did find out, and she ... My missus said she took men up there, but seeing's believing. If I'd caught 'er at it, I'd 've 'ad 'er out, but I never did. I wish I'd got rid of 'em before."

George nodded, and turned to the door. "Don't bother to come up," he said. "I'll have a look round and then talk it over with you."

The old man grunted. "I ain't coming up," he assured him. "Can't manage them stairs. You'll find the place in a mess. The missus' been cleaning it up, but it ain't quite finished. The way those two lived ... like pigs."

George's heart was thumping as he sank the key into the lock. He pushed open the front door and entered the tiny hall. The flat had obviously been cleaned, but there was still a faint smell of sandalwood in the air. It affected George. He felt alone, miserable.

He went into the sitting-room. Now that the curtains had been washed, the carpet swept and surrounds scrubbed, it looked quite a homely little place. He went through the drawers, looked into the empty waste-paper basket, and the cupboard, but he found nothing. He went into Sydney's bedroom. He found nothing there, nor did the kitchen reveal anything. He purposely left Cora's room to the last. When he opened the door, a vein in his temple began to pound. The room had not been touched. He could tell that by the dust on the mantelpiece, the rubbish piled in the grate, and the soiled towel with a trace of lipstick that hung over the back of the chair.

He entered the room and closed the door. He remained still for a few minutes, trying to sort out the various odours that hung in the stale, stuffy atmosphere. There was sandalwood and tobacco smoke, stale perspiration and dirt. There was an elusive smell which, although scarcely perceptible, excited him. It was Cora's own intimate smell – a heady, slight smell, feminine, yet fleshly.

He pulled open the drawers of the dressing-table. They were filled with empty jars, sticky tubes, cigarette cartons, and bottles. Eye-black mingled with a spilt box of face powder. A tube of toothpaste oozed over a pair of sunglasses. A bottle of witch-hazel – the bottle he had given her – had leaked, filling the drawer with a layer of white grease. He had never seen such a disgusting mess.

The second drawer was empty except for a soiled handkerchief. He closed the drawer with a grimace. Then he went to the fireplace and examined the scraps of paper, newspapers, a sheet of greasy brown paper that smelt strongly of decaying fish.

He was very patient, and at last he found what he was looking for: a business card of an estate agent in Maida Vale.

He stood up, his eyes bright and excited. Maida Vale! Yes, they would fit in in Maida Vale. It had either to be Russell Square, or Soho, or Maida Vale. He slipped the card into his waistcoat pocket, pleased with himself.

Then he locked the door and went downstairs.

"I'll think it over," he said to the greengrocer. "I'd like my wife to see it."

His wife! He thought of Cora, and there was a bitter taste in his mouth.

From the top of the bus he watched the crowded street. Then suddenly his heart gave a lurch. At the corner of Southampton Row and High Holborn he saw Nick, the Greek. He was standing on the kerb, a cigarette hanging from his thin lips, reading a newspaper. George shrank back.

He remained uneasy and alarmed until the bus began to crawl up Baker Street, and then his fears quieted. The Greek hadn't seen him. It was a near thing, of course, but he hadn't seen him.

He got off the bus at Maida Vale and went immediately to the estate agent. It was a small office, and a fat little man, behind a shabby desk, was the only occupant.

He seemed startled when George opened the door and entered, as if he seldom had callers.

"Good afternoon," he said, fingering a heavy silver watch chain. "Is there something …?"

"I don't know," George said, and smiled. He was anxious for the little man to like him. "I don't want to waste your time, but I believe you can help me." He took out the card and studied it. "It's Mr Hibbert, isn't it?"

The little man nodded. "You're lucky to find me here," he said. "Most places close on Saturday afternoon, but I thought I'd hang on a little longer …"

"I'm looking for a couple of friends," George explained. "It's important I should find them." He smiled again. "You see, I owe them money."

Mr Hibbert scratched his head. "I don't know," he said. "Perhaps you'll tell me how I can help …"

"Oh yes," George said eagerly, taking out a crushed packet of Players. "Will you smoke?"

Mr Hibbert took a cigarette rather doubtfully. "I don't usually smoke in office hours," he explained. "But seeing it's Saturday ..." He had a trick of not finishing his sentences.

They lit up.

"You see," George went on, "they were looking for a place. I've been away for some time. As a matter of fact, I've been in the States. I traced them to a flat near Russell Square, and now I learn they've moved to Maida Vale. I think they came to you for a place."

"The States?" Mr Hibbert's eyes grew dreamy. "Often thought I'd go there myself. Wonderful place, I believe."

George nodded. "It's all right," he said with assumed indifference. "But I suppose I've seen too much of it. Give me England any day." He dropped ash carefully into the tobacco tin lid that served as an ashtray. "These two," he went on, anxious not to stray from his purpose. "They were young – brother and sister. Brant is the name. The fellow had a bad scar: a burn."

Mr Hibbert's face darkened. "Oh yes," he said, frowning. "I remember them. Hmm, yes, I remember them quite well." He conveyed that he did not approve of them, and that because George knew them, he wasn't sure whether he should approve of him.

"It's just that I owe them money," George said apologetically. "They did me a good turn once." What was he saying? A good turn? But he went on, "They're not friends of mine, you understand; but one must honour one's debts."

Mr Hibbert nodded. He looked at George with sudden warmth. "Those sentiments do you credit. I like to hear a man talk like that. Wouldn't think *they'd* honour anything."

George shook his head. "A wild pair," he said. "Did you fix them up?" He waited, his heart thumping dully against his side.

"Against my will," Mr Hibbert told him sadly. "Business is not what it was. A year ago I'd 've sent them packing. As it happened, I had a place. A couple of rooms over a garage. There were rats in the place; no one seemed to want it, so I let them have it. They can be as wild as they like there. They'll have no neighbours." A sly, lewd look came into his faded eyes. "The girl's remarkable, isn't she? No better than she makes out to be, I shouldn't wonder. Her figure …" He shook his head. "Wants a mother, I shouldn't doubt … brazen …"

A hot flame of desire flickered in the pit of George's stomach. He knew what Mr Hibbert meant.

"I'm most grateful," he said, after a pause. "Could you write the address down for me?" He stubbed out his cigarette and added bitterly, "It'll be a surprise for them."

Mr Hibbert wrote the address on the back of his card.

"It's a turning off Kilburn High Street, a mews. It's easy enough to find."

They parted warmly.

While George waited for a bus to take him down the long, straight road to Kilburn, a man with a bundle of evening papers passed, and George bought one. He glanced down the columns, scarcely concentrating. An item of news caught his attention for a second. An unknown man had fallen on the live wire at Belsize Park Station. A train had entered the station a moment later, and the hold-up had caused a considerable delay on the line. George was glad he hadn't been there: a beastly, messy death. He looked down the road impatiently. A bus was in sight, but it was taking its time. Then George stiffened, spider's legs ran down his spine. He looked at the newspaper again. The small print swam before his eyes. The unknown man, the reporter wrote, was about twenty-two. He had a scar – a bad burn – on the right side of his face, and a shock of straw-coloured hair. He wore a dark blue shirt, a red tie, grey flannel trousers and a tweed coat. The police were anxious to identify him. There was nothing in his pockets nor on his clothes to say who he was and where he had come from.

The bus passed George. He made no attempt to signal to it. He stood reading the notice over and over again. Could it be Sydney? The description was exact. Were there other men with scars, straw-coloured hair, who wore dark blue shirts and red ties? It seemed unlikely.

He had to find out. The trip to Kilburn could wait. He had to find out whether Cora was now on her own. It might make a tremendous difference.

He began to walk towards Kilburn, not knowing where he was going, but anxious to think. What a death! How unlike Sydney to fall in front of a train! Was it suicide? He thought of the cold, ruthless face, and decided that Sydney most certainly would not have taken his own life. An accident, then? But how did people fall in front of trains unless they deliberately jumped or were pushed? Pushed? His mind began to crawl with alarm. Was he pushed? Suppose Emily and Max and the two Greeks …? He gritted his teeth. Was this the beginning of their revenge? He looked furtively over his shoulder, and quickened his pace. It was the kind of clever, ruthless trick they would stage: a murder that looked like an accident. Of course, the dead man might not be Sydney, and in that case he was getting alarmed over nothing. But he wouldn't rest until he knew for certain. He supposed the body would be in some mortuary, but he hadn't the vaguest idea which one. He was scared to go to a police station. The memory of Crispin now filled him with nervous dread.

Farther up the road he saw a policeman coming towards him. He forced down his natural fear of the uniform and with misgivings planted himself in the policeman's path.

"I think I know this man," he blurted out, pushing the newspaper at the policeman. "I believe he's a friend of mine."

The policeman gave him a quick, inquisitive glance, and then looked down at the newspaper. He frowned, chewing his moustache.

"What man's that, sir?" he asked patiently.

George pointed to the paragraph. His finger danced on the page.

The policeman ponderously read the item, then he glanced at George. "You think you know 'im, do you, sir?"

George nodded. "I suppose I ought to do something," he said helplessly. "I thought you could advise me."

The policeman brooded. "If you think you know 'im," he said at last, "it'd be your duty to – er – view the remains." He shook his head sympathetically. "Unpleasant job, sir, at the best of times, but seeing as 'ow you might identify 'im …"

"Where should I go?" George asked. The word "remains" made him feel sick.

"Well, the accident 'appened at Belsize Park Station," the policeman said. " 'E'd be at the 'Ampstead mortuary as like as not. If you come with me, sir, I'll 'phone. There's a police box just round the corner."

A few minutes later George was on his way to the Hampstead mortuary. It took him some time to screw up enough courage to ring the bell outside the double gates. After what seemed to him an interminable wait, a small door in the gate opened and a white-coated attendant looked at him inquiringly.

"I think I know this man," George said, offering the newspaper. "The man who fell under the train this morning."

"Then you'll 'ave come to identify 'im," the attendant said cheerfully. "This way, if you please, sir."

George ducked through the doorway, and found himself in a small yard. A low brick building faced him, and with a tight feeling in his stomach he followed the attendant across the yard into the building.

"If you'll wait 'ere a moment, sir," the attendant said, "I'll get PC White."

Left alone in the white-tiled passage, George looked round uneasily. There was a door at the end of the passage through which the attendant had disappeared. Near where George was standing he noticed a small window covered by a yellowing blind. He thought the place looked exactly like a public convenience, and because of the familiar association, his fears began to subside.

The door at the end of the passage opened, and the attendant beckoned. George entered a box-like room which served as an office. A police constable rose from behind a desk as George came in.

"Good morning, sir," the police constable said. He had a kind, understanding face, and he was obviously anxious to set George at ease. "Sit down, will you? You think you can identify the unfortunate gentleman who died this morning?"

George nodded. He was glad to sit down. He took off his hat and began to twirl it round between his sweating fingers.

"Distressing business, sir," PC White said, settling down in his chair again. "But you've nothing to worry about, sir. There won't be anything unpleasant. Perhaps you'd give me a little information; just to keep our records straight." He drew a sheet of paper towards him. "Your name, sir?"

George's mind went blank with fright. He hadn't thought

they'd ask questions about himself. It would be madness to let them know that he had anything to do with Sydney. If they ever found Crispin ...

A name jumped into his confused mind. "Thomas Grant," he blurted out, and then, tightening his control over himself, he volunteered, "247, North Circular Road, Finchley." He had once stayed at that address, a boarding-house, when he first came to London.

PC White wrote for a moment, his head on one side, taking pride in his neat, copper-plate handwriting.

"And what makes you think you know the deceased?"

"It's the description," George said, slowly recovering from his first fright. "The burn. I had a friend once who was fair and had a burn on the right of his face. I haven't seen him for some months. He used to live at my address – it's a guest house. Timson was his name. Fred Timson."

PC White did a little more writing. "You haven't seen 'im for some time?" he repeated.

"Well, no. Of course, I may be mistaken. But, I thought ..."

"Very good of you, I'm sure. We're grateful for any help. The gentleman had no papers nor anything to tell us who he is." He got slowly to his feet. "Well, sir, if you'll come along with me."

George suddenly felt that he couldn't go through with this ghastly business. PC White noticed how pale he had gone.

"Now, don't worry, sir," he said. "We try to make this sad business as pleasant as circumstances allow. You'll only need to take a quick look at 'is face. You won't see anything unpleasant."

George did not trust his legs. He sat still, gripping the arms of his chair, uneasy, frightened that he was going to be sick.

"All right, sir," PC White said, sitting down again. "Take

your time. It takes people like that sometimes. Of course, we're used to it. I've been on this job now for fourteen years. You'd be surprised 'ow some people react. Some of 'em are as callous as can be; others get unnecessarily upset. It depends on their temperament, I always say. Why, only an hour ago we 'ad a young lady in to see the same gentleman wot you're going to see. She was a cool card all right. I knew I wasn't going to 'ave trouble with her, soon as I sets eyes on her. Cool as a cucumber; in her trousers and sweater. Don't 'old with that get-up for a girl myself, but, then, I suppose I'm old-fashioned. A bit too immodest, if you takes me meaning. Well, this young lady comes in, looks at the remains, and although she didn't know 'im, I had difficulty in getting her away. She stood there staring and staring, and she made me and Joe feel a bit uncomfortable: don't mind admitting it. But, for all that, she never turned a 'air – not one blessed 'air."

George licked his dry lips. "Did she say who she was?" he asked in a low, tight voice.

PC White hesitated. "Well, it don't matter to you, does it, sir?" he said. "I mean we don't ... You see, it wasn't as if she knew him."

So Cora had already been here. If she didn't know the dead man, then he wasn't Sydney. George's nausea went away.

"I'm all right now," he said, getting slowly to his feet. "I'm sorry, but this business has upset me."

"Don't you worry about that, sir," PC White assured him. "Take your time. Now if you feel like it, just step out into the passage. I'll be right with you."

George moved slowly into the white-tiled passage. PC White took his arm and led him to the blind-covered window that George had noticed when he had been waiting to go into the office.

"All right, Joe," White called. "Now, sir, just a quick look. It'll be over in a few seconds."

George braced himself as the white-coated attendant, from behind a partition, pulled up the yellowing blind. A light clicked on. Close against the window, on the other side of the partition, stood a cheap, brown-stained pine coffin on trestles. The lid was drawn back a foot from the head of the coffin. George started back with a shudder of horror as he recognized Sydney Brant.

A comforting hand gripped his arm, but he was scarcely aware of it. He stared down at the waxen face. There was a sneering half-smile hovering on the bitter mouth. The eyes were closed. A lock of straw-coloured hair lay across the scarred cheek. Even in death, Sydney Brant seemed to jeer at him.

Almost in a state of collapse, George turned shudderingly away.

"It's a mistake," he said in a strangled voice. "I don't know this man. I've never seen him before in my life."

And out of the corner of his eye, he saw the blind come down in silence, slowly, almost regretfully, like the curtain of the final act of an unsuccessful play.

# 15

It was growing dusk when George left the Heath. From the mortuary he had walked along the Spaniards Road and had cut across the Heath to Parliament Hill. His mind was blank during the walk, and it wasn't until he reached the deserted bandstand perched on Parliament Hill, with its magnificent view of the City of London, that he realized that he had been wandering to no purpose, with no idea where he was going. He sat down on the grass under the shade of a big oak tree and lit a cigarette.

He had sat there brooding for nearly two hours. Sydney was dead. There was no doubt about that. How he met his end was a mystery. George was sure that he hadn't killed himself. And another thing, why was Sydney in Belsize Park Station? Where had he been going when he met his death? No one seemed to have seen him die. At that time in the morning – George had discovered that Sydney had died at ten-thirty – few if any people used the station. It was a convenient place for murder.

George shuddered. If it had been murder, then Cora and he were in danger. Would Emily and Max and the two Greeks be content with one life? He doubted it.

The obvious thing to do would be to leave London, but he had no intention of doing so, even if they were really hunting for him. He would not bring himself to believe that they were. It was all too fantastic. Anyway, he was not going to leave Cora. She might need him.

He thought about her, his mind confused by fear and desire. What was she going to do without Sydney? How was she going to live? He had to see her. Pity stirred in him. He might save her from herself. Without Sydney, surely she would wish to get away from the evil life they had led? George would be only too happy to leave London if she would go with him. All this beastliness could be forgotten in a year or so.

It worried him that she had not identified her brother. What strange, sinister motive prompted her to do that? Didn't that point to murder?

He went on thinking and brooding for a long time along these lines. Each train of thought always finished at the same place. He must see Cora. If he didn't see her soon, it might be too late. She might again move somewhere where it would be impossible to find her.

He left the Heath, walking quickly past the Hampstead ponds, and cut through into Haverstock Hill. It was eight-thirty by the time he reached Belsize Park Station. He bought a tuppeny ticket, and only half certain what he had in mind, descended to the platform.

The platform was deserted except for a porter, who glanced at him without interest.

The urge to know the truth forced George forward. He rattled his loose change in his pocket suggestively. The sound caught the porter's attention.

"Excuse me," George said. "Perhaps you can help me. It's about the man who was killed here this morning. He was a friend of mine. I'm trying to find out how it happened." He took out two half crowns and let the porter see them. "Was there anyone on the platform at the time?"

"There wasn't anyone on the platform when my mate found 'im," the porter said, eyeing the half crowns with interest.

"You don't know if anyone bought a ticket about the time he did? I mean someone might have seen what had happened and dodged across to the other platform. They might have done that, mightn't they?"

The porter turned this idea over thoughtfully. "They could an' all," he said, nodding his head. "Never thought of it like that. Might not want to get themselves mixed up with the inquest, like."

"That's what I thought. I wonder who could tell me."

"I was on duty upstairs," the porter said. "I remember some people. S'matter of fact, I remember the bloke what did 'imself in. I saw 'im come into the booking 'all and buy a ticket. I noticed 'im because 'e seemed a bit upset like."

"How do you mean – upset?" George asked sharply.

"Well, I dunno," the porter said, scowling in an attempt to concentrate. "Sort of worried, kept looking over 'is shoulder like 'e expected someone to meet 'im."

George went cold. "You say you remember some other people?"

"That's right. Two foreign-looking blokes came into the station and bought tickets a few minutes before your friend arrived. I particularly noticed them. Little blokes in black, wearing cloth caps."

"Go on," George said in a husky whisper.

"Well, your friend came in, and about a couple of minutes after – by the time 'e'd got down on the platform, I should say – a big woman arrived. She 'ad a lot of yellow 'air, and I noticed 'er because she was a bit like my old woman, fair busting out of 'er dress she was."

"I see." So it had been murder, after all. "And none of

these people were on the platform when he was found?"

"That's right, but of course they could 'ave taken the up train on the other platform. It don't mean because they were down 'ere they saw anyfing."

A sudden thought dropped into George's mind for no apparent reason. "Was my – my friend carrying anything?" he asked.

The porter scratched his head. "Carrying anyfing?" he repeated. "Well, now you comes to mention it, 'e was. 'E 'ad a black leather case under 'is arm. Now, that's funny, I don't believe they found it. Now I come to fink of it, 'e 'ad it with 'im when 'e was getting 'is ticket. I remember that distinctly although it'd gone clean out of me 'ead until you mentioned it."

"Oh, I expect the police have got it all right," George said hurriedly. "Don't worry about it. I'll ask them."

He gave the porter the two half crowns and left the station. He was frightened now. For all he knew, they might have got onto him and were planning his death. He thought of his gun. There wasn't a moment to lose. He must never be without the gun again. He must get it immediately.

Back in his room, he took the gun from under his shirts. It still smelt of gunpowder. What a careless fool he had been! That alone could have hanged him. He spent ten feverish minutes cleaning the gun, and then, without hesitation, he pulled out the magazine and filled it from the box of cartridges. He was careful not to jack a bullet into the breech, and he was careful also to make sure that the safety catch was down. He put the gun into his hip pocket and picked up his hat. All right, he thought, if they start being funny with me, they'll find they've bitten off more than they can chew. They weren't going to scare George Fraser! And they'd better not get ideas about Cora either.

Cora was his girl now; she was under his protection.

He paused, frowning. This is extraordinary, he thought. I don't feel frightened any more. He looked at himself in the mirror. He saw a great, bulky figure; the scarred face looked tough and hard, the eyes were cold and steady. It was the gun, of course. It had given him a sudden, quite mysterious confidence in himself. He wasn't poor old George, the cat-loving lonely book tout any longer. He was George Fraser, millionaire gunman. He had killed a man, hadn't he? At this moment they were hunting for him, seeking revenge. Why, he was every bit as good as the gangsters he had read and dreamed about. He was better, in fact: he wasn't frightened; the *Front Page Detective* had always described the gangsters as frightened, yellow rats.

Deliberately he took out his battered cigarette case and selected a cigarette. Then he found a match in his pocket and flicked it with his nail. It flared up. That was a trick he had seen on the movies, and which he had tried again and again to imitate, but had never succeeded. He stared at the match, his face lighting up, then he lit the cigarette and tossed the match away.

All right, he thought, buttoning up his coat, I'm ready for them. They'll be damn sorry they started anything with me. Now for Cora; and he wasn't going to stand any nonsense from her in the future. She was going to be his girl. "I'm your gun moll," she had said. Well, that's just what she was going to be!

It was almost dark by the time he reached the garage mews off Kilburn High Street. He moved cautiously, aware of a feeling of excitement, and that his nerves were steady. As he stepped through the gateway and crossed the builder's yard, he drew the Luger, holding it down by his side.

The mews was in darkness. It was an ideal place for

murder, he thought. The noise of the traffic in the High Street would drown any cry for help. It might even drown the sound of a shot.

He paused outside the flat. At first it seemed in darkness, but a second glance revealed a chink of light coming round the curtain of the front room.

There was no bell nor knocker, so he rapped sharply on the door with his knuckles. He waited, his ears pricked, his breathing deep and steady.

No one answered. He waited, and then rapped again. Perhaps she was out. It would be like her to leave the light on: typical of her indifferent carelessness.

He stepped back so that he could look up at the window. The hair on the nape of his neck bristled. The light had gone out.

He stood hesitating. So she was in there. Why had she turned off the light? Why wasn't she answering the door?

He flicked his fingers impatiently. Of course; she was taking precautions. She would have been insane to have come down and opened the door in such a lonely alley, not knowing who it was who was knocking.

He returned to the door and rapped again, then he pushed open the letter-box and called.

"Cora! It's George. Let me in."

Almost instantly, as if she had been waiting for this assurance, she jerked the door open.

"You frightened me," she said. "Come in quickly."

The sound of her voice, the smell of the sandalwood and the nearness of her presence had an overpowering effect on him. He stumbled forward into the darkness, and the front door closed behind him. He heard her shoot a bolt home.

"Can you find your way up?" she asked. "I don't want to show a light. They're watching this place." Her small, warm hand took his, and she drew him up a steep flight of stairs.

A moment later a light sprang up. He blinked round. The room was large and poorly furnished. A big divan bed stood in one corner. A table and armchair and a cupboard made up the rest of the furniture. A worn carpet covered only the centre of the floor.

He turned and looked at her.

She was still wearing the blue sweater and slacks. They looked as if they could have done with another wash. Her hair was untidy, and her lipstick put on anyhow. The blue smudges under her eyes had now turned to purple. She somehow looked older, more worn, more shop soiled.

"Good old George," she said in a low voice. "I was beginning to wonder what I was going to do."

"Do?" he repeated. "What do you mean?"

She giggled. It was a grating sound that made George's nerves recoil. "They're out there waiting for me," she said, jerking her head towards the window. "And then you turn up."

He suddenly realized that she was terrified, but her pride, her arrogance were holding her terror in check.

"Emily?" he asked, a little startled. "They killed him. You know that, don't you?"

She wandered across the room, pounding her clenched fists together.

"Clever George," she said. "How did you find that out? No one was supposed to know."

Her jeering voice stung him. "Sydney planned Crispin's death, didn't he?" he said, standing over her. "Sydney and you. You wanted to push it on to me."

She looked up at him.

"We have pushed it on to you," she said, and giggled again. Had he any understanding, he would have seen she was close to complete nervous collapse. "But they want us, too."

He took hold of her by her shoulders and shook her, snapping her head back, startling her.

"Sit down," he said, pushing her onto the divan. "It's nothing to giggle about. You're going to talk. You're going to tell me everything."

"Don't do that!" she said, suddenly angry. Her eyes flashed and she shifted away from him. "Keep your paws to yourself."

"Shut up!" he said, possessive and determined. "You've played around with me long enough. Now you're going to explain."

She stared at him. "My poor George," she said, "have you gone mad?"

"I'm not your poor George," he said angrily, and giving way to a blind instinct, he smacked her face. As his hand connected with her cheek, he pulled back, so that the blow was a light one, but even at that, her head jerked back.

She was instantly on her feet.

"How dare you!" she stormed at him. "You cheap, rotten – "

He smacked her again. This time he hit her hard, knocking her onto the divan.

He stood over her. "I don't like doing this, Cora," he said, breathing heavily, "but it's the only way I can show you I've changed. From now on I'm master, do you understand?"

She leaned back on her elbows, one side of her face red, the other side like wax. Then she giggled.

"You?" she sneered. "You haven't the guts of a rabbit."

Confident in his new-found courage and strength, George merely shrugged. He took out a cigarette, found a match, flicked it alight with his thumb nail. He lit the cigarette and forced a stream of smoke down his nostrils.

"Killing a man makes a lot of difference," he said shortly. "You may as well get used to the idea, Cora."

"We'll see," she said, twisting her hands in her lap. "We'll see how brave you are, George my pet. You're big enough to knock me about, but we'll see what you're like against them."

"Yes," George said, and he crossed the room and sat down in the armchair.

"I wonder why they let you come here," she went on, looking towards the window. "I should've thought it'd've been easier for them to have killed you in the darkness."

George stiffened. "Kill me?" he said. "You mean they're out there in the alley?"

"Nick is. I saw him not half an hour ago. Poncho, his brother, is round the back." She ran her fingers through her hair, and he knew at once why it looked so untidy. She must have been doing that for the past half hour.

"It's silly, isn't it? But I'm scared stiff," she went on. Her flash of temper had been short-lived. He could see she was sick with panic. "When I get frightened my tummy turns to water."

"Here, have a cigarette," George said, going over to her. "I won't let them hurt you."

She lit the cigarette. "I don't fancy going out there," she said, trying to control herself. "Nick's hot stuff with a razor." She shivered.

"Can they get in?" George asked.

She looked up sharply. "I suppose so. They could break a window if they really wanted to get in, couldn't they?" Her inside rumbled loudly and she giggled. "Collywobbles," she said. "I'm a yellow little bitch, aren't I?" And she squeezed her stomach with her crossed arms and scowled down at her feet. "I saw him this afternoon, all tucked up in a coffin. He looked filthy. I hope I don't look like that when I'm dead." A sob jerked in her throat. "I was terribly, terribly fond of him, George, although he was such a rotten bastard."

"I saw him, too," George said, not looking at her.

She sat for a little while as if she hadn't heard, then she said, "You're not such a fool, are you, George? They must have pushed him in front of the train. He was running away from me." She flicked ash onto the carpet and rubbed it in with her foot. "And I loved him so. I never thought he'd do that to me. He wouldn't let me touch the money. And I had helped him. If I hadn't 've helped him he'd 've never got the money. He never gave me a penny of it: not a damn penny. And as soon as he was sure they weren't after him, he skipped. He took the money and left me without even a word." She beat her clenched fists together. "After all I've done for him!"

George crushed out his cigarette and immediately lit another. He felt a little sick.

A cheap clock ticked excitedly on the mantelpiece. The distant traffic rumbled up the High Street.

"I told him he was playing with fire," she went on, after a pause, "but he wouldn't listen. He thought he was smart. Over and over again I told him they wouldn't stand for it. He never did think they had any brains. He was so pleased with his plan – his stupid, silly little plan. What a fool I've been! I should never have listened to him. But he was mad. I know he was mad. After Crispin burnt him, he was never the same. He brooded all day and half the night; looking at himself in the mirror, his hand to his face, planning revenge. I warned him! I told him it wouldn't succeed. But he wouldn't listen. And now he's dead." She got up and wandered round the room. "And I'll be dead, too, before very long. They won't rest until they've killed me, and they won't rest until they've killed you."

While she had been talking, George had been looking round the sordid little room, his mind listening to her words, his eyes unconsciously seeing the various articles in the room. He found himself looking at a cheap fabric suitcase; from it was hanging a luggage tag, and on the tag, printed in bold letters, was the name *Cora Nichols*.

It only wanted that to confirm his suspicions. Very quietly, suppressing the sick dismay that rose inside him, he said, "Then you're not his sister?"

"Sister?" she said bitterly. "Do I look like anyone's sister? I wasn't even his wife."

George shivered. So all the time he had been dreaming about Cora, all the time she had promised to be very nice to him, she had been sleeping with Sydney.

"I see," he said, clenching his fists. "Well, that accounts for it, I suppose."

"I loved him!" Cora exclaimed, "and he treated me like a dog. I love him still. If he came back to me this very moment, I'd forgive him. I'd forgive him taking the money; I'd forgive him leaving me without a word, if only he'd come back." She sat down, holding her head in her hands, her eyes like holes cut in a sheet.

"Who was he?" George asked, after a long pause.

"Sydney?" Cora said. "Who was he? A cheap thief. That's who he was. He stole cars for Crispin. Then one day he found a car with a case of jewellery in the back. He turned the car over to Crispin, but kept the jewellery. He thought he was being smart. The things he promised me when he had sold the jewellery! And then he was stupid enough to try to sell them to the fence who worked for Crispin. That's how smart he was! And the Greeks came after him. They got him in the end, and they took him down to Copthorne, and Crispin put a mark on his face. He said if he ever saw him again, he'd mark him again." She went back to the divan and sat down. "They didn't know about me, so I was the one to watch them. Sydney kept out of the way. That's why he took up selling those silly books. He had to earn money somehow, and he had to keep out of the West End. I fooled them all right. I found out that the fence was going down to Copthorne with seven hundred pounds to buy a collection of stuff from the various cars Crispin had stolen. So Sydney made his plans."

George listened grimly to all this. "Well, go on," he said bitterly. "When he met me he decided I was to be the stooge?"

"Yes," Cora said listlessly. "He saw his chance to kill Crispin and pin it onto you. I believed in him because I loved him, but I knew it wouldn't come off. I knew they'd be too smart for him. But he wouldn't listen."

"It meant nothing to you that I should be trapped into killing a man? You didn't care what happened to me, did you?"

She frowned. "Why should I? You meant nothing to me."

George flinched; then, stung to anger by her brutal callousness, he said furiously, "Well, I'm going to mean something to you now! And the sooner you realize it the better!"

But she wasn't listening. "Did you hear?" she said, a white ring suddenly appearing round her lips.

Somewhere in the building came the faint tinkle of breaking glass.

"They're getting impatient," she said, and ran her fingers through her hair. "I hope I don't start screaming, George.

I'm in an awful funk."

George sprang to his feet. "Barricade the door," he said, his voice quivering with excitement. "We ought to have thought of that before. Help me with the cupboard."

She did not move.

Without waiting for her, he pulled the cupboard towards him and began to drag it across the room. It was heavy, but with a tremendous effort he managed to wedge it against the door.

"They can't get in that way," he said, panting from his exertions. "Can they get in through the window?"

She giggled. "Not unless they've got wings," she said. "You are a scream, George. Why don't you go down and kill them, like you killed Wineinger, Barrow and Banghart?"

He stared at her, not understanding for a moment what she was saying. Then he flinched. He had forgotten about Wineinger, Clyde Barrow and Gustave Banghart. It seemed a long time, another age, since Cora and he had sat in that restaurant together and he had told her all those stupid lies.

"I thought you liked tough spots," she went on, watching him with frightened, jeering eyes. "I thought you were out for excitement, and you didn't care which side you were on, so long as you got into a scrap." Her inside rumbled again. "Well, there's a juicy scrap waiting for you downstairs. Why don't you get into it? You're not scared of two little Greeks and a fat old woman, are you?"

"Stop it!" George said, sharply. "I was lying. You may as well know now. I've never been to the States. I've never seen a gangster. I was a fool. A vain, stupid fool."

She beat her fists together. "Poor old George: as if we didn't know. It was easy, George: easy as falling off a log. As soon as you started bragging, Sydney saw how he could use you. Pretend you love him, he said to me, and he's ours."

George couldn't look at her. He wanted to hate her, but shame and desire seemed to be his only emotions.

She was listening again. Her eyes darted like those of a frightened animal.

The stairs creaked outside as someone moved cautiously up them.

"It's Poncho," she whispered, bending forward. "He's got in from the back."

George started up. The heavy Luger bumped against his hip. He had forgotten the gun. Instantly he had it in his hand, and he thumbed back the safety catch.

"I'll kill him if he tries to get in here," he muttered.

"They'll be sure of you if they know you have a gun," she said, watching him intently. "They'll know for certain you killed – "

"Shut up!" he said. "I don't care. They know enough as it is." He faced the door, waiting.

There was a long pause, then they heard the handle of the door turn. The door opened an inch or so and then stopped, blocked by the cupboard.

George raised the Luger. His hand was steady. He pressed the trigger, lifting the cartridge from the magazine into the breech. Then he waited, tense, sweating.

There was another long, ghastly pause. Cora was holding her head between her hands, her mouth was open, and her smeared lips formed a soundless scream. Someone outside was breathing softly, making a faint, whistling sound. Then footsteps went away. The stairs creaked. Once more there was silence except for the hum of distant traffic along the High Street and the excited ticking of the clock.

"He's gone," George whispered, lowering the gun.

Cora lit another cigarette. "Not far. They're used to

waiting."

"Let them wait," George said. "We'll see who gets sick of waiting."

She lay back across the divan. "I didn't think you had the nerve," she said, a new note in her voice. "You looked fine standing up to him."

George scarcely heard her. He was staring up at the ceiling. "We could get out that way," he said. "You can't live here any more, Cora. We'll have to find some place where they'll never find us."

"We?" she said, rolling over on her stomach and looking at him. "So you're not going to desert me?"

"Did you think I would? I may be a fool, but I love you. I don't know why, because you've always been rotten to me. But I love you, and I'm going to look after you."

She held up her hand. "What's that?" she asked, her eyes dilating. He listened. A murmur of voices floated up from the alley: whispering, hushed voices of people in church. He went over to the window, and without moving the blind, he listened. He heard a woman's voice and then a mutter of men's voices.

"Turn out the light," he said. "It's Emily."

Cora stiffened; she remained where she was. She beat on the pillow with her clenched fists.

George crossed the room and snapped off the light. Then he returned to the window and cautiously lifted the curtain.

The moon was rising above the roofs of the buildings, and part of the alley was no longer in darkness. Immediately below him he could see Emily, Max and Nick. They were standing before the front door. As he watched them he heard a bolt slam back and heard the front door open. Emily said something, and then they all entered and the front door closed.

As George put on the light again, they could hear footsteps moving about in the garage below. They made no attempt to conceal their presence now. They talked. They opened and shut doors. Once Nick laughed. The noise they made was more menacing than their previous stealth. They were confident that they would be undisturbed, and that they had George and Cora in a trap.

"We've got to get out," George said. "They're up to something. We can't stay here any longer."

Cora sat up. She was shivering, and she chewed her knuckles until one of them bled.

George went over to the window and opened it. He leaned out. The gutter above him was out of reach; the ground below was too far away. There was no escape through the window. He turned and looked up at the ceiling.

Footsteps came up the stairs and along the passage. The door handle turned and the door was opened until it was stopped by the cupboard. There was a fumbling sound at the door that sent a cold shiver of excitement down George's spine. He sprang across to the fireplace and snatched up a poker. Then he climbed up on the table and began to hack at the plaster of the ceiling.

"Turn it on," Nick's voice called.

A hissing sound filled the room.

Cora screamed.

The sharp point of the poker sank into the plaster, and a large part of the ceiling came down with a crash. George was choked with fine white dust, and almost blinded. He went on hacking at the ceiling, tearing at the wooden laths with his hands.

A strong smell of gas filled the room. So that was what they were up to, he thought, not pausing in his efforts to make a hole in the ceiling. Well, they were too late. The window was open, and it would not be possible to build up a strong enough concentration of gas to suffocate them. But suppose they set the place on fire? It'd go up like a powder barrel!

He worked for a few seconds like a madman. Voices sounded in the alley. They had left the garage. Any moment they might set fire to the place. The hole was big enough to get through now. He shouted to Cora, but she just sat on the divan, coughing and wringing her hands.

He jumped off the table and grabbed hold of her. She resisted weakly, but somehow he got her on the table.

"Through the hole," he gasped, "it's our only chance."

He caught hold of the back of her slacks and hoisted her up. She clutched at the torn edges of the hole and he bundled her through. Then he hoisted himself up.

They crouched between the plaster and the tiles. He smashed at the tiles with the poker, and a moment later he saw, through the hole he had made, the cloudless sky and the bright moon floating serenely above them.

"Up," he panted, grabbing Cora round the waist, and he shoved her onto the roof which sloped gently to the flat roof of the next building. He followed, and together they slithered down the warm tiles, ran across the flat roof, dodged round a chimney-stack and paused at the foot of the next sloping roof. Then suddenly a huge yellow flame shot into the air, followed by a violent rush of air and a tremendous bang. The blast tossed them against the roof. A great wave of black smoke engulfed them: the sound of flames and crackling wood roared up in the night.

# 16

They came out of a little shabby pub into the darkness. Away to their right, the sky glowed red where the fire still raged, burning the row of garages, flaring up every now and then as the flames reached a reserve of petrol.

They stood for a moment in the shadows watching the glow in the sky, the whisky they had swallowed steadying their nerves, bolstering their courage.

"When they hear we weren't found," Cora said, pushing her hands deep into her trouser pockets, "they'll begin looking for us again."

George glanced up and down the dark, deserted street. It was just after ten o'clock. His legs ached and his body sagged. The exertion of breaking out of the flat, the wild scramble over the roofs with the flames pursuing them, the nightmare climb down a water pipe had exhausted him. Dust and grit scraped his skin every time he moved. His clothes were white with plaster, his face streaked with smuts. Cora was no better off. She had a triangular tear in the knee of her slacks, and her elbows had burst through the woollen sleeves of her sweater. The smell of smoke still clung to her hair.

But she had recovered her nerve. She had swallowed three double whiskies in rapid succession, and George had seen the terror drain out of her like dirty water out of a sink.

"Plans," she said, and took out a crumpled packet of

cigarettes from her pocket, stuck a cigarette between her lips and lit it. She drew hard on the cigarette, and then forced a stream of smoke down her nostrils. "We've got to go somewhere tonight." She cocked her head at him. "Got any money, George?"

He pulled out a handful of loose change. He had twelve shillings and a few coppers.

She grimaced. "That's no use," she said. "Any money at home?"

He shook his head.

"I don't think it'd be safe to go to your place. We've got to duck out of sight, and keep out of sight."

He thought in dismay of his clothes, his books, his personal belongings.

"I'll have to go back," he said.

She shrugged. "Go if you want your throat cut, but you'd better wait until the morning."

"We've got to go somewhere," he said helplessly. "Look at the mess we're in. If the police spot us, they may ask questions."

She brooded into the darkness. The red glow of her cigarette bobbed up and down.

"Little Ernie," she said, at last. "He'll put us up."

Immediately George became uneasy. "He knows too much," he said. "I don't think we should go to him."

"You don't know anything about him," Cora returned shortly. "Ernie's all right. He'll help us." She began to move down the road. "He's had his eye on me for some time."

George fell into step beside her. "I don't like him," he growled. "He'd better keep his hands off you."

Cora didn't say anything.

They walked on in silence until they reached a bus stop. While they waited, George watched her out of the corners of his eyes.

Her grey-white face was hard and expressionless, but she held her head high, and she moved with a jaunty swagger.

The bus took them along Piccadilly, and they got off at Old Bond Street. The passengers on the bus gaped at them in undisguised astonishment. George, embarrassed, kept his eyes fixed on his dusty, cut shoes. Cora looked round with arrogant indifference, staring with jeering contempt at anyone who looked at her.

They walked up Old Bond Street towards Burlington Street: an odd couple in one of the richest streets in the world. Four prostitutes waited at the corner of Old Bond Street and Burlington Street. Their harsh voices chattered excitedly in broken English. Their French accents reminded George somehow of the Parrot House at the Zoo.

Cora paused, gave them a quick glance, and said, "Eva about?"

The four women stopped talking and stared at her. One of them, tall, hideous, fox furs hanging from her gaunt frame, seemed to recognize her.

"What a mess you're in, darling," she said, with a harsh laugh. "What have you been doing with yourself?"

"Seen Eva?" Cora repeated, her hard little face tightening.

"She went back with a client about ten minutes ago."

Cora nodded and walked on.

George hadn't stopped. He crossed the road and waited on the opposite corner.

"Come on," Cora said impatiently. "I hope Ernie's at home."

They paused outside a tall building in Clifford Street.

"This is it," Cora said, pushing upon the front door. They began to walk upstairs. On every landing was a front door with a card set in a brass frame. George read the lettering on the cards as they passed. "Frances", "Suzette", "Marie", "José".

As they turned to mount the last flight of stairs, they heard a door open, and a moment later, an elderly, well-dressed man came down the stairs, whistling softly. When he saw them, alarm jumped into his eyes and he stopped whistling. He paused, uncertain, and gripped his stick.

"Well, make up your mind," Cora said contemptuously. "Either come down or go back. We want to come up."

He came scuttling down, his mouth working with fear. He shot past them like a startled rabbit.

"I bet we put the fear of God into him," Cora said, and laughed.

George sympathized with the man, he knew how startled he would have been to see two such filthy, wild-looking people if he were coming from such a place.

They reached the top landing. The card on the door read "Eva". Cora banged on the door with the little brass knocker.

There was a pause, then the door opened and a young woman in a smart grey tailored coat and skirt gaped at them. She had a mass of red hair, and her face was a mask of make-up.

"Ernie in?" Cora asked shortly.

"Well, my dear!" the young woman exclaimed. "Whatever have you been up to? What a surprise! Who's your boyfriend?"

They stepped into a well-furnished hall. The floorboards gleamed, the big brass tray on ebony trestles glittered, and the thick rug on which they stood tickled their ankles.

"This is George," Cora said, waving her hand carelessly in George's direction. "I want Ernie."

The young woman smiled at George. She had big, strong white teeth. "I'm Eva," she said. "I've heard so much about you. And what a mess you're in! But don't stand there, come in, come in."

She took them down a passage and threw open a door.

"Look, my precious, what's blown in," she called.

Little Ernie glanced up. He was lying in a big armchair, his small feet up on a padded stool. He looked completely out of place in the lavishly furnished room.

George had never seen such a room. It was too big, the ceiling was too high, and the white carpet that went from wall to wall looked like a fresh fall of snow. The ivory furniture had chromium on it, and the enormous scarlet drapes hung from the tops of the high windows and tumbled on to the white carpet. Four big white suede armchairs stood about the room. A vast cocktail cabinet, filled with dozens of bottles of every conceivable drink, stood by the window.

If he had been told that he had strayed into Buckingham Palace, he would have believed it. The room was exactly his idea of a Queen's boudoir.

Little Ernie scrambled to his feet. His eyes gleamed with sudden excitement and eagerness.

"For cryin' out loud!" he exclaimed. "Cora, my ducks, and me old pal, George. Well, well, fancy you coming 'ere." He turned to Eva. " 'Ere, get 'er cleaned up, and then we'll 'ave a nice little chat. Come on, palsy," he went on to George, "you come along with me. You two've been in trouble, I can see that."

He took George out of the room and down the passage. He pushed open another door and led George into a small bedroom. It was elegant and well furnished.

"There you are," Little Ernie said. "The bathroom's just

through there. Make yourself at 'ome. Sorry I can't give you a suit, but you and me ain't quite in the same class, are we? Feather weight and 'eavy weight, eh?" He smirked. "You 'ave a clean up, and I'll get a drink for you. Could you do with a bite to eat?"

George suddenly realized that he was famished. "It's good of you," he muttered, embarrassed, worried. "If it's not putting you out ..."

Little Ernie winked. "Leave it to me," he said, and moved to the door. He could not resist saying, "Posh place, ain't it? D'yer like it?"

George nodded. "I've never seen anything to touch it," he said frankly envious.

Little Ernie jerked his thumb to the door. "She works like a nigger," he said, lowering his voice. "Never no trouble. Takes a pride in the place. A gold mine," and, nodding, he left the room.

Twenty minutes later George returned to the big sitting-room. He had made himself as tidy as he could and brushed his suit. He had had a bath, and his big face was shiny and red from the hot water and soap.

He found Little Ernie busying himself before the cocktail cabinet. A small table was laid with a snowy white cloth and glistening silver. Eva was perched on the arm of a chair, a cigarette in her full red lips, her eyes expectant and curious.

"What'll you have?" she asked George as he came into the room. "A dry martini?"

" 'Ave a whisky, chum," Little Ernie said. "You don't want cissy drinks like them French cocktails." He came across the room with a tumbler a third full of whisky and clinking ice. "Ain't Cora ready yet? You women ... you'll be the death of me."

While he was talking, George noticed that Eva did not once take her eyes off his face. She looked at him with open admiration and expectancy. He suddenly realized that Little Ernie had probably told her he was a killer. It gave him an exciting feeling of power.

"Come and sit down," Eva said, patting the chair next to hers. "I've been dying to meet you ever since Ernie told me about you."

"That's right," Little Ernie said, grinning. "Meet Frank Kelly's gunman. He's tough, but 'e don't like talking about it."

George sat down. The gun dug into him, and deliberately he pulled it from his hip pocket, and then glanced at the other two, tightening his mouth and scowling.

They both froze at the sight of the gun. Eva's eyes dilated and her lips parted. Little Ernie stiffened, his face expressionless.

"Do you mind if I put it on the mantelpiece?" George said, carelessly, getting to his feet. "It's a bit in my way."

"That's all right, chum," Little Ernie said, his voice a trifle husky. "You make yourself at 'ome."

As George put the Luger on the mantelpiece, the door opened and Cora came in. George looked at her; a shiver of pleasure and desire ran through him. She had washed her hair, which was now soft and fluffy; she was cleaner than he had ever seen her before, and she was wearing a scarlet wrap which enhanced her strange beauty. Her feet and legs were bare. George suspected that she wasn't wearing anything under the wrap, and the thought sent his blood racing through his veins.

Nor was he the only one. Little Ernie, too, looked at her with frank admiration and lechery.

"Come on in," he said, turning to the cocktail cabinet.

"What'll you 'ave? Doesn't she look a beauty, Eva?"

"Wonderful," Eva said, without any sign of jealousy. She reached forward and rang a bell. "I've got to leave you now," she went on, gathering up her hat and bag. "Ernie'll look after you. And keep your voices down, won't you? My gentlemen friends are ever so nervous. They like to think they're all alone with me, the poor darlings." She waved her hand and went off, blowing a kiss to Ernie on her way out.

"What a gal!" Little Ernie said, sitting down. "See what I mean? It's work all the time with 'er."

The door opened and a thin sad-faced woman in black came in pushing a small trolley. She manoeuvred the trolley near the table, and went out without even a glance at any of them.

"There you are. Just 'elp yourself," Little Ernie said, beaming on them. "Eat as much as you like."

There were bowls of jellied soup and lobster salad, a pile of chicken sandwiches, and a plate of finely cut, lean ham. A silver bucket containing a bottle of champagne on ice completed the meal.

While they ate, Little Ernie took charge of the champagne.

"Only the best," he said, smirking at George. "That's Eva all over. Beats me 'ow she picks everything up. Must be 'er posh friends. You wouldn't believe it, but I found 'er in a smelly little restaurant in Pimlico washing dishes. I took one look at 'er shape and took a chance on 'er. Like a monkey, she is. Picks up everything. Talks posh even. Best day's work I ever done."

He kept up a ceaseless chatter during the meal, and when the woman had taken the trolley and table away, he poured fresh drinks and sat down.

"Well," he said, stretching out his short legs, "don't tell me if you don't want to, but you two certainly were in a state when you came in."

Cora looked at him mockingly. Now that she had eaten and rested, she was once more her old self.

"That's our secret," she said, with a short, hard laugh. "If you really want to know, Ernie, we had a fire."

Little Ernie picked his nose. "I 'eard the fire engines going," he said. "So you 'ad a fire, did you?"

Cora nodded.

"Burnt your 'ouse and 'ome, eh?"

"Everything went up in a gorgeous bonfire."

"Hmm."

There was a long pause.

" 'Ow's Syd?" Little Ernie asked, looking at Cora sharply.

She looked away, her mouth tightening. "Didn't you see in the newspapers?"

Little Ernie's eyes narrowed. "Was that 'im? I wondered. Gawd love me … what a death! 'Ere, Cora, I'm sorry. You know that, don't you? I'm sorry. I liked Syd. 'E'd got guts."

Cora moved restlessly. The wrap slipped, and both men caught a glimpse of her naked thigh. She adjusted the wrap impatiently.

"I didn't identify him," she said tonelessly. "They may as well bury him. I haven't any money."

George shivered. It sounded so brutal, and yet he realized that it was only the sensible thing to have done.

" 'Ow did it 'appen?"

"He slipped," Cora said, looking Ernie straight in the eyes.

"Wasn't pushed?"

"He slipped."

There was another long pause. George felt that these two had forgotten him.

"Ain't seen Crispin about for some time," Little Ernie said thoughtfully. " 'Ave you?"

"I can't be bothered with him," Cora returned, her eyes watchful. "He's around, I suppose."

"I wonder." Little Ernie lit a cigarette and tossed the match into the fireplace. "I did 'ear that 'e'd come to a sticky end. Marvellous, ain't it, the way I 'ear things?"

Cora continued to stare at him watchfully.

"Listen, Ernie," she said. "I want a place for a week."

"Do you now? What makes you think I've got a place for you?"

"Come off it, Ernie. You must have dozens of flats in the West End."

"And they cost me a packet, too," Little Ernie said darkly.

"I only want it for a week."

" 'Ow much can you pay?"

"Nothing."

" 'Ave an 'eart."

She looked at him. He seemed to read something in that look, because his ferrety eyes lit up.

"Why don't you get wise, ducks?" he said. "You ain't got any dough. Why don't you get in the game?"

While this conversation had been going on, George sat listening, a dull, brooding expression on his face. He was trying to imagine how Frank Kelly or any of the other big shot gangsters would have handled Little Ernie. He was sure they wouldn't have stood a rotten little pimp like him for five seconds. All the same, Little Ernie knew too much: he might also be useful. It wouldn't do to get too tough with him. But it wouldn't do, either, for him to think that George was a stooge who sat and listened and was not consulted.

His contempt for the little man was so great that he felt no diffidence in handling him.

He surprised them both by barking, "Cut that out!"

When they jerked round to stare at him, he went on, sitting forward, his heavy face congested with blood, "She's not going on the game, and you can keep off that subject if you know what's good for you!"

Little Ernie's eyes opened. "That's all right, palsy," he said hastily. "I was only having a bit of fun," but he glanced at Cora uneasily and looked away.

Cora's mouth tightened. "Don't get excited," she said, giving George a long, cold stare. "Ernie's only trying to be helpful." She looked at Little Ernie. "Don't worry about him. He's a bit jumpy. Now, be nice, Ernie. How about a flat?"

Little Ernie opened his mouth to say something, but caught the look in Cora's eyes. He hesitated and then said, "For a week, eh? Well, per'aps. I'll think about it."

George bunched his great shoulder muscles. "You'd better do more than that," he said. "We want a place. You'll get your money all right. I've got plans."

Little Ernie scratched his head. He was suddenly not quite sure of George. The gun, which continually caught his eye, lying on the mantelpiece, disturbed him. This big, hulking fellow could be dangerous. It might be wise to get in with him, rather than antagonize him.

"You leave it to me," he said. "I'll fix you up tomorrow." He got up and went over to the cocktail cabinet. " 'Ave another drink?"

George shook his head. "No," he said shortly. "I've had all I want."

Cora was watching George with a puzzled expression in

her eyes. "Can we sleep here tonight, Ernie?" she asked.

Little Ernie nodded. "Sure," he said. " 'E can 'ave my room and you can 'ave the spare room, unless you and 'im want to kip together."

George felt the blood rush to his face. He got up and walked over to the mantelpiece and picked up his gun, keeping his back turned to them so they should not see his embarrassment. He wanted to say that Cora and he would share a room, but his nerve failed.

"I want a bed to myself," Cora said in a cold, tight voice.

George drew in a quick breath. What else had he expected? he thought angrily. There was time for that when they got a place of their own.

"That's settled, then," Little Ernie said. "Well, I've got to shoot off. Must 'ave a word with the girls before turning in, you know. Gotta encourage 'em, bless their sweet 'earts. I'll be seeing you. Make yourself at 'ome," he went on, looking at George. "I'll see you tomorrow." He nodded, gave Cora a quick, searching glance, and went off, moving softly, like a ghost.

George and Cora stood silent until they heard the front door click shut, and then Cora said sharply, "You dotty or something? Ernie can help us. What do you want to bark at him for?"

"He's a filthy little rat," George said, clenching his fists. "I saw the way he kept looking at you."

"So what?" Cora said, sitting on the settee. "Why should you care, if I don't?"

George stood over her. This was the time. It was now or never. One of them had to be master, and if he were to have any peace in his life, it must not be Cora.

"Because you're my girl," he said. "I love you, Cora.

240

You're on your own, and you need someone to look after you. Well, I'm going to be that someone."

She leaned back and crossed her legs. "You?" she said. "Don't make me laugh. What have you got to offer me? Why, you can't even look after yourself."

"We'll see about that," George said grimly. "If Ernie tries any funny stuff, he'll be sorry!"

Cora's jeering expression suddenly changed to blazing rage.

"If you interfere with me," she exclaimed, jumping up, "I'll make you sorry! I'm going to do what I like! I'm in the market. The man who offers most gets me."

Again George's slow mind groped for inspiration from Frank Kelly. Kelly always kept his women. He treated them tough and loaded them with jewels. But how could he do that? Now he had got Sydney out of the way, he wasn't going to lose her. Little Ernie could give her the world. He had just got to compete with Little Ernie.

"What do you want?" he asked abruptly, struggling to conceal his doubts and fears.

"What do you mean?" she demanded.

"You're in the market, aren't you?" he said, clenching his fists. "Well, then, what's the price?"

"I think you must be drunk or mad," she said angrily, and turned away. "What can you give me? Leave me alone and peddle your silly books!"

George sat down. He took out a cigarette and lit it. His hands were steady, his mind coldly determined.

"I've got nothing now," he said, "but I can get it. You don't want to throw yourself away on a little rat like Ernie. Name something and you shall have it."

"Oh, shut up!" Cora snapped. "You're nothing but a cheap bluffer. You live in dreams. I want more than dreams, and I'm going to have more than dreams."

The Luger dug into George's hip. It gave him extraordinary confidence in himself. Thoughts crowded into his desperate frustrated mind. He had killed a man! Nothing else that he could do could be worse than that. Even if he killed another man, it wouldn't be worse than the first killing. *Once a gangster kills there is no stopping him.* He had read that somewhere, and it was true.

Sooner or later Crispin's body would be found. Bodies were always found. Then the hunt would be on.

If the police didn't get him, then Emily and Max and the two Greeks would. Well, until then he was going to live his life to the full. He was going to have Cora. He wasn't enduring this black, ghastly frustration any longer. If he had to buy her, then he'd buy her, no matter what the cost.

He reached out suddenly and caught hold of Cora's arm. He jerked her down beside him on the settee. The silk wrap parted, and he had a momentary glimpse of her that tipped the scales of his sanity. He caught her to him and held her, his great strength crushing her, frightening her.

"What do you want?" he said, her hair against his face. "I mean it. There's nothing I can't get for you."

"Let me go!" she said. "Will you let me go!"

He released her and sat back.

"Well?" he said. "What do you want?"

Cora could scarcely believe this was the same man. The hard face, the wild, desperate eyes, chilled her. But she was quick to see that she must call this ridiculous bluff. In his present state of mind, she felt he was dangerous. He might do anything unless she provided an outlet for his pent-up, violent repression.

"I want a complete outfit," she said. "And I want it now. Give me that, if you can, you cheap bluffer."

George looked at her steadily. "You mean clothes?"

"Of course, I mean clothes. I want something to wear when I go out tomorrow morning. I want a complete outfit. And don't think I can't get it. I've only to ask Little Ernie."

"I'll get you the money," George said slowly.

"I don't want the money, I want the clothes. I want something decent to put on when I get up tomorrow morning."

George hesitated. She had purposely asked for the impossible. There were no shops open at this time, but, of course, Little Ernie could get an outfit from one of his girls. It would be the simplest thing in the world for him to do. But George had no girl to borrow anything from. She had laid the trap and he had walked into it.

Cora, studying his face, saw doubt and dismay there, and she got up with a laugh.

"Now shut up, you bluffer," she said. "I've had quite enough from you for one night. I'm going to bed." She went to the door, and looked back over her shoulder. "I don't think you and I have much in common, do you, George?" she went on. "I think you'd better go back to your cat and your book selling."

George sat brooding for some little time after she had gone. She was slipping through his fingers. He had to do something.

Tomorrow would be too late. She had asked for a complete outfit of clothes: well, she must have it.

He got to his feet, picked up his hat and stood staring down at the thick white carpet.

Getting an outfit of women's clothes at eleven-thirty at night might set even Frank Kelly back on his heels. He must prove to himself that he was a better man even than Frank

Kelly.

He crossed the room and quietly let himself out of the hateful little flat.

# 17

In the network of narrow streets that lie behind Shaftesbury Avenue there is one particular street where taxi drivers leave their cabs while they have a meal after the theatre rush.

It was to this street that George made his way. He moved along Piccadilly, past the Piccadilly Hotel, threading his way through the crowd of men and women lingering outside the hotel for a final word before dispersing to their homes. He stood on the kerb, his back turned to the darkened windows of Swan & Edgar, while he waited impatiently for the traffic lights to stop the flow of traffic towards Regent Street. There was an apprehensive feeling, like a lead weight, in his stomach. He had conceived a desperate, reckless plan. It depended for success on one thing: the strength of his own nerves. A week ago he would have shied away from such an idea as any person in their right mind would have shied away from touching a red-hot stove. It was the kind of thing he had read about, the kind of desperate act that, at one time, American thugs used to commit in the wild, dangerous days of prohibition. It was a plan conceived by desperation, the only possible solution of Cora's demand.

At first he had thought of breaking into one of the big stores, like Selfridges or Swan & Edgar. Here, he knew, he would be able to steal some women's clothes. But even if he succeeded in breaking into the store, he had still to select the right clothes, the right size, the right match. Cora had said she wanted a complete outfit. It was no use making a mess of it. She must have something that she could put on, complete to the last button, and that went for hat, shoes, stockings and bag as well as the clothes. He couldn't possibly go from counter to counter picking the right things. That was out of the question.

There was only one thing to do. He had to find a girl of Cora's size and take from her her clothes and everything that went with her outfit. Only in that way would he be sure that he had forgotten nothing, that everything fitted, that everything matched.

His great shoulders hunched, his head down, he walked across the Circus, pausing for a moment under the statue of Eros, before gaining a foothold on the crowded pavement of Shaftesbury Avenue. He went on past the Windmill Theatre into Archer Street, where chorus girls in their street clothes were coming out of the stage door.

The next street brought him to a long line of taxis. He slowed his pace, looking sharply at each taxi as he passed. They were all empty, and through the lighted door of an eating-place a few yards farther on came the sound of men talking and laughing. Without stopping he glanced through the glass door. A crowd of drivers sat over their food at long, wooden tables in a room hazy with tobacco smoke.

He stopped before the eating-house, turned and began to wander back again. He continued on to where the first taxi headed the long row of deserted vehicles.

Once more he paused. He fished out a cigarette and lit it. As he did so, he glanced up and down the street, his eyes watchful, his face expressionless.

Satisfied that there was no one coming, he got quickly into the driver's seat. It was some time since he had driven a car. His feet fumbled, feeling for the accelerator, the foot-brake and the clutch. His hand grasped the gear lever, and pushing out the clutch, he manoeuvred the lever through the gate. It worked smoothly, and he was surprised and pleased that he made no mistake.

This begins it, he thought, his heart thumping against his side, and he pressed the starter. The engine growled, but nothing else happened. He caught his breath sharply, and stabbed at the starter again. The whirring, frustrated sound of the engine trying to start made a tremendous racket in the silent street.

His nerve wilted. In a few seconds they would be out after him. He cursed the engine feverishly as he stabbed at the starter again. Then he cursed himself. He hadn't switched on! What a damn, stupid, frightened clod he was! He turned on the ignition with fumbling fingers, pressed the starter and immediately the engine sprang to life.

Somehow he got the cab moving, and turned the corner. He was now in such a fever that he clamped down on the accelerator, yet the cab moved slowly, making a terrific din. He clung to the wheel, his eyes bolting out of his head, terrified, wild. Then, as no one shouted after him, he gained control of his nerves and managed to change into second and then into top.

The cab went on. Ahead was Oxford Street. George swung blindly into the busy thoroughfare. He nearly collided with a bus, and he realized with alarm that he had crossed against the red traffic light. The bus driver shouted at him, but he accelerated and left the bus behind.

He was coming to Oxford Circus now. The lights changed to red when he was a few yards away, and he pulled up so sharply that he stalled the engine.

He sat in a heap, sweat running down his face, his ears

pricked. He felt he was experiencing some horrible nightmare.

He became aware that cars behind him were blaring with their horns and klaxons. Without his noticing it, the traffic light had changed to green. Hurriedly he started the engine, forgetting he was still in gear. The taxi jumped forward and went bounding down the street like a startled frog.

People were staring at him from the pavement. Another taxi overtook him, and the driver leaned out: "Make it waltz, mate," he pleaded as he passed. "You've done everything else."

Gritting his teeth, George changed down. He turned right and drove on, past the BBC, up Portland Place and into Regent's Park.

There was scarcely any traffic in the Park, and he became calmer. He must get used to this cab, he thought, before he ventured again into the wilderness of traffic lights and heavy traffic. He drove round the inner circle several times, stopping and starting, changing up and down, until he had regained some of his confidence. Then he stopped and lit a cigarette and tried to make a plan. He decided that he would go down Park Lane, along Piccadilly to Berkeley Square, up the square to Bruton Street, into New Bond Street and down into Piccadilly again. It was getting late, and his best chance was to catch some girl coming from a nightclub.

He would have to be quick, because the theft of the cab would be reported very soon and the police would be looking for it. He had, at the best, a half an hour in which to find the girl and get her out of the West End.

He started the cab again and headed for Park Lane. A number of people hailed him, as he drove along, hugging the kerb, but after a quick glance in their direction and seeing that they were all in parties, he kept on.

Without stopping, he drove along the route he had planned. His nerves began to ease as he went on. There seemed to be no unescorted girls waiting for a taxi, and he began to hope that the plan would fizzle out.

But as he drove down New Bond Street for a second time, he saw a girl standing on the kerb, and she waved to him.

One look was enough. She was about Cora's build, and she was wearing a dark coat and skirt; a smart little hat was perched on her head, and as she waved at George a gold bangle glittered in the street light.

George pulled up, eyeing the girl, his mouth suddenly dry, his nerves tingling.

The girl was a typical Mayfair deb – the kind of girl whose picture appeared regularly in the *Bystander* and *Tatler*, and who seemed to spend their lives either smiling vacantly at some sleek young man in tails and white tie at Lady Someone or other's ball, or resting their hard little sterns on shooting-sticks while attending a shoot in Scotland.

"Chunks!" she shouted excitedly. "I've got one. Chunks, do come on!"

Oh, hell! George thought in a fever, she's not alone! He wanted to engage gear and drive away, but the girl had already jerked open the cab door, and was standing looking over her shoulder at the open door of a building, partly obscured by the darkness.

"Do come on, Chunks," she called again. She turned to George. "He won't be a minute. I want to go to Highgate Village."

At this moment a tall young man came running down the steps. "You *are* marvellous, Babs," he said. "I don't know how you do it. You're just too nauseatingly efficient. Why couldn't you let the porter find you a taxi?"

"I like doing things for myself," the girl said.

"Are you *sure* you don't want me to come?" the young man asked. "I don't mind. I don't mind a bit."

George stiffened. He looked quickly at the girl, willing her to refuse.

"Of course, I don't," she returned. "Besides, you always get a bit hectic in taxis, Chunks, and it's too hot to wrestle with you all the way to Highgate."

The young man giggled. "All right, darling," he said. "Have it your own way. I'll see you tomorrow."

"Thanks for a terrific evening," she returned, climbing into the taxi.

The young man slammed the door.

"Manor House, Parkway," he said to George. "Do you know it?"

George nodded, keeping his face in the shadow. He was shivering with excitement, and he let his clutch in with a jerk and roared away towards Hyde Park Corner. What a bit of luck! he thought. She's just right. I'm sure she's just right. Now, what's the next step? Highgate Village lay beyond Hampstead Heath. That was a good spot to do what he had to do. At this hour it would be unlikely that anyone would be about. He gripped the steering wheel tightly. He had perfect faith and confidence in his gun. He felt positive that all he had to do was to point the gun at this girl and she would obey him. There was nothing the Luger couldn't get for him – and for Cora.

He turned up Park Lane and slid to a standstill as the traffic lights changed. As he sat waiting, he noticed a policeman at the corner, watching him, and his heart lurched. Were they looking for him already? The light turned to amber, and he hurriedly drove on.

He heard the girl singing to herself. She seemed a pretty lively type, he thought. Rich, and spoilt, without a care in the world. What a different world Cora lived in! He went on up Orchard Street, past Baker Street station and on towards Swiss Cottage.

It wouldn't be long now. A distant clock chimed the quarter past midnight. He'd have to look slippy. Any moment now the police might be looking for him. He sent the cab whizzing up Fitzjohn's Avenue, and in a few moments he was on the Heath.

A bright moon hung in the sky, lighting the trees and the scrub, throwing heavy black shadows. The place seemed completely deserted. He kept on until he saw a large clump of trees standing by the roadside, then he reached forward and cut the ignition. The engine died with a splutter and the cab coasted towards the trees, finally coming to a standstill in the deepest shadows.

George sat for a moment, screwing up his nerve, then he climbed down stiffly onto the road.

The girl poked her head out of the window.

"Why are you stopping?" she asked. "Is there anything wrong?" She seemed quite calm and mildly interested.

George pulled his hat farther down over his eyes.

"Petrol," he grunted. "I'm sorry, miss; I thought I'd filled up."

"What a bore!" she exclaimed, opening the cab door. "Now, I suppose I'll have to walk. Well, it's not so far. What are you going to do?" George was startled that she should think of him. It was not what he expected from the upper classes.

"I'll manage," he said, his hand on the cold butt of the gun.

"If you like to walk along with me," she said, "I'll give you a tin of petrol. You've got miles to go back."

He wished feverishly that she hadn't been like this. He

251

wished she had flown into a temper and had upbraided him. It would have been so much easier. Now she was making him feel like a rat. His mind flew to Cora. He had to go through with it. He couldn't return to the flat empty handed. He eyed the girl's clothes furtively. They were expensive and well cut. He was sure they would fit Cora. He could imagine her face when she saw them: that thought decided him.

"Would you like to do that?" the girl was saying. She had opened her bag and was lighting a cigarette. "You can leave the cab ..."

"Don't be frightened," George said, pulling the Luger from his hip pocket, and pointing it at her. "This is a – a hold-up."

She stood staring at him, the match burning in her fingers. Her eyes went to the gun and then back at him. She flicked the match away.

"Oh," she said, and stood very still.

George kept the muzzle of the gun pointing at her. He looked at her for signs of fear, a change of expression, any reaction which would give him courage to complete this beastly business. But her expression didn't change. She seemed very calm, and she took the cigarette from her lips as if she were in a drawing-room full of her own kind.

"I'm not going to hurt you, if you do what you're told," George went on, making his voice gruff.

"Well, that's a blessing," she said quietly. "I most certainly don't want to get hurt. What do you want?"

George gulped. This was going all wrong. She ought to be frightened, she ought to be grovelling before the menacing threat of the gun.

"I want your clothes," he said.

A look of complete astonishment crossed her face. "My

clothes?" she repeated. "Oh, come. How can you have my clothes? I want them myself; and besides, what in the world would you do with them? You can have my money – not that I've got much – but I really can't let you have my clothes. Do be reasonable."

"I see," George heard himself say feebly. He stood baffled. The calm tone of her voice, her obvious disregard for the Luger, the quiet reasoning of her argument, flummoxed him.

She opened her bag and took out several pound notes. "That's all I've got. Four pounds. I suppose I'll have to give it to you, but it'll make me beastly short. You've no idea how close Daddy is. He won't give me a penny more than twenty pounds a month. That's not much, is it?"

"Well, no," George said, gaping at her. "I suppose it isn't."

"Of course it isn't," the girl went on, holding out the money, "but I suppose you want it more than I do, otherwise you wouldn't be taking such a risk. I do think you're being awfully silly, you know. You could get six months' hard for this."

This was quite fantastic, George thought. I must control this situation. But he made no move to take the money. The girl was so reasonable, so unafraid. He wondered wildly what Frank Kelly would have done in such a situation. He would probably have shot the girl, but George couldn't do that. Besides, he admired her. She'd got more guts than he had. He had the gun, but he was flustered, near panic, while she was cool and at ease.

"Look here," he said desperately. "I'm sorry about this, but I've got to have your clothes. I don't want to hurt you, but if you don't give them to me, I'll have to …"

She looked at him intently. "You're not a sex maniac, or

something, are you?" she asked, then, before he could say anything, she answered her own question. "No, I'm sure you're not. Would you like to tell me why you want my clothes so badly. It sounds interesting."

George stared at her helplessly.

"Do tell me," she went on. "Let's sit down." She went over and sat on the running-board of the car. "I might be able to help you. Don't look so worried. I'm not going to run away."

Slowly, bemused, George lowered the gun. It was going all wrong. He knew now that he would never be able to attack this girl, he knew that he was not going to get her clothes, and the reaction of the excitement and strain made him feel giddy. He came over and sat limply down by her side.

"You've never done this kind of thing before, have you?" the girl went on. "Not that you're bad at it. You fooled me completely, but I think you're a bit too kind really to make a success of it, aren't you?"

George nodded miserably. "I suppose so," he said. "No, I've never done this kind of thing before. But I was desperate. I'd better drive you home now. I – I'm sorry if I frightened you."

"Well, you did give me a bit of a turn," the girl admitted, "but now you're being nice, I don't mind. But do tell me why you wanted my clothes. I can understand you wanting my money, but why my clothes?"

George hesitated. Then he blurted out, "They were for my girl," he said. "She's got nothing to wear ..."

"Your girl?"

George nodded. "I promised her I'd get her anything she wanted, and she thought I was bluffing. She said I could get her a complete outfit. She wanted it tomorrow morning."

"How romantic!" the girl exclaimed. "Why, if I asked

Chunks to get me a complete outfit in the middle of the night, the poor lamb would commit suicide. He'd do anything for me. I think I must really try this one on him."

George clenched his fists. She didn't understand! And he was so hoping that she would.

She noticed the change of his expression. "I say, I am sorry," she said quickly. "I didn't mean to be funny. I suppose you're pretty badly in love?"

Instantly George warmed to her. "Yes," he said.

"Is she very lovely?"

George nodded. "She's marvellous," he said, looking across the limitless expanse of the Heath. "You see, she doesn't think I've got any guts. She – she won't have much to do with me. She deliberately laid this trap, knowing that I couldn't do anything about it. That's why I tried." He drew in a deep breath. "I – I stole that taxi."

"Are you quite sure she's the right one for you?" the girl asked, looking at him curiously. "She doesn't sound your type at all."

"She isn't really," George admitted, "but sometimes one can't help that. A girl like that gets in one's blood and there's not much one can do about it. I can't, anyway."

The girl thought about this for a moment, then she nodded. "Yes, I can understand that," she said; "but you ought to be careful. A girl like that could get you into a lot of trouble."

Trouble? George thought bitterly. She had done that all right, if you could use such a word for murder.

"Well, I can't help it," he returned tonelessly. "I can't do without her."

The girl stood up. "All right," she said. "I'll help you. Take me home and I'll give you an outfit. I'd like to surprise your girlfriend. I only wish I could be there to see her face when you give it to her."

George stared at her, scarcely believing his ears.

"You'll give me an outfit?" he repeated stupidly.

"Yes. I'd much sooner give you one than have to go home without a stitch." She suddenly laughed. "I have to think of Daddy. It would give the poor darling a stroke; and think what the servants would say!"

Was this a trap? George wondered, suddenly suspicious. Was she going to get him to the house and then send for the police? Why should she give him the clothes? She had never seen him before. What was behind this?

She seemed to read his thoughts.

"It's all right," she said, looking down at him. "I'm not going to trap you into anything. It's just that I have a lot of clothes and it pleases me to help you. What do you say?"

Still George hesitated. The suggestion was preposterous. He had set out as a desperate bandit, and now the girl he had planned to rob was actually going to give him what he wanted.

"Do make up your mind," she said, throwing away her cigarette. "It's getting late, and I ought to be home."

He got slowly to his feet. "I don't know what to say," he muttered, looking at her uneasily. "It's fantastic."

"No, it isn't. You're nervous I'll send for the police, aren't you? I won't. I promise."

He remembered Cora's promise. Women made promises lightly, he warned himself, but looking at her he was inclined to believe her. Anyway, if he became suspicious he had his gun ... and he'd use it, too!

"Well, thanks," he said. "I think it's awfully decent of you," and he opened the cab door for her.

"Has she my colouring?" the girl asked, sitting on the little turn-up seat so that she could talk to George as he drove.

Cora had her colouring all right, but that was as far as the resemblance went. She had a better figure, more character in her face than this girl – not that this girl wasn't nice looking. In a way, George preferred her to Cora. She hadn't Cora's sulky expression, nor the lines near her mouth. She had a better skin than Cora's, and her hair was more beautiful. But that didn't mean she was more exciting than Cora: she wasn't. There was something about Cora which tortured George. He knew this girl would never torture him.

"Yes," he said. "She's about your size, and she's got hair like yours."

"What do you think she'd like?" the girl asked. "Would she like a frock, or a costume, or a coat and skirt?"

Was she pulling his leg? George wondered. Had she got so many things to give away?

"Well, I don't know," he said. "I thought something like you're wearing."

She laughed. "Of course, that's why you picked on me, wasn't it? I think I've got something that'll do. I don't mind parting with clothes. It's money I hate parting with. You see, Daddy pays for my clothes, and gives me pocket money for extras. He doesn't seem to mind how many clothes I have, but he just won't part with any more cash."

George drove on, bewildered.

"We're just here," she called after a few minutes. "The gate's on the right."

George hesitated. Should he drive in? Should he risk a trap? Before he could make up his mind, he had reached the gates and had turned into a long, winding drive. But when he sighted a vast house through the trees, he slowed down and stopped the cab.

She jumped out.

"Stay here," she said. "I won't be long."

"All right," he said uneasily, and watched her walk swiftly towards the house.

As soon as she was out of sight, George left the cab and moved off the drive into the garden. He couldn't afford to trust her. He would give her ten minutes, and then he'd go. From where he stood, in the shadow of a big magnolia tree, he could see the house. He could see her run up the broad, white steps, open the door and go in. The ground floor was in darkness, but the windows of both the wings on the two upper floors showed lights.

He stood still, watching the house, his hand on the butt of his gun. A moment or so later a light sprang up in one of the centre windows, and he caught a glimpse of the girl as she passed to and fro before the window.

He relaxed slightly. Anyway, she wasn't telephoning, he thought. How astounding! He was sure if anyone had tried to hold *him* up, he would have given them over to the police at the first possible opportunity.

Scarcely ten minutes had gone by before he saw her coming down the steps again. She held a bundle under her arm, and George, convinced of her sincerity at last, went to meet her.

"I bet you had a bad ten minutes," she said, smiling at him. "I hope I haven't been too long. You'll find everything there. I duplicated the underclothes. The hat's the only thing I wasn't sure about. Does she wear hats?"

George blinked. "No," he said. "How did you know?"

"I somehow felt she didn't." She pressed the bundle into his arms.

George stood gaping at her, a prickly sensation behind his eyes. "I – I don't know how to thank you. I don't really."

"I've got to get in now. Good night, and please don't hold up any more girls. You know, we don't really like it."

He watched her go, then he turned and stumbled back to the taxi. People were kind! he thought. He would never have believed it. Never! To think that a girl like that, so rich, who had everything, should have been so damned decent, especially after the fright he had given her. It was terrific of her! It really was marvellous.

Driving back across the Heath, George had this girl Babs more in his mind than Cora. Cora had never been kind to him. She had always jeered at him. Babs was the only girl who had ever been decent to him except, of course, Gladys; but Gladys didn't count. It was her job to be decent to everyone. But Babs – why, she could have called the police, she could have trapped him easily enough; but instead, she had given him the impossible. She had done more for him – a complete stranger – than Cora would ever do for him, even though Cora knew he loved her.

He wouldn't wait for the morning, he decided. He would go into her bedroom and wake her up and lay the clothes on the bed for her to admire. He would stand over her and grin. It was something to grin about, wasn't it? "You cheap bluffer!" she had called him. Well, this would show her whether he was a bluffer or not.

A sudden stab of desire caught him. She might be so pleased that – well, it was no good thinking along those lines just yet. But she might feel that she could be nice to him. She might be very nice to him. After all, few people would have done what he had done. He wouldn't tell her about Babs. He'd just say he kidnapped a girl and stripped her of her clothes. That'd startle her. That'd show her he had guts!

He was so excited at the thought of bursting into Cora's

room that he threw caution to the wind and drove right through the West End to Hanover Square. There was no difficulty in leaving the cab on the cab rank there. It was nearly one o'clock and the Square was deserted.

He hurried down George Street, across Conduit Street and into Clifford Street. He ran up the stairs to the top flat.

There was a light on in the hall, and he could hear Eva's voice coming from the sitting-room. A moment later, Little Ernie answered. He wondered if Cora was with them; then he remembered she said she was going to bed. Well, he'd look in her bedroom first. He went down the passage very quietly, and opened the door.

The room was in darkness, but the heady, exciting smell of sandalwood greeted him.

"Cora?" he called softly. "Are you awake?"

"Who is it?" Cora's voice asked sleepily, then she said more sharply, "What is it?"

"It's me, George."

"What do *you* want?" She sounded irritable, and a moment later she snapped on a light over her bed.

George looked at her, feeling a great rush of love and tenderness to his heart.

She's wonderful, he thought, looking at her. She was wearing a pair of satin, peach-coloured pyjamas he guessed she must have borrowed from Eva.

"What is it?" she repeated, looking at her wristwatch. "Why, it's after one. Haven't you been to bed?"

"May I come in?" George asked, still standing awkwardly in the doorway. "I've got a surprise for you."

Instantly a quick, calculating expression jumped into her eyes.

"A surprise? What is it?"

"I've got you some clothes," George said, showing her the bundle. Now he was in the light he saw that Babs had put the clothes in a pillowcase.

"Are you mad?" she said blankly. "What clothes?"

"You wanted an outfit," George said patiently. "I – I've got you one."

Cora sat up in bed. "You've got me one?" she repeated.

It was just as George had hoped it would be. He had staggered her. She was excited. She had never looked at him like this before.

He nodded. "I said you had only to ask and I'd get it for you."

"But how?" Cora demanded. "Don't stand there like a dummy. Come in, shut the door." She slid out of bed, now thoroughly awake and excited. "How did you do it?"

This was George's moment. This was the sweetest moment in George's life.

"Well, it wanted a bit of thinking out," he said, coming into the room and shutting the door. "I couldn't rob a store. I hadn't any money. So I decided to take the clothes off someone about your size."

Cora gaped at him – actually gaped at him! "You didn't!" she exclaimed. George nodded. Tears of elation pricked his eyes. "I had to pinch a taxi. That wasn't too easy, and then I cruised around the West End until I spotted a well-dressed girl. I offered her a lift. She lived in Hampstead somewhere and – and I took her up on the Heath and made her take her clothes off and – well, here I am."

"George!" Cora gasped. "I don't believe it."

But she believed it all right; he could see the look of startled admiration in her eyes.

"You did that for me?" she said, jumping up. "Why, George! Why, it's wonderful!"

For a moment he thought she was going to throw her arms round his neck, but instead, she ran past him to the door and threw it open.

"Eva! Ernie! Come here! Come here at once!"

He didn't want the other two. He wanted to hear Cora say over and over again that he was wonderful. He wanted her to be very nice to him in that lovely peach-coloured suit. He wanted to be able to hold her in his arms and feel her hair against his face.

Eva and Little Ernie appeared in the doorway. They looked startled.

"Wot's hup?" Little Ernie asked, looking from Cora to George.

"You must hear this," Cora exclaimed, excitedly. "I asked George to get me a complete outfit of clothes. Of course, I was fooling. I knew he couldn't get them at this time of the night, but I wanted to pull his leg. I pretended to be dead set on having some clothes for tomorrow ..."

"Well, I could have fixed you up," Little Ernie said, leering at her. "I've got tons of clothes. It's me job to keep my girls smart, ain't it, Eva?"

This was a triumph for George. Well, he'd beaten the little rat! In the morning Cora would have gone to him, and George would have had the humiliation of seeing her wear clothes from a pimp.

"Shut up, Ernie," Cora said sharply. "George has actually done it! It's the most fantastic story I've ever heard. He pinched a taxi, picked up a girl, took her on the Heath and pinched her clothes."

George could feel Eva's admiring gaze. Even Little Ernie's mouth fell open.

"For Gawd's sake!" Little Ernie said. "The old Chicago stuff! Wot 'appened to the girl? Cor luv me! I'd given me eyes to 'ave seen 'er. She must 'ave been 'opping mad."

George smirked uneasily. "I didn't bother my head about her," he said, shrugging his shoulders. "I told her to scram, and she scrammed!"

"I bet she did," Little Ernie giggled. "And pinching a taxi! Wot an idea! That's brains! Lolly Cheese! I wouldn't 'ave thought of that one meself."

"Let's look at the clothes," Eva said. "What has he got you?"

"Of course!" Cora cried, snatching the bundle from George. "Let's see if his taste is good."

George giggled with excitement. He couldn't help it. Suddenly it seemed he was one of them. They were smiling at him, nodding at him. They said he had brains. Cora was like a kid in her excitement.

The two girls took the pillowcase over to the bed, while Little Ernie sidled up to George.

"Wot was she like, palsy?" he whispered. "Orl right?"

George winked. He suddenly quite liked this red-headed little man, and when Little Ernie nudged him in the ribs and put the obvious question, George shoved him off playfully and said, "That's telling."

There was a sudden silence that made him turn his head. Cora and Eva were looking at him. They were no longer smiling. There was a look of suppressed rage and disappointment in Cora's eyes that startled him.

"Do you like them?" he asked, with a catch in his voice.

Little Ernie moved forward. "Wot's hup?"

"Nothing," Cora said viciously. "I might have known the fool was pulling my leg. What are you trying to do, George? Get even?"

George suddenly went cold.

"What do you mean?" he said, feeling the blood leave his face.

"What I say," she said, pointing to the bundle on the bed. He pushed past her and turned the things over. At first he couldn't believe what he saw. He held up one garment and stared at it stupidly. It looked like a pair of black combinations, only it had a long tail. He dropped it as if it had bitten him and stared down at the rest of the stuff.

"It's a Mickey Mouse outfit," Eva cried suddenly. "My God! It's Mickey Mouse!"

Little Ernie started to laugh. Eva joined him. Together they shrieked at George and Cora.

"Wot a card!" Little Ernie spluttered. "In the middle of the night! Stone me! 'Ad our Cora properly. Oh dear, oh dear, this'll kill me!" He collapsed howling in an armchair.

George turned away. He wanted to be sick. He wanted to die.

He heard Cora say in a voice hoarse with frustrated rage, "Get out! Do you hear! Get out, both of you!"

And when Little Ernie and Eva, roaring with hysterical mirth, had stumbled out of the room, Cora turned on George.

"You rotten rat!" she said. "Do you think that's funny? Do you think you can make a fool out of me?"

George wasn't listening. He picked up a scrap of notepaper that he had just noticed lying on the bed. It seemed to be a letter written in small, neat handwriting:

*Dear Dick Turpin,*

*You really shouldn't trust a woman, and you should never threaten if you can't go through with it. I hope the girlfriend likes the costume. From the sound of her, I shouldn't trust her either. It's not April 1st yet, but remember this when it comes round. You did frighten me, you know. And I don't like people frightening me.*

He became aware that Cora was standing at his elbow, reading over his shoulder. He screwed up the note and turned away, crushed and dazed.

Cora suddenly burst out: "So you weren't lying! You did it! And she made a fool out of you! God! What a sucker you are! What a damn, stupid, dim-witted fool!" And she suddenly went in peal after peal of jeering laughter. "Go away, you chump," she cried, throwing herself on the bed and rolling backwards and forwards, holding her sides. "Oh, it's the funniest thing I've ever heard. You sucker! You big tough, stupid sucker!"

George opened the door and went slowly down the passage to his room.

# 18

The following night the first of three robberies took place at a garage on the Kingston Bypass. The police stated that the robberies were the work of one man, described by the three garage attendants as a big, powerful fellow with shoulders like an ox. They could give no better description than this, since the man had masked his face with a white handkerchief.

This fellow had walked into the Kingston garage just after midnight. He seemed to know exactly what he was doing. He threatened the attendant with a Luger revolver, and before the attendant could gather his startled wits together, the man had given him a crushing punch on the jaw. When the attendant recovered consciousness, he found the till had been rifled and nearly twenty pounds were missing.

The following night a similar crime was committed at a garage on the Watford Bypass. The big man again succeeded in getting away, this time with thirty pounds.

Another attendant was attacked the next night in a garage on the Great West Road by the same man, and forty-five pounds were taken.

Then, as abruptly as they had begun, the garage robberies ceased.

George, with a net gain of nearly a hundred pounds, decided for the time being, not to tempt Providence further.

He had told no one what he had done; but Cora, reading of the robberies, knowing that the man who had been responsible for them was big and had carried a Luger, looked at George questioningly.

She was uneasy about George. Since the night she and the other two had laughed at him there had come over him a subtle change. He was hard now, and his temper inclined to fly up. There was a cold, bitter, brooding look in his eyes that Cora didn't like.

He had left Eva's flat before anyone was up on the morning following the scene with the Mickey Mouse costume. Cora, awakening to find him gone, hoped that she had seen the last of him, but he returned in the afternoon just as she was going out.

She was wearing a silk frock, silk stockings and high-heeled shoes borrowed from Little Ernie's wardrobe. Little Ernie and Eva had gone off to the dog-racing at Wembley, and she was alone in the flat.

George came in and stood looking at her, the brooding expression in his eyes.

"What do you want?" she snapped, uneasy, and wondering why he had come back.

"Here," he said, thrusting an envelope at her, "buy yourself some clothes."

She took the envelope, and found inside five ten-pound notes. She knew the wise thing to do was to throw the money at him and tell him to go to hell, but fifty pounds impressed her, and she could not give up such a sum, no matter what the consequences might be.

"Where did you get this from?" she asked.

"I've had that sum by me," he returned, watching her. "I got it out of the post office for you. There's more where that came from."

"Well, thank you," she said, wondering just how much there was. Perhaps it would be as well, she thought, to wait a little while before getting rid of him.

"Now, come on," he said; "you're going to get yourself some clothes."

They went together, and when they returned, having spent all the money except for a pound or two, George pointed to the bedroom.

"Get out of that outfit," he said grimly. "You're not wearing clothes from a pimp."

She showed a flash of temper. "Who do you think you are?" she snapped. "I'll wear what I like."

Before she could stop him, he had reached out and had laid hold of the front of her dress in his thick fingers. He jerked her forward, and with a twisting movement he ripped the dress right down.

"Get out of those things or I'll tear them off you," he said, white as clay.

"You must be cracked," she gasped, startled out of her temper, but she went into the bedroom and changed into the clothes he had bought her.

When Little Ernie returned, he told them that he had a flat for them.

"How much?" George asked, staring with hot, intent eyes at the little man.

"Don't worry about that," Ernie said, shooting a quick glance at Cora. "You're my pal ..."

George walked over to him and caught him by his coat front.

"I ask no favours from you," he said between his teeth. "And listen, I don't like the way you look at Cora. She's my girl. If you try anything with her, I'll kill you. I shan't warn you again."

And Little Ernie, looking into the brooding eyes, suddenly went cold.

The flat that Little Ernie rented them was on the top floor of a block of offices in Holles Street, off Oxford Street. It was secluded and, after business hours, as lonely as a shepherd's hut on a Welsh mountain. It was vacant only because it was some distance from the usual haunts of the street-prowlers.

George liked the place. It was his first proper home, and he took pride in it. He did everything in the house, including the cooking.

Cora, still in two minds as to whether she should stay or not, was influenced by the money that George had so suddenly acquired. She could ask him for anything and she got it. At first, it was clothes, and then it was jewellery. She was already brooding about a car; but she hadn't quite made up her mind what kind of a car to have.

She wasn't giving him anything in return. When he came to her room one night, a look of pleading hope in his eyes, she played a card which she was certain would keep him out of her room in the future.

She invited him to sit down; she even took his hand. Then speaking in a quiet voice, a sad expression on her face, she explained about Sydney. He was, she said, the only man she had ever loved. If George wanted payment, then she wouldn't resist him. But he would be making a prostitute of her, because, at the moment, she had no feelings for him. But if George were patient, if he let her recover from the shock of losing Sydney, then she might grow to love him. She was quite clever about this, and the look she managed to get into her eyes – a look of promise of wonderful things to come – completely fooled George.

He was crazy about her, and the thought of forcing his

attentions on her was unthinkable. So it was agreed that she should have her own room, George should do the housekeeping and pay for everything, and Cora – well, they didn't come to any decisions about Cora. It seemed rather obvious that Cora wasn't to do anything.

And Cora did nothing. She stayed in bed most of the morning, reading the books George got for her from a twopenny library. She spent a long time before her mirror preparing herself for the day. They lunched together and loafed away the afternoon. In the evenings they either went to a movie or a theatre and had dinner out.

This kind of existence dragged on for a few days, and then George discovered his money was running out again. It was frightening how quickly money went, living in the West End with Cora as a companion.

He decided that he would have to stage another robbery. He viewed the prospects quite calmly. He had a lot of confidence in himself now. It seemed as if he were living a charmed life. He had killed a man, and no one had arrested him. He had attacked three garage attendants, and the police were still floundering. It would be all right, he decided, after some thought. He would leave garages alone this time and pick on a bank. That was dangerous, of course, but there was a lot of money to be found in banks: the prize was worth the risk.

He was sitting by the open window. It was eight o'clock in the morning, and Cora was still asleep. He sat there, making his plans, his hands caressing Leo's thick fur.

It was odd how he had brought Leo to the flat. The morning he had left Eva's place, after going to the post office to draw out the fifty pounds, he had returned to his room off the Edgware Road. He had hastily packed his things, paid his rent and told Mrs Rhodes that he had been unexpectedly called out of town. He had said goodbye to Ella. She had known that something was wrong, and she had asked him outright.

"You're in trouble, ain't you, Mr George?" she said. "Is it that gang you was telling me about?"

George nodded. He wished he could tell her the gang that was troubling him was a girl far more dangerous than any make-believe gang he had bragged about in the past.

"I'll keep in touch, Ella," he said. "If anyone asks for me, tell 'em I've gone to Scotland on business. It's important that no one should know where I really am."

Leaving Ella thrilling with intrigue, he had picked up his bag, slung his mackintosh and overcoat over his arm and ran down the steps. It was while he was waiting for a taxi that Leo suddenly appeared. George put down his bag and stroked the cat. He suddenly realized that he was going to miss Leo. Leo meant so much to him: understanding, companionship, love even – odd things like that.

A taxi drew up, and George opened the door, put his bag and overcoat on the seat and gave the driver Eva's address. Then, without stopping to think, he picked Leo up, and got into the taxi.

He was glad now that Leo was with him. He had hoped that Cora would have filled the hollow loneliness of his life, but somehow, although they were together so much, she seemed like a stranger. She talked, but her talk meant nothing. There was no love nor understanding in her look. She might really not be there.

Leo did not like Cora, and whenever she was in the room the cat would creep under the settee; but alone with George it would reveal an affection for him which did much to comfort the big, wretched man.

Sitting in the armchair, Leo on his knee, George made

plans to rob a bank. It would have to be a village bank, he decided. There was only one way to discover the right kind of bank. He would have to hire a car, and he would also have to leave Cora for a few days. He must never incriminate her. He guessed she knew that he was the mysterious robber who masked his face with a white handkerchief. But they had reached a silent understanding that they should not mention the fact. If he were caught, she must know nothing about the robberies.

So it was arranged. George explained to Cora that he had to go off on business. She gave him a quick look, read his expression correctly, and agreed without protest. He hired a car, and after putting Leo in a cat's home for a few days – he did not trust Cora to feed the cat – he set off for Brighton.

It took him three days to find the bank he was looking for. It was a tiny place in a village a few miles from Brighton. The staff consisted of only a branch manager who opened the bank twice a week. It did not take George long to obtain the information he needed. It was extraordinary how easy it was to rob the place. Of course, he had thought out a plan and had spent a lot of time on the ground, but somehow he felt it shouldn't have been quite so easy. He entered the bank at a few minutes to three, just as the branch manager was closing the door. There was no one else in the bank, and the manager, a red-faced, cheerful man of about sixty, shut the door and bolted it before attending to George.

"You're the last customer, sir," he said, rubbing his hands. "I want some golf this afternoon."

George hit him with his clenched fist in exactly the spot where he had hit the garage attendants. The manager slumped to the floor, and that was all there was to it.

George helped himself to two hundred pounds. If there

had been more he would have taken it, but two hundred pounds wasn't to be sneezed at. He left by the back way, drove to London without incident and handed the car back to the garage where he had hired it.

He returned to the flat after four o'clock. It was pretty obvious that the place hadn't been touched since he had been away. It was in a complete mess, and George felt suddenly depressed and a little irritated. He put Leo on the settee. He had collected the cat on his way back to the flat, and set to work to tidy up. Cora wasn't in. Her bedroom was dirty, and hopelessly untidy, and there was cigarette ash over everything.

It took him until almost six o'clock before he had straightened the flat, then he made himself a cup of tea and sat down. Leo got onto his lap.

George wondered where Cora had got to. He wondered hopefully if she had missed him. Perhaps tonight she would decide that it was time to be nice to him. Somehow he didn't think he could go on indefinitely like this. The strain was beginning to tell on him. He could understand her feelings for Sydney. Though how she could have loved a fellow like that defeated him. Sydney had been very firm with her. Perhaps he had better be firm, too. Perhaps … he clenched his fists. It was no good thinking now. He would see her tonight.

Cora returned at half past six. George heard her come in and go to her bedroom. Almost immediately she came into the sitting-room.

"So you're back," she said, looking at him curiously.

He looked at her, aware of a tightening in his throat. She was wearing wine-coloured slacks and a white silk-and-wool sweater. Her long black hair curled to her shoulders and partly hid her right eye.

George drew in a quick, deep breath. The sweater and

slacks set off her sensual little figure. The sight of her in these new clothes fired his blood. He pushed Leo off his lap and went to her.

"Cora!" he said, taking her in his arms. "Can't you be kind to me now? Do I have to wait much longer, Cora? Look!" He pushed her away and took out the roll of notes. "Two hundred pounds! Think what we can do with that! I can get more. But can't you give me just a little...?"

She studied him, a strange expression in her eyes. "I think so, George," she said at last. "Yes, I think so. I think you've waited long enough."

He took her in his arms again and kissed her. She stood quite still, her eyes closed, cold, indifferent. He tried to move her by his kisses, but her mouth was a hard line. He let her go at last, and sat down.

"I've got to get used to the idea," she said gently. "It's no good rushing me. George, will you do something for me?"

He stared up at her, his face congested. "Aren't I always doing something for you?" he said hoarsely.

"This is such a little thing," she said, smiling. "Will you leave me for an hour? I want to think. I want to get used to the idea. I have a feeling that when you come back ..." She turned away. "Well, you'll be surprised, George. I promise you that."

He had gone at once, and he had spent the next hour tramping the back streets, continually looking at his watch, his hunger for her deadening him to any other feeling.

When he returned to the flat, she had gone. She had packed her clothes, taken her jewellery and gone. There was no personal thing of hers left in her room except the faint smell of sandalwood.

He stood looking round the room for a long time, and then he wandered into the sitting-room. He glanced almost indifferently at the mantelpiece where he had left the two hundred pounds. That had gone too.

He was angry. This was the last time a woman would make a fool of him! He didn't blame her in a way. He should have guessed that she still loved Sydney too much to have any feeling for him. It wasn't that that made him angry. It was the knowledge that she had deliberately thrown dust in his eyes, sure of her ability to fool him as she had fooled him before, as Babs had fooled him. What kind of a man was he, that women could fool him so easily? He clenched his fists, cursing himself for being such a simple, trusting weakling.

No doubt she hadn't expected him to return so soon. She had probably been getting ready to leave when he had returned. So she had got rid of him with a promise, and instead of keeping the promise, she had packed and gone.

He lit a cigarette and, taking Leo on his lap, he stared out of the window. He remained like that until it grew dark. While he sat there, he decided that he would wash his hands of her. He would pack and go. He would go to Eastbourne. He had always wanted to go to Eastbourne, and now he would see what the town had to offer him. He would put all this behind him and go back to his bookselling. It wasn't much of a life, but anything was better than this ghastly, reckless existence.

He was still sitting there in misery, trying to bolster up his spirits, when he heard someone rapping on the door. At first he wasn't going to answer, but the rapping went on and on, so he got up finally and jerked open the door.

Eva was standing there.

He stared at her blankly, wondering what she wanted.

"Yes?" he said, blocking the way. "What do you want?"

"Is Cora here?" Eva asked. There was a cold, spiteful

look in her eyes.

He shook his head.

"Where is she?" Eva asked.

"I don't know."

"You mean she's left you?"

He nodded. "Please go away," he said, and began to close the door.

"Perhaps you don't know she's been sleeping with Ernie for the past four days," Eva said.

George looked at her. "I don't know why you've come here," he said. "But I don't intend to listen to your lies."

"Lies?" Her voice shot up. "Why, you dumb fool, why should I lie about a thing like that! I want you to do something about it. Do you think I want a bitch like that to steal my man?"

George went cold. "I don't believe you," he said. "She's in love with Sydney. She wouldn't ..." And he stopped. Was this another of Cora's little tricks? Was all that talk about being in love with Sydney just an excuse to fob him off?

"She's been after Ernie for months," Eva said. "I've watched her. But until now Ernie hasn't been having any. But she's got money now. She's giving him things. She promised to give him a car! He's not satisfied with the car I gave him. Oh no, he wants another! She's been working for him all this week. Making money ... big money! Well, you've got to stop her! Do you hear? You've got to stop her!"

George clenched his fists. A red curtain hung before his eyes. So that's what she had been doing with his money. Giving it to Ernie, winning Ernie's attention.

"Working?" he said. "What do you mean?"

"He's given her a beat," Eva returned, her voice hoarse with suppressed fury. "And a flat in Old Burlington

Street."

"Where's her beat?" George heard himself ask.

"Sackville Street," Eva returned, suddenly frightened by the ruthless, hard face before her.

"All right," George said, and closed the door in her face.

Fifteen minutes later he left the flat and walked across Hanover Square towards Sackville Street. Street-walkers moved slowly along the back streets, paused to talk among themselves, looked at George hopefully and went on.

George walked down Sackville Street, along Vigo Street into Bond Street. He turned and retraced his steps. He had been doing this for over half an hour when he suddenly saw Cora. She was walking just ahead of a tall, well-dressed man in his middle fifties. She was loitering, a contemptuous expression on her hard little face.

George stepped into a shop doorway where he could watch, without being seen.

The well-dressed man overtook Cora, glanced at her and went on. She did not increase her pace, but kept on, swinging her hips, her head in the air.

The man walked as far as the street corner, and then stopped. He looked round furtively, noted that Cora was still coming towards him, and then looked up and down, as if to assure himself that no one was watching him.

Cora came on. She looked at him enquiringly as she paused before crossing the street.

The man raised his hat and said something. Cora smiled. She waved her hand towards Old Burlington Street. From the doorway, George could see the man eyeing her figure. He said something, and then looked away.

Cora turned and began to walk casually towards Old Burlington Street, her hands in her pockets, her hips swinging.

After giving her a start, the man followed her.

George came out of the doorway and followed them. They entered a tall building half way down the street, and when he was sure that they were safely out of the way he went up to the front door. There were three bell-pushes on the door. One of them had a little card: "Miss Nichols".

George stood looking at the card for several minutes, then he crossed the street and waited. He waited until the well-dressed man had left the building, and then he approached the place himself. As he was crossing the street again, he saw a man coming towards him. He thought it looked like Little Ernie, and he darted into a doorway, his hand flying to his gun.

It was Little Ernie.

George watched him coming down the street. Ernie called out cheerfully to a woman who was walking in the opposite direction. " 'Ullo, ducks; don't loiter. There's still an 'our before bye-byes."

George gritted his teeth. The little rat had made Cora into one of these women! All right, he'd fix him. The world would be well rid of a filthy little brute like Ernie.

He stepped out of his doorway as Little Ernie turned into Cora's building. A few quick steps, and George was on him, as he was opening the front door with a key.

"Hello, Ernie," George said softly.

Little Ernie gave a squeal of terror. He spun round, throwing up his hands.

George rammed the gun into his side.

"I warned you, you rotten little rat. You won't get a car this time," and he pulled the trigger three times.

The noise of gunfire crashed down the empty street. The flash blinded George. But he wasn't nervous nor frightened.

He watched Little Ernie flop on the steps of the house and then, bending over him, he shot him again.

A woman began to scream at the other end of the street.

George slipped the gun into his pocket and stepped from the shadow of the doorway. There was still no one about. Without hurrying, he walked to Clifford Street and stopped a passing taxi.

"Hyde Park Corner," he said, and got into the taxi.

He glanced through the little window at the back. People were appearing now. A policeman was running down Old Burlington Street. It was going to be all right. His luck was holding. In another few seconds he'd be out of danger. He sat back in the cab and closed his eyes.

He did not allow himself to think until he had paid off the taxi and was walking towards Knightsbridge. He had no horror at what he had done. It was as if he had stepped on a beetle, no more, no less.

What would Cora do? Would she tell the police? If she did that it would be the end of him; but he somehow didn't care. He was tired of this business, sick and tired of it. He wanted a little peace. Better keep away from the flat tonight, he thought. He wanted one more night of freedom. He'd go back the next morning. If the police were waiting for him, then he'd let them take him. But not tonight. He'd walk and walk, because he wanted to think. He wanted to make plans.

He woke the next morning in a Salvation Army hostel off the Cromwell Road. He remembered walking until he could walk no more, and had crawled into this place at three o'clock in the morning. Now it was just after seven o'clock, and he decided to return to his flat immediately.

On his way back he tried to think about Little Ernie, but what had happened the previous night had a dream quality about it, and he could not get his mind to believe that it had happened.

Even when climbing the stairs to the flat high above Holles Street, he could not believe that the police might be waiting for him. He was so tired, anyway, that he couldn't care one way or the other.

He pushed open the door, and for a moment hesitated, listening. There was no sound in the flat. He went into the sitting-room. There was no one there, but there was a distinct smell of sandalwood in the room. He stood very still, trying to remember whether the scent had been there before Eva came to see him. He couldn't remember. Anyway, Cora wasn't likely to have returned. But the thought disturbed him, and he went quickly to his bedroom. Then he paused and looked blankly round the room. His cupboard and chest of drawers were open and empty. His clothes were scattered all over the room. One look at them was enough. They had been systematically ripped to pieces. His flannel trousers were in shreds. His tweed coat was armless and ripped down the back. His shirts were a mass of holes. Even his shoes were cut with a knife. Everything he owned was torn to pieces, as if it had been set upon by a wild animal.

Cora! Of course! She had come back to revenge Little Ernie.

Then he remembered Leo, and he felt so sick and faint that he had to sit on the bed. As he did so, he became aware of something in the corner, half hidden by the dressing-table. He saw red streaks on the wall. He peered forward fearfully. In the shadowy light he could make out fur, blood, and then a squashed paw, and he closed his eyes.

He sat there shivering. After a while, he began to cry.

# 19

Light rain began to fall, and islands of sullen grey clouds knitted together to form a depressing curtain of mist that blotted out the watery moon.

George stood in a shop doorway, his collar turned up and his hat well down on his ears. He carried Leo, wrapped in a bath-towel; the bundle felt hard, a wood carving, against his side. He remained in the shelter of the doorway for some time, a lonely motionless figure, merged into the darkness, unseen.

One by one the lights behind the big window opposite, screened by the yellow muslin curtains, went out like the eyes of a robot figure closing in sleep. Several times the green-painted glass-panelled door with the gilt letters "Restaurant" on it, opened, and men and women, in pairs or singly, came out. George watched them disperse, their heads down, some arm in arm, moving rapidly to another more distant shelter.

There was only one light burning now. He could see the shadowy outlines of the big blonde woman, Emily, and the white-coated Hebrew, Max, through the curtain. The woman sat at the cash desk. He guessed she was emptying the till. The Hebrew seemed to be clearing up at the bar, washing glasses, drying them and putting them away.

It was time to talk to them. George crossed the street, pushed open the green-panelled door and entered the restaurant. The long room was stuffy, and smelt of food, cigars and coffee. The shaded light above the cash desk threw off an isolated yellow pool in the dim, smoky room.

"We're closed," Max said, continuing to put the glasses under the counter.

George looked first at the Hebrew and then at the woman, Emily. He closed the door and moved further into the light.

Emily recognized him.

"Max …" There was a quick, urgent note in her voice. She put her hand under the desk, and a bell began to ring somewhere in the building.

Max was bending down behind the counter, arranging the glasses in an orderly row. As he heard the bell and caught the sharp note in Emily's voice, he clashed the glasses together. One of them slipped from his fingers and dropped with a little thump on the carpet. He raised his head and peered at George, his pebbly eyes blank with alarm.

George waited. It was no use talking to them until they were ready to listen. At the moment their attention was concentrated in keeping him there, in trapping him.

"It's all right," he said, wanting to reassure them. "I've come to explain."

The two Greeks, black shadows, threatening, slid out of the darkness and stood between him and the door. The shaded light glittered on their razors.

"You mustn't let them touch me before I explain," George said quickly, not liking the expressions on the Greeks' faces. "That's why I've come."

Max straightened slowly. He put his veined hands on the counter, and his pale tongue touched the corners of his lips.

"Leave him be," he said to the Greeks.

There was a long pause. They did not seem to know what to expect or what to do with him now that they had got him.

George looked uncertainly at the Hebrew, and then at the woman. It seemed to him that since she was in charge of the cash, she should be the one he should address.

"May I tell you about it?" he said, looking at her anxiously.

Again there was a long pause, then Emily leaned forward. "You know what will happen to you, don't you?"

George nodded.

"Then why have you come here?"

He offered her the bundle. Immediately she drew back, suspicious, alarmed. The two Greeks made a slight movement: two blades of light danced on the ceiling as they lifted their razors.

The Hebrew said, "Wait." George's white face, the sharp etched lines of misery, his despairing eyes puzzled him. "What is that?" he asked, nodding at the bundle.

George put the bundle on the counter. "It's my cat," he said unevenly.

The woman looked at the bundle and then at George.

"What's he talking about?" she asked impatiently.

Max touched the bundle with two bony fingers. He felt the hard body and he grimaced.

"Is this a trick?" he said, not believing it was a trick, but bewildered.

"Would you mind looking?" George said. "Could you look so that I don't have to see him again?" His mouth tightened. "I'm sorry to be so upset, but he was really the only thing that meant anything to me."

"Perhaps he's mad," Emily said, half to herself.

Reluctantly, the Hebrew lifted the corner of the towel.

His face revealed an impersonal disgust, but he turned the bundle so that the woman could see.

"She did that," George said.

Both Emily and Max seemed to know whom he meant.

"Ah," Max said, dropping the towel. "It was your cat?"

George nodded. "I didn't think she'd do such a thing. I knew she might do anything to me, but I didn't think she would touch Leo. I suppose I ought to have thought of it, because there was nothing else she could have done which would have hurt as much as this."

"Is that what brought you here?" Emily asked abruptly.

"Oh yes," George said. "She can't be allowed to go on and on. She might hurt too many people. That's why I've come to you."

"You killed Crispin, didn't you?" Emily said, in a flat, cold voice.

"That's what I mean," George returned steadily. "I've come to explain. Then you must decide what to do."

"You were foolish to come," Max said softly. "You know what happened to Sydney?"

Again George nodded. "It doesn't matter about me," he said. "I don't care what happens to me. I just want to be sure that she won't escape."

Max glanced over at Emily.

"I think we should hear what he has to say," he said. "It might save a lot of time."

Emily nodded and walked round the cash desk. She crossed to a table and turned on the lamp. She sat down and pointed to a chair opposite her.

"Sit down and talk," she said.

George sat down. The two Greeks moved nearer so that they were immediately behind him. The Hebrew left the bar and joined them at the table.

"Perhaps one of you would take the gun," George said. "It's in my pocket. I don't suppose you would like me to take it out. Be careful how you handle it, it's loaded."

He felt the gun being lifted from his pocket. Nick slid it across the table towards Max, who put his hand on it.

"I want to tell you exactly how it happened," George said. "It'll take a little time, but it's important."

Emily shrugged. "Take as long as you like," she said indifferently. "It'll probably be the last time you'll talk to anyone."

George considered this. He found it strange that he was unmoved. He knew they were killers, but he was so tired and sad that nothing really mattered any more.

It was a relief to tell them about it. It was extraordinary how easy it was to tell once he started. He began by explaining about his parents.

"You see," he said, folding his hands on the table and looking at the woman's hard, fat face, "no one ever bothered with me when I was a kid. My parents were on the stage. They didn't want a child. I used to envy them. They had their names in the newspapers and on hoardings. I wonder if you can understand why I pretended to be someone quite different from what I really am? It was foolish, but I wanted so badly to be someone ... to impress people."

The woman nodded, understanding. She thought sadly of her son, Crispin. He also had wanted to impress people. "Go on," she said, "I understand that part of it."

"When I told Sydney about the gun he changed towards me. I know why now. I was just the fool he was looking for, but I didn't know then. It wasn't until after I shot Crispin that I knew."

They all stiffened when he said that. Nick reached

forward and seized him by the back of his neck, but Max struck his hand away.

"Wait," he said.

"So you did shoot him?" Emily said, her eyes snapping.

"Oh yes," George returned, "it was an accident, but I shot him all right. It's something I'll never forgive myself for."

He told them about Cora.

"I don't understand women," he explained. "I've never had anything to do with them. It all happened so quickly. She rather swept me off my feet. I've been very stupid, I'm afraid."

He went on, explaining every detail, showing them the gun. He explained how Sydney had fixed the trigger and had stolen the cartridge. He pulled out the magazine and demonstrated how easily the gun fired. He told them how careful he had always been never to put a cartridge into the breech.

"I was afraid of accidents," he said, "but they loaded the gun without telling me. You see, they were determined to make me a murderer."

The woman and the Hebrew sat listening, their faces intent. The two Greeks wanted to have done with it. George could feel their restlessness. He knew they were not interested in what he had to say. He sensed that they were planning how to get rid of his body when they had finished him.

He told them about the whip and the visit to the cottage.

"I don't really know how it happened. She gave me the gun. I heard her slip back the safety catch, but it all happened so quickly that I had no chance to do anything. As soon as I touched the trigger, the gun went off."

Max blew his nose.

"I don't think there's anything else to tell you," George went on, leaning back in his chair, suddenly tired. "A lot has happened to me since then, but I won't bother you with that. I don't know what you want to do with me, but I know what I want you to do with her."

They looked at him.

"What do you want us to do with her?" Emily asked softly.

"I want justice," George said simply.

"Sydney's gone," Max said, looking down at his veined hands. "No one can touch one of us without paying the price. Crispin was one of us, you know."

Emily touched his arm. Her eyes reached George's face. "Where is she?"

George told her.

She got to her feet. "We'll go and see her."

"What about him?" Nick said, speaking for the first time.

"He'll come with us."

"It would be better ..." Nick began, but Emily shook her head.

"He'll come with us," she repeated.

She went over to the desk and put on a light coat.

"Get a taxi," she said.

Max changed his white coat for a black one, put on his bowler hat and picked up an umbrella.

"It's raining," he said gloomily.

While Poncho went for a taxi, Nick stood over George, threatening him with the razor. Somehow George felt no fear. He was hollow, without feeling, disinterested.

They waited, while the rain fell outside, and the sound of distant traffic vibrated the big windows.

A taxi drew up outside.

"All right," Emily said, picking up the Luger and putting it into her bag.

George stood up. "If you please ..." he began and stopped.

They looked at him.

"It's my cat," he said. "Could he be buried?"

Max nodded. "We'll bury him," he said, almost kindly.

George touched the bundle. He didn't want to leave Leo like this, wrapped in a soiled bath-towel on a bar counter. Leo deserved something better than this, but there were other things to do. Besides, George was tired. He had no idea where to bury Leo. Cora must have felt the same way about Sydney. It was better, perhaps, to leave the cat in the hands of strangers.

A clock was striking eleven as they got into the taxi. Max and Emily sat on the turn-up seats. George, between the two Greeks, sat opposite them.

It did not take them long to reach Old Burlington Street.

"Shall I tell him to wait?" Max asked.

"We'll be some time," Emily said, "better not."

They watched the taxi drive away, and then they walked into the building and up the stairs.

George went first, then Nick, then Emily, then Max, clutching his umbrella, and finally Poncho. They were quiet. The soft scraping of their shoes on the coconut matting sounded like the scamper of rats.

George paused outside the flat door.

"This is it," he said. "Shall I ring the bell?"

Nick pushed him aside, looked at the lock, took something from his pocket, and a moment later there was a soft click as the door opened.

The light was on in the lobby, and a door opposite was

ajar. There was a light on in the room.

Emily touched George's arm and motioned him forward. He shook his head, but again she pushed him. So he went into the room, leaving the others outside in the lobby.

The room was large and well furnished. Cora was sitting in an armchair. A cigarette dangled from her thin mouth. She was still wearing the white silk-and-wool sweater and wine-coloured slacks. There was a scraped-bone look on her face, but her lips were twisted in a humourless smile. She was holding a packet of pound notes in her hand, counting them with rapt concentration.

George stopped just inside the doorway, looking at her.

Her fingers ceased moving and she raised her head, fear jumping into her eyes. When she saw who it was, her mouth tightened.

"Get out!" she said, folding the notes quickly and slipping them into her pocket.

George continued to stare at her.

"Get out!" she repeated, her eyes wary. "We're quits, aren't we? Don't stand there looking at me. I'm not frightened of you."

What's the matter with me? George asked himself. Why am I feeling like this? I'm not still in love with her. I hate her.

"I wouldn't have done this if you'd let Leo alone," he said in a small voice. "Animals are so helpless. I suppose that's why I like them."

She got to her feet, an ugly expression in her slate-grey eyes. "What are you drivelling about?"

"I want you to know why I've done this."

"Done what?" she asked sharply.

"You see, you might do an awful lot of harm if you were allowed to go on and on. It's got to stop, Cora. I can't trust you any more," and he turned to the door and threw it open. "Will you come in, please?"

Emily and Max walked in. The two Greeks followed them. Nick slid across the room to the window, while Poncho closed the door and set his back against it.

Cora's hand flew to her mouth. "No!" she screamed, and her eyes rolled up, so that only the whites showed.

Emily marched over to the armchair and sat down. She opened her coat and fluffed up her untidy hair.

"Before we get down to business," she said, ignoring Cora, "I'd like a cup of tea. Can you make tea?" She looked at George.

"Oh yes," he said blankly, "but don't you think ...?"

"I don't," Emily snapped. "Get me a cup of tea, there's a good fellow."

George turned and looked helplessly at Poncho, who stared back at him with menacingly dark eyes.

"Let him make some tea," Emily said, watching them.

"He'll run away," Poncho argued, a little angrily.

"I don't think he will," Emily returned, taking out a packet of Woodbines from her bag and lighting one. "If he does, it won't matter." Poncho shrugged and stood away from the door. George went out through the lobby into the little kitchen across the way. Not quite knowing what he was doing, he put on the kettle and laid a tray. He was glad to have something to do. Every now and then a tiny spark of horror flared up in his mind, but instantly it sparked out. He knew now that Emily was going to let him go free. By telling him to make the tea, she had shown that she had believed his story and she wasn't holding him responsible. It was justice. He had no pity for Cora. There would be nothing to worry about, not the way Emily would do it. Although he did not know how she would do it, he was sure that it would be as efficient and undetectable as Sydney's death.

He made the tea and carried the tray into the sitting-room.

Max had sat down. His bowler hat and umbrella lay at his feet. He was glancing through a notebook, absorbed. Emily sat in a heap, her fat little feet stretched out before her, the cigarette dangling limply from her lips. She was looking round the room with a blank look in her eyes, her mind far away.

Cora still stood against the wall, her face twisted in a mask of frozen terror. She did not look up as George entered. The room was silent, and he distinctly heard the rumbling of her insides. She coughed nervously, as if to hide the sound, but George knew how frightened she was.

Poncho closed the door after George. He seemed startled to see him again.

George put the tray on the table. He was surprised to find how indifferent he was to all this. He felt cold, pitiless, and he realized then what real hatred meant. The discovery shocked him.

"Will you have some?" he asked vaguely, looking round.

No one said anything, and he looked helplessly at Emily for guidance.

"I want a cup," she said. "Never mind about anyone else."

He poured out the tea and handed the cup to her.

"I think ... perhaps ... I'll have a cup myself," he said apologetically.

Emily stirred her tea, added sugar and sipped. Then she nodded to George. "It's good tea."

"Don't you think ...?" Max said, glancing at Cora.

Emily's hard little eyes snapped. "We don't have to talk to her," she said. "It's a question of how it's to be done."

Cora pointed to George. "He did it," she said breathlessly. "You can't blame me. He did it. He shot Crispin."

Emily smiled. "We know all about that," she said. "He told us." She looked Cora up and down. "No one can harm us without paying. You were in it as deep as Sydney. You must go too." She glanced at Poncho. "Arrange it, and be quick. An accident with an electric iron … if there is one here."

Poncho came back after a few minutes with a portable ironing board, an electric iron and some underwear he had found in Cora's bedroom.

"Everything," he said, with a triumphal grin.

He worked quickly and methodically, setting up the ironing board and plugging in the iron. Then he produced a penknife and began working on the flex.

Emily noticed George's blank gaze.

"He's clever," she said, smiling. "In a moment that iron won't be safe to touch." She leaned forward. "They'll find her some time, and they'll think she died because of a faulty flex. The joke is, it will be because of a faulty flex."

Cora crossed the room slowly and stood before George. Her eyes were dark with terror.

"You're not going to let them do this to me, are you?" she said. "You can't do it." Then her voice suddenly rose to a scream. "George! You can't let them. Don't you understand what they're doing? They're going to kill me. Save me! I'll do anything! I swear I'll do anything if you'll only stop them! You can do it! You're big enough! Save me, George!" And she rushed forward, putting her arms round his neck, her face against his. "I'll never leave you, George," she went on wildly. "Forgive me! Don't let them touch me."

The feel of her slight body against his, the smell of her

perfume, her hair against his face suddenly weakened him. He felt sick and faint.

Nick snatched her away from him, twisting her arms behind her.

"Have you forgotten your cat so soon?" Emily said, looking at him thoughtfully. "You'd better go. You needn't bother with her or us any more. You're lucky. You tell a good story, and I think it's true. I'm sorry about your cat. You mightn't think it, but I like animals myself."

"George!" Cora screamed. "Don't go! Don't leave me!"

Nick put his hand across her mouth. His fingers dug into her cheek.

"Go now," Emily said.

George walked unsteadily to the door. He hesitated, then went on out of the flat to the stairs. As he began to walk down the stairs a dreadful cry of terror and despair tore through the door past him into the dimly lit confines of the building. He shivered, the bleakness in his heart frightening him; but he kept on. Then there was a bright flash of blue light from the fuse box at the bottom of the stairs, and the lights went out. He knew that Cora would never worry him again.

For a moment he stood still, trying to see in the suffocating darkness. Thoughts flashed through his mind. Where was he going? What was he going to do? He would be lonely. There was no Leo now. There was no Cora either. He would have nothing. The future loomed before him: dark, empty, ageless.

He reached the front door, opened it and stepped into the rain. Men appeared from out of the darkness and crowded round him. He saw the glistening capes and the police helmets.

"What ...?" he began, weak with fear.

"I'm Detective Inspector Tuck," a voice said, and George could just make out a tall man wearing a bowler hat pushing his way through the little crowd of policemen. "I think you are George Fraser. It's my duty to arrest you and charge you with the robbery of a garage near Kingston."

George blinked at the detective, then his fear went away and he sighed with relief. In his bones he had felt all along that they would get him in the end. Well, now they had him. It was a good thing that all this ghastly business was ended.

"Oh yes ...?" he muttered, aware that two policemen were running their hands over his clothes.

"Stop," the detective said quickly. "I have also to caution you that anything you say will be written down and may be used in evidence at your trial."

"I understand," George said. "Thank you, but I want to tell you everything. You want me for murder too." He drew himself up feeling a sudden sense of pride. "I killed Crispin and Little Ernie."

They took hold of his arms, but they were quite gentle with him, and when the detective spoke again he sounded kind.

"Little Ernie? You did that? Hmmm, well, all right; it's a good thing to get everything off your chest. You come along with me. Who's this fellow Crispin you're talking about?"

"Oh, it's a long story," George said, suddenly feeling tired. "But the others are up there. They've just killed Cora. You'll find them all up there: Emily, Max and the two Greeks. You mustn't let them get away."

Four of the policemen pushed past him and entered the building. He could hear them running up the stairs.

"I don't know how you found me ..." George said, moving towards the car. "I've always read how clever you are. I thought somehow ..."

"You were identified," the detective said, getting into the car and sitting beside him. "The fellow at Kingston saw you about an hour ago. He telephoned the Yard, and here we are. We've had our eye on you for some time. We didn't like the company you kept. Here, have a cigarette." He offered a crumpled carton.

"I don't think I'll smoke," George said slowly. "I didn't drink my tea. Do you think I could get a cup where we are going? My mouth is very dry."

"That's all right," the detective assured him. "That's all we do – drink tea. There'll be a cup for you all right."

George nodded. "I suppose they'll hang me," he said. "You know, I'm not afraid. I've been awfully lonely all my life."

"Now don't talk like that," the detective returned, looking at him sharply. "While there's life there's hope, you know. You don't have to get depressed."

"Oh, I'm not depressed," George returned. "I'm really quite happy now."

A moment later the car took him away to meet his destiny.

# James Hadley Chase

## An Ace Up My Sleeve

When three very different people come together, all out for the same thing and prepared to go to any lengths to get it, the stakes are likely to be high. But, for a wealthy middle-aged woman, an international lawyer and a young American, games of bluff and counter-bluff quickly develop into a dangerous and deadly battle. As the action hots up, Chase weaves a fast-moving story of blackmail, intrigue and extortion with a hair-raising climax.

## The Fast Buck

International jewel thief, Paul Hater, knows a secret that everyone wants to know – and will go to any lengths to uncover. How long can he remain silent?

When Hater is arrested in possession of a stolen necklace, the police use every possible means to persuade him to reveal the location of the rest of the collection. He remains silent and so begins his twenty-year prison sentence. Having exhausted all their leads, the International Detective Agency, acting on behalf of the insurers, must patiently await Hater's release before they can hope to find out more. But just as his day of release approaches, Hater is kidnapped by a ruthless international gang determined to force the secret from him and prepared to go to any lengths to do so...

# James Hadley Chase

## Have a Change of Scene

Larry Carr is a diamond expert in need of a break. So when his psychiatrist suggests he has a change of scene, he jumps at the opportunity to move to Luceville, a struggling industrial town, and become a social worker. This, he thinks, will give him all the rest he needs…until he runs into Rhea Morgan, a ruthless, vicious thief who also happens to be extremely attractive. He falls headlong into the criminal world and embarks upon a thrilling, rapid and dastardly adventure in true Hadley Chase style.

## Just a Matter of Time

An old lady's will seems to be causing quite a stir. Suddenly everyone wants to get in on the action, everyone that is, including a master forger, a hospital nurse, a young delinquent, a bank executive and, to make matters worse, a professional killer. With such ingredients, a showdown seems inevitable and James Hadley Chase adds enough suspense to keep you guessing right up to the very last page.

# JAMES HADLEY CHASE

## MY LAUGH COMES LAST

Farrell Brannigan, President of the National Californian Bank, is an extremely successful man. So when he builds another bank in an up-and-coming town on the Pacific coast, he is given worldwide publicity, and this new bank is hailed as 'the safest bank in the world'. But Brannigan's success came at a price and he made many enemies on his way up the ladder. It seems that one of them is now set on revenge and determined to destroy both the bank and Brannigan himself.

## YOU'RE DEAD WITHOUT MONEY

Joey Luck and his daughter Cindy were small-time criminals going nowhere fast...until they joined forces with Vin Pinna, a hardened criminal on the run from Miami. They began to set their sights higher and turned their hands to kidnapping. But their hostage, ex-movie star Don Elliot, seemed to have different ideas. He wanted in so they formed a 'quartet in crime' and this time the stakes were higher still – eight Russian stamps worth a million dollars.

'realistic and suspenseful' – *Observer*

Printed in Great Britain
by Amazon